ANY GIRL BUT YOU

DANA HAWKINS

Storm
PUBLISHING

Ebook ISBN: 978-1-83700-060-9
Paperback ISBN: 978-1-83700-062-3

Cover design by Rachel Lawston
Cover illustration © Rachel Lawston

Published by Storm Publishing.
For further information, visit:
www.stormpublishing.co

ALSO BY DANA HAWKINS

Not in the Plan

In Walked Trouble

So Not My Type

The Ex Effect

I Will Always Love You (Maybe)

To my family for putting up with me during the holidays. If you know, you know.

ONE
QUINN

I am totally convinced nobody actually *likes* Christmas.

And before you get your garland-covered pitchforks out, hear me out. Throughout the year, people glamorize the holiday and view it through a sparkly bow filter where everything looks like a sweet, magical winter wonderland. Parents picture themselves in their matching flannel pajamas, sipping spiced eggnog and watching the little ones tear into their gifts. Friends laugh at the memory of exchanging goofy white elephant gifts while competing in the office's annual ugly Christmas sweater contest. Kids remember ripping through shiny wrapping paper and pulling out the gift they begged Santa Claus for at the mall. Thinking about Christmas, *that's* the fun part.

But come *actual* Christmas time, those parents spend the week swearing like drunk frat boys while assembling presents, friends stress over fighting traffic and coming up with a "clever" white elephant gift while grinding at their jobs, and kids throw temper tantrums when Santa doesn't bring the toy they want.

The holiday is loud, chaotic, and the same damn song plays over and over (*can we all agree there are some solid Mariah Carey fans out there?*) During the season, there's too many people at the store, too many screaming toddlers, and too much sugar.

Wait. That last one I take back. The sugar is one of the best parts of the season. Especially when co-workers bring in their butter toffee and I bet a trip to the dentist that I can make it through one without a cracked tooth.

But that's it. The music sucks. The people suck. They think they're excited, but they're not. They're stressed-out. They're angry. Last year, I saw a grandma throw a candy cane at a man at a store. Maybe he deserved it, who knows. The guy did look like a dick. Point is, an *actual* candy cane. Lobbed through the air and smacked him square on the cheek.

So, why the hell did I choose to buy a Christmas tree farm?

Yes, that's right. Seven months ago, I went from Quinn Lee, Wall Street Executive Assistant of Vice President Asshat, to Quinn Lee, Tree Farmer in Spring Harbors, Minnesota. And I've been asking myself this exact question every day since I purchased this place. I'll probably keep asking it until I die. Or sell. But my stubbornness rivals a bulldog's, so I'll say die.

These are the thoughts that consume me as I step out of the shower and scrunch my hair in a towel, being careful not to rub. My curls can be a temperamental little bitch, and the slightest deviation from my coconut hair creamer and wet-diffusing process will fray the strands. Trust me—nothing can ruin a day like suboptimal coils.

Was the dead of January the smartest time to decide on buying a run-down tree farm outside of my small hometown of Spring Harbors, Minnesota? Probably not. But the emotion of that weekend seven months ago overtook me, grabbed me by my North Face jacket lapel, and made me jump headfirst—the stresses of my New York job had reached nightmare levels and I missed Frankie, my sister (and New York roommate) who'd moved back here to our hometown to be with her girlfriend, Morgan. And honestly, I felt a little lost. Not that I'd admit that to anyone, not even my sister. So, last year when I returned for the holidays and saw the magic of the snow, trees, and holiday lights, a stirring started deep in my core and I thought, *This is it*. My calling.

Must. Buy. Tree. Farm.

I tug my robe over me, unravel the diffuser, and tip my hair to the side.

Was getting out of New York the right decision? Definitely. When I moved back to Minnesota, I told myself I would not give another thought to my old job. That place stripped me of a decade. Constantly being told I was being dramatic, or had misunderstood instructions, or was too sensitive (*I assure you, I'm not*) killed bits of my soul. For years I put up with a boss who wouldn't show up for a meeting and then blamed me for getting the times wrong on his calendar or berated me in front of an audience and an hour later convinced me he never screamed or... Nope. See? I'm doing it again.

I will *not* think about what happened at my former job.

After my curls reach the appropriate bounce level, I cross the hall into my bedroom of the house that I share with Frankie and Morgan. Besides the job, so many things have changed from my New York days. I inherited a house with my sister (thank you, Grandma Peaches), that has a *garage* and a *shed* and a *lawn*. A freaking lawn. In New York, Frankie and I had a seven-hundred-square-foot two-bedroom apartment with a barely functioning elevator.

Not only do we have a lawn, though, we also have matching furniture and nice pictures on the wall, and Frankie has an actual bedroom furniture set. Of course, courtesy of Morgan, who's the type of woman that always has her shit together. Morgan keeps things around the house tidy, fresh smelling, and homey.

Me... Well, I contribute by taking off my shoes at the door, and keeping my bedroom door closed so she doesn't have a heart attack when she passes by.

A muffled phone buzzes from somewhere. I dig under the pile of clean laundry in the corner, the pile of dirty laundry in the other corner, and finally grab it from the pocket of the jean shorts I wore yesterday. "What?"

"You don't live in New York anymore," Frankie says. "When someone calls you, it's customary to say hello."

"Customary, my ass." I tap my phone onto speaker and open the closet. "I've never said hello to you before, and I'm not starting now." I slide over a box with the side of my foot, step on my tiptoes to look on the shelf, then kick over a pile of jackets. *Seriously, where are my Converse?* "And I'm not changing the way I talk just because I moved from the city."

"People around here are different. I have to deprogram you before you assimilate too much into Spring Harbors' society. You can't be all direct and in their face like on the East Coast," Frankie says. "Here, there's like... conversational foreplay. You have to ease into it."

Frankie acts like I've never lived here before. We grew up here, not more than ten miles from the house we now own. But it's different, being here as a thirty-two-year-old than as a child. "Being direct is not rude. It's efficient." In New York, people value directness. Back there, everything is on a clock. The quicker you get your point across, the quicker you can move on. It's a societal norm cherished by everyone, from the servers to the executives.

But here in the beautiful, lush, sleepy town of Spring Harbors, instead of saying, "I'll have an Americano, little cream, thanks," I need to flash a toothy smile, and say things like, "Good morning! Beautiful day. Can you believe this weather? I'll have an Americano with just a splash of cream. Thank you so much," or people will think I'm a snob.

So annoying. Who's got time for that? Not me.

"Speaking of being direct, what do you need? I'm just about to leave." *Oh, there are my shoes!* Buried under my pile of sweatshirts. Sure, it's been over half a year since I've been back, but I haven't had a chance to fully unpack. Who knew revamping a failing Christmas tree farm business would take so much time?

"Don't kill me," Frankie says.

Oh no. I freeze at the tone. "This means I'm going to actually kill you. What did you do?"

A sharp inhale comes through the speaker. "I can't fly back tonight anymore."

"What?" A flicker of panic rushes through me. Tomorrow's the "Christmas in August" event in Duluth—my first-ever vendor event where I'm getting word out that a new Christmas sheriff is in town, ready to knock the striped red-and-green socks off everyone with her new and improved Christmas tree farm. My sister is supposed to sit with me, flash her dimples, flex her absurdly fit biceps, and charm customers into coming to my place. "Frankie, *you promised* you'd sit with me."

"I know, I'm really sorry. Long story short, but some major stuff blew up at work and I can't leave. I'll fill you in later. But Morgan will be there with you, and we both know she's friendlier than both of us combined."

I push my fingertips into my temple and sit on the edge of the bed. It's not Frankie's fault, but it doesn't mean I won't be unfairly irritated with her for a solid day. Last year, Frankie landed the job of a lifetime to be a photographer for the high-end lifestyle brand Birch & Willow, with its beautiful website, product line, and New York flagship store. So now she divides her time between Minnesota and New York. Her job is seriously demanding, and in all fairness, she told me last month there was a possibility that she wouldn't make it to the vendor event. But I can't shake the memories of when our parents did shit like this—leaving us at the last minute to fend for ourselves. A lifetime of not coming to choir concerts, or school programs, or forgetting teacher conferences fills my mind. Heat rises in my chest, and I blow it out before I say something snarky.

"I swear to God, if you don't ask Morgan to marry you, I'm going to. She is literally saving you from me kicking your ass." Clearly, I'm joking. Where I'm more the soft, curvy kind, with boobs bigger than my head, my sister's the kind of woman who does real push-ups, drives a Harley, and takes absolutely no shit. There is no way I could actually kick her ass.

My sister knows exactly who she is. Frankie left home at eighteen to become a successful photographer in New York. Now she's reunited with Morgan, the love of her life, and has a job at one of the most coveted magazines in the world. Everything she puts her mind to, she makes happen.

Me? I'm chasing Frankie around the country 'cause I'm too scared to be alone, and still figuring my crap out, day by day.

"Seriously, Quinn, I'm super bummed, and am really sorry," Frankie says. "But you got this. I believe in you."

Do I actually have this? I'm not sure. When my aunt and uncle decided to sell their Christmas tree farm, they were so desperate to keep it in the family that they offered it to me at a great price. After spending a month getting tarot card readings throughout Manhattan, manifesting for hours in my journal, and following all the recommendations for each layer in my astrological profile, I thought the price was a sign from the universe, saving me from having security drag me out of the office after I stabbed my boss in the eye with one of his overpriced gold pens. Warm sleigh-filled memories, probably way too much wine, and the idea of having Frankie beside me again inspired me to pull the plug.

Frankie had warned me, had said that the farm was not how I'd remembered, how much work it would be. But I knew that she and Morgan—who's a local wedding planner—had spent the previous summer remodeling the barn for a wedding. So really, how bad could it be?

In January, when I stepped onto the property for the first time. I got my answer. *Bad*.

Although the trees were in good shape, and the rustic barn looked great from the remodel, everything else was a complete shit show. From the cracked fence, to broken-down machinery scattering the field like tombstones in a graveyard, to boxes and boxes and more boxes of junk filling every space, I nearly passed out. After months of chipping and limbing, cleaning every part of the property, a crash course on irrigation, planting, and seedlings... finally, I'm in a place to recreate the Christmas magic.

"You are marginally forgiven, but I'm still debating what your betrayal will cost you." I toss the phone on my bed and tie my shoelaces. "You'll be happy to know that I'm going to Zoey's today."

"*Finally.*"

Not sure how much I love the pep in Frankie's voice. She and Morgan have tried to get me to meet Zoey, of Zoey's Bakery—apparently the best baked goods this side of Lake Superior—since I moved here. And I've done everything I can do to *not* meet Zoey.

Sure, they've told me about Zoey. And I've picked up that she's sweet, funny, and kind, and exactly *not* the type of woman I need in my life. I know what they're doing—trying to get me to settle down. Frankie tried this in New York, too. But settling down is not for me. I don't have time for relationships. For anyone, really. Besides, a holier-than-thou snow angel is not my type. I like my women messy, unhinged, and definitely not looking for attachment —a mirror image of myself. Relationships are so low on my priority scale they don't even register. I've got things to do. Which, currently, is finding my purse so I can leave.

"I actually stopped in there a few days ago to put in my order, but she was gone," I say, marching through the house looking for my purse. *Linen closet, maybe? Bathroom? Kitchen?*

Zoey's Bakery is super cute. All pale pink, white, and rose gold with such beautiful, artistic cupcake arrangements, I couldn't believe they were real at first. From the pink-and-white-striped awning outside the door, to the pale gray hardwood floors, to the couple of white café style tables and chairs, the place almost reminded me of something I'd find back in New York. And the cookies Frankie mentioned a million times deserved the hype. Sure, Frankie and I share the same Lee family sweet tooth, but she nearly pants like Pavlov's dog every time someone brings up the shop. After I sunk my teeth into a cupcake, I understood why.

"She wasn't there? I think she works like twenty-four-seven. Must've been urgent," Frankie says. "Make sure you have one of her lavender and vanilla macaroons when you go today."

"Yeah, yeah." *Oh! There's my purse.* Hanging on a rack outside the coat closet which can only mean one thing—someone way more responsible than me hung it up. "Okay, I really do have to bounce," I say, strapping the purse around myself.

"For real, though, be nice," Frankie says with a caution in her tone that I really, really don't appreciate. "She's one of the good ones."

Whatever. Doesn't matter if Zoey is one of the "good ones." It wouldn't even matter if Zoey is a real-life angel floating from heaven. I'm in town for one reason only—recreate the Christmas magic for our town, one tree at a time.

TWO

ZOEY

For the past six years, every time the little silver bell on the door to my bakery rings announcing a new customer, a jolt of dopamine rushes through me. I'm not immune to how very lucky I am that I live out my dream every day. After living in Spring Harbors, Minnesota, my entire life—the best town in America, mind you—and opening my dream bakery, I usually need to pinch myself.

Today, sadly, is not one of those days. It's not quite as bad as the day six weeks ago, when I recreated every cartoon-banana-slipping scene from my childhood. But instead of a banana peel, it was loose flour on the kitchen floor. And instead of doing the splits and having stars and birds flutter above my head, my glasses flew off my face and skidded across the floor, I landed on my butt with one leg sky-high, and the other leg going exactly where it shouldn't.

Caleb, the flour culprit and my part-time employee, felt so terrible I was sure he was going to cry into a rack of fresh pistachio macaroons. After some uncharacteristic swear words (including the f-bomb which I never, *ever* use) had slipped from my mouth, I hobbled up on my fractured foot and assured him it was okay.

It wasn't okay, of course. I had reminded him several times that morning to sweep up the floor and he hadn't. But making him feel bad would not fuse my bone back together, so I sent him funny

GIFs from the ER, and the next day brought him a coffee so he knew I wasn't mad.

So today is not *quite* as bad as that. As I pull on gloves and start carefully packaging up the eight-dozen red and blue cookies for Quinn Lee, the sister of one of my regulars, Frankie, I try to focus on the methodical boxing, and not the poop-tastic morning I've had so far. It began with Mrs. Pinkerton. She's very sweet, but her snappy Pomeranian is not, and it got loose once again and tore around my shop. I'd promised myself if it ever happened again, I'd enforce a service-animal-only rule.

Instead, I sent her home with a free cupcake.

And then my sister called, needing my help with babysitting my nephew, Noah, this weekend. Yes, I love Noah more than almost any human in the world, and yes, my sister is a single mom who works hard and needs a break, and yes, my mom helps a lot and wasn't free on Sunday. But this is the last weekend of the summer. After having a cast on since mid-June, it *finally* got removed yesterday and I really wanted to take a proper day off.

So, what did I do? I offered for Noah to not only hang out with me but sleep overnight.

My former therapist would be very, very disappointed in me. I *hate* disappointing people.

"Hey, I just double-checked the delivery, and it looks like the driver left a five-pound bag of hazelnuts off the order," Luna, my part-time employee, says as she bounces into the back room.

She reminds me of what a little sister would be like if I had a little sister, although we look almost completely different. Her short pink pixie cut, facial piercings, and full sleeve tattoos are almost my alter ego. However, if I ever attempted any of those things, I'd look like I was dressing up for Halloween as someone way cooler than me.

"Do you want to talk to him?" Luna asks.

Ugh. I really need to be firmer. The delivery guy, George, is the nicest man, but he often forgets things, and the following week, when he remembers what he forgot the previous week, he forgets something else. I take a tentative step with my new walking boot, pull my shoulders back, and lift my chin.

Be strong, be firm, set boundaries. George will still like me even if I make him go back and get the order. *Be strong, be firm, set boundaries...*

"Hey there, Zoey!" George says. "So sorry, looks like I forgot the hazelnuts. I'm going to be making a run back through town later this week, on Wednesday. Is it okay if I swing by then and drop it off?"

I swallow a way too big of a lump in my throat and thumb my glasses back up my nose. "Oh yikes. Gosh. Um, you know I really need those. They are, well, a key ingredient to so many of my items. And tomorrow is a heavy baking day," I lie. Every day is a heavy baking day.

His mouth twists, and I see it in his eyes. He's disappointed. In the situation, in me. And then he won't like me. And if he won't like me, his deliveries might get worse, and people will think I'm terrible. Word will spread around town that I'm unreasonable, that this guy made one mistake, and I'm forcing him to work extra hours.

George taps his clipboard against his leg. "They're all the way back in Duluth, and it's the end of my shift. To go there, back here, and back... we're looking at ninety minutes, easy."

Don't do it. Stay strong. He is the one that messed up the order, not me. "Oh yes, of course. Next week is totally fine! I'll just scoot right over to the grocery store and pick up what I need in the interim." *Ugh.* Now I'm so disappointed in myself I might deny myself dessert tonight. My old therapist would officially fire me as a client.

Two years ago, after Josie and I broke up after a decade together, I started therapy. Sure, I learned some communication skills, fleshed out some things that led to our breakup, and tried to build empathy for myself for having a failed relationship. The therapist guided me in discovering why I have this deep, intrinsic need for people to like me, why I avoid hard conversations, and encouraged me to take the lessons I learned from my last relationship into any new relationships.

So, what lessons did I learn? For that first year, the one I held on to most was that I will never, ever open myself up the way that I did with Josie. That the pain was so deep, so profound, and that singlehood was a blessing from the gods.

But this last year, I spent my downtime really evaluating what I want and need and concluded that as painful as Josie's and my breakup was, I'm not giving up my fairy-tale dream. Some people are meant to travel this world alone, and some are not. I'm one of those not slated for singlehood. I want to fulfill my life partner, rescue dog, picket fence dreams. My soulmate is out there. I just need to find her.

I blink away those thoughts and focus on George.

"You're the best, Zoey!" he says, tucking the clipboard under his arm. "I promise I'll bring it on Wednesday."

"Sure thing. Have a great weekend." I smile brightly and wave. When I turn back, I shake my head. I might not be in therapy anymore, but I know I've got to do better. Starting now, I'm not taking any more poop from anyone today, no matter how hard it may be.

I hobble behind the counter to help with customers but wish I could bake bread. A perfect creative outlet is when I work with our custom cupcakes, cookies, and cakes. Adding edible glitter edging on my cookies and designing chocolate stilettos with gold bow tops fills that need in me. But working with dough, flexing my fingers, kneading out my frustrations into a ball of gluteny goodness is heaven.

The door rings and a couple of giggling teens pop in with beach bags stuffed with towels and hats. After they order cake pops and a cupcake, one girl leans towards me. "You're Zoey? The owner?"

"Sure am," I say with a proud smile.

She plants her hands on top of the display case with a soft smack. "Oh my God, has anyone told you that you look like Zooey

Deschanel? It's so crazy. Like, you really, *really* look like her. I know the show is super old, but I am *obsessed* with *New Girl*. The Jess and Nick story... I mean, classic, right?"

Have I heard before that I look like this actress? Maybe only a hundred times. I'm not sure if it's because I have long brown hair with bangs and glasses, or the blue eyes, or the fact that my name is actually Zoey, but it's a compliment, so I'll take it.

Once I send the teens on their way, I return to the kitchen, grab my Sharpie, and scribble *Quinn Lee* on top of the four oversized cookie boxes.

Quinn Lee... I'm actually pretty excited about meeting her. I've known Morgan Rose for years. She owns a wedding and event planning business in town and is one of my top customers for her clients. And when she reconnected with her high school girlfriend, Frankie, last year, I met her, too. Within a short while, they both started chatting to me about Quinn. *A lot.*

Spring Harbors is a small-enough town. Everyone heard about Pete and Patty's Christmas tree farm getting sold to Quinn Lee. For so many years, that farm had served this town. But, from what I understand, it went downhill fast. Josie and I went there maybe five or six years ago to pick out a tree. But it was so depressing, like the place where Christmas dreams go to die, that we never returned.

So yes, I know about Quinn Lee. But every time Frankie and Morgan chat with me about her, I get this underlying impression that they're trying to set me up. "You two have so much in common," "Can't wait for you guys to meet each other," and "We should all hang out some time," are common themes through our conversations.

Last year, when they started talking about Quinn, I thought the Josie scars on my heart would never heal and would forever taint any potential relationship. So, for my safety and sanity—and any potential mate's—it was simply best not to engage. As politely as I could so they didn't get mad at me, I told them all my time goes into my shop, and I have zero social life. Which was not a lie.

However, now that I'm in a better place emotionally, and those scars have mostly faded, maybe a new... friend... is exactly what the doctor ordered. Things have slowly settled around my shop, and fall—my favorite season—is right around the corner. Walking hand in hand with mitts on and a shared pumpkin latte while watching the leaves change colors sounds wonderful. Besides, I just got off crutches and cannot wait to do something outside.

Speaking of my foot, my gosh, this walking boot is not comfortable. I sit in a chair by the prep stand and elevate until the throbbing stops.

A moment later, Caleb pops into the kitchen through the swinging door. "Hey, Zoey? Quinn Lee is here to grab her items. Need some help carrying them up front?"

I could probably manage, but I'm getting used to the new boot, and the last thing I need is to trip and spill the contents of these pink boxes. "Yes, that'd be great."

When I step out to the front, I take all of five seconds to scan the small crowd in front of the large display case and pick out the woman I've never seen before. Because had she ever been in my shop, I definitely would've noticed. *Wow*. Red curly hair that reaches just below her shoulders with coils that seem to spring with reckless abandon. Freckles that I can see all the way from across the room. Short, ripped denim shorts and an off-the-shoulder summer knit sweater holds in curves that I'd give just about anything for.

Quinn Lee is *beautiful*.

THREE

ZOEY

Wow.

I stare at Quinn Lee in front of my counter, looking at her for the first time, and try to recall everything Frankie and Morgan told me about her this past year. Smart, yes. Funny, yes. Moved back from New York, yes. Setting up the farm, yes. But both of them failed to warn me that Quinn is *stunning*. Like gut-wrenchingly, from-a-different-era, pinup-worthy, stunning.

I set a box of her cookies at the edge of the counter and fumble with the stack. I really hope she likes these cookies, but it'd surprise me if she didn't. There are many things in my life that I'm not confident about, but my baked goods are on point.

Be cool. I clear my throat. "Quinn?"

She looks up, and uff da. That smile. It's so wide and beautiful it takes up almost her entire face. Maybe it's the way the sunlight is hitting the room, bouncing off the gold strip on the display case, and ricocheting to her, but everything about Quinn Lee darn near glows.

"Hey! Zoey. *Finally*, my sister can get off my ass. We're actually meeting," she says, her hair bouncing like a drumbeat with her as she hops closer to the counter. "I'm telling you now, I'll absolutely not live up to any expectation you may have about me. Frankie likes to lie and exaggerate and is never to be trusted."

Her voice is fun, lively, and raspier than I would've expected for someone so... springy.

"I won't tell her you said that." I smile and breathe my bangs out of my eyes. "Your sister is great. So is Morgan. I think I see Morgan more than my own family sometimes."

"Morgan is the best. But don't cover for Frankie." She leans closer like she's about to tell me a secret and hikes an eyebrow. "We all know she's in here more than she lets on."

Quinn grins. I really, really like her grin. It's warm and bright, like a citrus cookie. Her lips are dark pink, highlighted by her heavy dusting of freckles, and maybe... just maybe... Frankie and Morgan were on to something when they said me and Quinn should meet. "I will not confirm or deny her consumer habits," I say. "But I will say since she moved to town, I go through product quicker than before. Might just be a coincidence, though."

When Quinn shakes her head, a few of her beautiful red coils smack her in the face. "Frankie is a sugar addict, and the more we can support her, the better her health journey will be. But... I'll let her know that you're not a narc. That'll score you some points."

I giggle. What is happening, here? I am a serious business-woman who is polite and kind, definitely not a giggler. And yet, here I am, yep, *giggling*, like I'm a teenager. It's like I've never been around a pretty woman before. I swear, this is what happens when you live in a small town your whole life, you know everyone, and there's only a handful of queer folks. *Pull it together*. I grip the edge of the display case as I shuffle over to the side, away from the other customers.

Quinn dips her head around the corner and looks at my feet with a twisted mouth. "Ouch. That looks like it hurts like hell."

"Well, I'm finally off crutches, so I've officially entered my 'winning phase.'" I reach out my hand and give Quinn's a shake. Her hand is warm, firm, and I very much try to ignore the tiny tingle that flies up to my elbow. "I'm glad I get to meet you in person. Frankie and Morgan have tried their darndest to set up a time for us to hang out, but it's just been so bananas around here. I promise I'm not as antisocial as I may appear."

Quinn waves away the words. "Ah. No sweat at all. Frankie has big ideas, but I haven't had a day off since February, so we're probably in the same boat."

I really want to ask her how it's going revamping the tree farm, but the line is steadily growing, and Caleb is fumbling to both fill orders and do the register. "Sorry I wasn't here the other day when you stopped in to order these. Had a follow-up doctor appointment for my mangled foot."

"No worries. Foot definitely takes precedence." She loops her thumb under her purse strap and bounces back on her heels. "Your employee, Luna, I think, helped me out."

I rarely get nervous around women. Mostly because I'm not interested in anyone, so there's no need for sweaty palms and a dry mouth. But here I am, my heartbeat kicking up, and words fumbling from my tongue. In all fairness, Frankie mentioned us all getting together at least a half dozen times, so there's a little bit of pressure for me to perform. I really like Frankie and don't want to let her down, which means I want her sister to like me.

Which must explain the nerves.

I carefully tuck the boxes into two large bags and drag them up to the counter, gripping the counter to not slip.

Quinn's fingertips eagerly tap together, her stacked rings tinkling like a chime. "Oh, I'm *so* excited for these cookies. Legit, Frankie doesn't shut the hell up about the stuff you make."

My cheeks grow warm. I hate that I'm such a blusher. Every emotion displays on my face like a neon sign, and the only way to hide what I'm feeling is by burying my head in my hands. "That's really *sweet* of her to say, a heavy amount of pun intended." Oh gosh, that was an epic level of cheese. So embarrassing. Am I trying to flirt here? It's been a decade since I last flirted with anyone, so my rustiness is probably justified. But this is painful.

"Not sure if Frankie or Morgan told you, but I'm doing the

huge Christmas in August event in Duluth tomorrow." Quinn tugs her credit card from the wallet and hands it over. "I'm so freaking nervous. I've held a few weddings at the farm this past spring, but this is my first big event. Trying to get the word out that the Christmas tree farm is back and better than ever."

I definitely know about the vendor event. In fact, a few times in the past, I sold treats there. But it was so much work that I prefer to stay in the safety and comfort of my shop. Besides—and I'm picturing myself knocking on wood—I don't really need that event to garner more business. The community is great, and my shop is usually full.

Funny how so much of the rest of the country does Christmas in July events, but this town started a unique tradition. The weekend before Labor Day, Duluth throws this extravaganza, enticing the last of the summer tourists to spend their money in our town. It's like the summer bookends, kicking off with Grandma's Marathon, where tourists and runners tear through our streets, and ending with this massive Christmas event. The event is super fun, like a pop of Christmas color while dying under the Minnesota humidity. "I'm sure people will be excited to know the farm's being revamped." When Caleb finishes ringing up the next customer, I swipe Quinn's credit card. "I bet that's a ton of work."

"*Soooo* much work," Quinn says. "From the irrigation system to fixing the fence, it's like a bottomless well of shit I need to do. In the spring, me and the crew planted five thousand seedlings. Five *thousand*. I never want to see another seedling in my life."

"Whoa. That is a ton. I can't believe you will have so many trees."

Quinn sidesteps a couple of kids who plaster themselves against the display case to look at the cupcakes. Mental note to wipe that baby down after Quinn leaves.

"Just a few short eight years and I'll be the proud owner of thousands of Christmas trees," she says.

"Yikes, that's such a long time." I hand the credit card back. "What do you do in the interim?"

"Thankfully, my aunt and uncle, who owned the place before me, maintained the other trees, so all of them are in various stages of growth. It's more everything else on the property that went downhill in a hurry." The kids run away, and she steps back towards me. "This year I'm going to bring in precut ones from a different farmer. So really, it's all the *other* stuff I'm trying to do... I want to create a gift shop with ornaments, wreaths, have a huge fire pit outside, those kinds of things."

This sounds like so much fun. Christmas season is my absolute favorite time of the year, and crafting is my favorite hobby. During the holiday season, I make my bakery snowflake- sparkly, like you're transported directly into a Hallmark movie. Quinn reviving that space and bringing back the holiday spirit is just what Kris Kringle ordered himself. When I was younger, that tree farm was magical—hayrides, Santa Claus, jolly music, and fun gifts. I cannot wait to see what she can pull off.

"That sounds like a ton of work," I say, tugging at the strings of my apron. "Thankfully, since you live with Morgan, she can give you a lot of ideas and help you out."

Quinn's smile drops, and it feels like someone just siphoned all the air in the room. "I don't need her help. I've got this."

Oh whoa... I so didn't mean it like that. "Oh, I just meant she's such a great decorator and designer that she's a good resource to have... since you live with her and all..." My cheeks are warm. Too warm. I should sit.

Quinn tugs her lips into her mouth and sighs. Well, this has been fun. Until I blew it. My therapist was right—my communication skills are clearly terrible. How am I ever going to find a life mate when I can't even hold a ten-minute conversation?

I move to stuff the last box in a bag, when Quinn holds up a hand with a smile.

"Hey, can I grab one of those really quick?" she asks. "I haven't had breakfast yet, and we all know that's the most important meal. Nothing better than a few cookies to kick off the day."

My chest lifts. Whew. Maybe I didn't totally blow this. "Of course!" I open up the box and spin it towards Quinn.

Her face drops. Again. Like, *really* drops, with a look that sinks my belly all the way to my toes.

"No…" Quinn's eyebrows wrinkle. She glances down at the box, at me, and back again. "These are blue and red."

A heaviness lodges in my throat, and I swallow. I know they're blue and red. I'm the one who packaged them up. "Yes, they're blue and red. That's what you ordered."

"No. I didn't." All smiles are gone from her voice.

I push up my slipped glasses and double-check the order slip. Yep, right there, printed across the top—*blue and red*. I read it once, twice, three times, and swallow. "This definitely says you ordered eight dozen blue and red cookies."

A thin pink stripe grows across Quinn's neck. "*No, I didn't.* I know what I ordered."

Her tone switches to tense, which makes me tense, and now we're in a bottomless bucket of tension. My belly twists, hard, and stays knotted. Any moment now, I'm going to stop breathing. "I'm really sorry, Quinn. I don't know what to say. But here." I hold the order form out to her and point to the clearly printed *eight dozen blue and red cookies*. "It says blue and red cookies."

"Why would it say that? Why would I have possibly said I wanted *blue* and red cookies for a Christmas event? I even talked to that Luna girl about it. She said her parents go to it every year and I'm going to love it." Quinn crosses her arms across her chest, and her fingers tap against her biceps. "So, if that slip says *blue* and red, not *green* and red, it was her mistake, not mine."

My shoulders brace. I blow air up my face to fan myself. It's definitely warm in here. I'm pitting out and will need an extra swipe of deodorant any moment now. But Luna is a great employee. She's been with me since she was in high school, and I don't take too kindly to outsiders from the big city coming in here and berating my staff.

"You… signed it," I stammer, then straighten my back. "You

signed it," I say, not quite matching the firmness in Quinn's tone, but at least inching towards it, and point at her signature. "Right here."

Quinn stares at the order slip, her face flushing into a myriad of colors. "No... there must be something wrong. I wouldn't have done that..." She exhales through her nose and a few terrible, excruciating moments pass. "It's okay. I just... I just need you to fix them."

I almost laugh. Does she see around my shop? As lovely as the first few minutes of this interaction have been, the line has doubled since we started chatting, and my customers expect a certain level of speediness. "I'm really sorry, Quinn. We can't just fix these. We've shut down the ovens for the day and—"

"Well, turn them back on." Pink stains Quinn's cheeks, and splashes across her freckles.

My breath tightens, turning my pulse heavy and thick in my throat. "That's not how it works." I mean, obviously, we can turn them back on, but we prep at night, bake in the early morning, serve customers during the day. It's our rotation. I might be a pushover on some things, but I am not changing my entire business model because Quinn thinks she ordered green cookies. "We do not have time to fix these. It took us hours to make these."

Quinn softens only a fraction and pushes her palm into her forehead. "I'll come back in the morning, so you have time to redo it."

My anxiety is currently through the roof. Like surpassed the building, out the chimney, heading on its way to the North Pole, through the roof. We have an overcapacity prep schedule tonight, and the morning baker is already coming in an hour early. I'm not adding eight dozen additional cookies to that list.

How is Frankie so very nice and cool, and Quinn is decidedly *not* cool? At all. She's not even that nice. And I really, really, do not like not-nice people. "We won't have time. I'm sorry, we already have more orders tomorrow than what we can handle." I'm trying so hard to keep a smile on my face that I'm gritting my teeth. All the moisture in my mouth catapults to the back of my neck and any moment now, a gross sweat trickle is going to bead down my spine.

"Are you actually serious right now?" she fumes, her cheeks even more red than before. "You don't have time? That is not my problem. That's for you to sort out."

The idea that anyone, especially Frankie's sister, won't like me grinds at me and will most definitely keep me awake tonight. And since Quinn's a local business owner, there's always an opportunity for collaboration. But I refuse to take any more of this nonsense, regardless if I work with her sister and roommate. "There is nothing we can do."

"But I need these for tomorrow," she says, dropping her crossed arms to rest her hands on her waist. "Your employee is the one who fucked up, not me."

This earns Quinn a hard look from the woman in line and an even harder twist in my stomach. "Now... just a second here." Who the heck does Quinn think she is? She comes into *my* place of business and talks smack about Luna—the girl who works her butt off for me every day—and then drops the f-enheimer right here in the middle of my family friendly shop? No. I absolutely am not standing for this. Between the dog that got loose, and the delivery guy who forgets my things, and my broken foot, and Josie... I have let way too much go today, this past week, this last decade, and I. Am. Done.

"Luna is an excellent employee. She's here before everyone, stays late, and I'm... I will not let you talk about her like this." My hand winds the apron string so tight around my fingers I may cut off circulation.

A long, icky moment stretches between us. An unfamiliar and uncomfortable standoff ensues, and something in me clicks. I refuse to be the one who breaks first.

Quinn shakes her head, and this, *this!*, is a look of disappointment that makes my insides cry. But right now, I'm so heated, it's only slightly affecting me.

"This is completely unacceptable," she says. "And you need to make it right."

"I'll take these back and refund your money." I'll take a hit, for sure. But I can put them in the display case today and tomorrow, half price them, and chalk it up to never doing business with Quinn Lee again.

"I can't do that. I need these cookies for tomorrow," she says with a deep frown, and an even deeper sigh. "This really sucks."

Enough! "Well, perhaps you should get your cookies from somewhere else from now on."

Oh no, I didn't.

But yep, I sure did. Yes, I said it with a calm voice and forced smile, but I said it, nonetheless. My therapist would give me a gold star for the day for this one.

Quinn cocks her head, her freckles darkening along with her eyes. "Perhaps I will."

She grabs the large bags. She's so much shorter than me that I almost offer to help, to make sure she doesn't trip as she juggles the cookies out the door. Thankfully, a customer steps in and holds the door open. Quinn bolts down the sidewalk with a very heavy, very annoyed stomp.

I let out a ragged sigh.

And *that* is my introduction to Quinn Lee. Which never, ever, has to happen again.

FOUR

QUINN

From the less-than-fifteen minutes I was inside Zoey's bakery, the late August summer sun heated the inside of the truck so much it smells like burning vinyl. I cautiously set the boxes of the *definitely wrong* cookies on the seat and roll down the windows to let out the trapped air.

I jump into the front seat, and fire up Truck Norris—the family truck with a very long history, starting with my grandma Peaches, who gave it to Frankie, who then gave it to my dad, who then, after a bunch of negotiation and some cash, gave it back to me so that I can use it for work.

My knuckles turn white from vise gripping the steering wheel. How did I make that mistake? How, how, how? *I know* I asked for green and red cookies. I can't believe I signed that order without validating the details. For the last decade, I've double, then triple-checked everything, partly for fear of my boss laying into me, partly because it was my job to make sure everything ran efficiently, partly because even if the state of my bedroom and house shows the Queen Chaos side of my personality, my business side is type A to the extreme.

Tears spring to my eyes. This is exactly what happened in

New York—the VP yelling at me because I made careless mistakes like this, even though I swore I didn't.

When I was in Zoey's a few days ago putting in this order, it was so hectic. Customers packed the shop like the A train during commuting hours, kids were running around, some dog got loose and terrorized the ankles of everyone, including me. I frantically signed the order slip just to get the hell out of there.

I push my palm into my forehead and squeeze my eyelids to contain the tears. So stupid. I'm smarter than this. I'm a business owner now, and should never, ever sign a contract without rereading the fine print. If I'm making these kinds of careless mistakes when I order cookies, where else am I going to fail?

But Zoey told me I should get my cookies elsewhere? I mean... *what*? Really? Okay, maybe I shouldn't have said that her employee effed up. That wasn't nice, but everything was accurate, direct, and to the point.

Whatever. I can get my cookies from anywhere... like the only other two options that exist. *Shit*. And really, is this anger about the cookies? No, it's not. I've been in a constant state of freak-out mode since moving here, and this, coming before the big event tomorrow, was the final nail in the coffin.

I ease out onto the road, hands clutching a firm ten and two, keenly aware that I've splashed my door with the logo LEE'S CHRISTMAS TREE FARM AND EVENT CENTER. No matter how gratifying it'd be to rev the engine and peel out of here, I can't. Thankfully, I had the foresight when I showed up earlier to not parallel park this beast. After taking the New York City public transportation for the last fifteen years, I probably couldn't even park a Fiat right now.

The cranked-up air-conditioning is barely making a dent in the heat. I roll to a stop in front of a crosswalk, and peek at the half dozen or so people walking on the sidewalk on Main Street. *Half dozen*. Not hundreds. Not the sardine-packed sidewalks in the Financial District where I could feel people's breath on me and smell the coffee in their hands when I hustled from the subway to my office building.

A woman scurrying across the crosswalk waves to me. I squint out the windshield. *Do I know her?* Ah... the thank-you wave—for doing the bare minimum as a driver and not plowing her down in the middle of a crosswalk. I wave back and smile. Driving is taking me a little bit to get used to. But the thank-you waves will take even longer.

The fresh, heated Minnesota air streams through the windows as I bump down Main Street and wait for the air-conditioning to kick in. Another thing I'm getting used to, being back in Spring Harbors? The air. New York has a different smell than Minnesota. Exhaust, the savory smoke from restaurants and vendors, some days the tangy garbage smell of too many people occupying a space until the sanitation workers clear the streets. Here it's clean. Pure. Like freshwater, pine trees, and freshly mowed lawn.

"I can't believe that happened," I mutter. I can't blame my actions on New York directness, either. My stomach knots. I pop open the cookie box and sink my teeth into the blue and red cookies.

And, of course. Sigh. They're freaking delicious. I polish off one in three bites and before I reach the end of the block, I'm going in for a second. I cannot make enemies of someone who can bake like this.

Or... who looks like that. For God's sake. At the red light, I push my thumbs into my forehead and pull in a heavy breath. Sure, Frankie and Morgan made an offhand comment about Zoey being cute if you're into the nerdy-sexy librarian vibe (which I absolutely am). But they failed to mention that Zoey was *gorgeous*. Messy bun, bangs sweeping to her crystal-blue eyes, chunky black eyeglasses, gorgeous.

At the house, I kick off my shoes at the mat and slump on the couch. I have a million things I need to do, but right now I'm itchy, restless, and feeling pretty shitty about the whole Zoey situation. Maybe I should apologize?

Or maybe she shouldn't have blamed me for something her staff screwed up. At least, I *think* they screwed up. Ugh.

When I left the city, I thought the whole blame thing was done. Clearly, I was wrong.

God, this sucks. I rub the corner of my shoulder with a thumb and try some deep breathing exercises, but it's useless. Before I meet hundreds of strangers tomorrow at the Christmas event, I need to release this pent-up tension. I grab my phone and start swiping through a dating app, going directly to the "looking to keep it light" and "casual vibes only" posts. I drop a couple of "hey, love your profile, you around tonight?"-type messages and wait for a few bites. It's Saturday after all. Someone within a sixty-mile radius must be looking to let off some steam.

The phone buzzes against my palm. *Yes!* That was quick.

Grrr. Buzzkill. My sister.

Did you meet Zoey?

She follows with a raised eyebrow emoji message. Did I meet Zoey? Yes. Did the woman with the softest, sweetest voice and eyes as big as sugar cookies essentially kick me out? Also, yes.

Sure did. Not great. Probably won't go back.

The phone rings immediately. "What do you mean it didn't go great? How can it *not* go great? She's literally one of the nicest human beings in the world."

I punch the pillow behind my head and lower myself into the couch. "Really? That wasn't my experience. She told me from now on I should get my cookies from someplace else."

"What... Oh no. What did you do?"

Heat flashes across my chest. "Really? How about defending me for once? Maybe *she* did something. I swear to God, I am always the one taking the blame for everything." Silence meets me and my snarky tone. I take a deep breath and slowly exhale. "I told her that her employee effed up my order."

"You didn't. Did you actually use the f-word?" It's like I can hear Frankie clench her jaw through the phone. "I don't even think I've heard Zoey say anything stronger than 'gosh darn.' Seriously, Quinn? Come *on*. You've got to control that temper."

"Control my temper? Are you serious right now? It's not like I threw punches or anything." But *maybe* I went a tad too far. I retell Frankie the chaotic story of ordering on Wednesday and everything that happened when I stepped in there today.

I leave out, however, how this Zoey person my sister keeps talking about not only surpassed my expectations but flew to the freaking moon. Reading energy of others is a lifetime survival skill, and I instantly saw she's a good person. And still, I stomped out of there like a toddler not getting their prized Christmas present. Ugh. I'm such a dick.

"You're still letting your old boss win. This isn't you, Quinn. At all," Frankie says. "Yes, you're a massive pain in the ass, but you're not someone who says that to people, especially when you first meet."

Frankie's words hit me, hard. I want to say that it's not true, that deep down I'm heartless and don't care about people, and it's not my responsibility to coddle those around me, but Frankie's right. This *isn't* me. I didn't recognize myself in that shop. When Zoey said I made a mistake, that the order was my fault, I saw red. Actually, I saw the former VP's face, saying this in front of a crowd of peers and leaders, then messaging me late at night retelling me what I did wrong. The amount of times he did that has blurred, but the humiliation still stings.

Frankie takes a long breath. "I'm sure things will get smoothed over. I know you're under a ton of stress with the farm and everything. Hopefully, you both can let this go," she says. "What are you up to now?"

A notification pings me from the app and I swipe it open.

"Currently, I'm fielding a message from the dating app about meeting up with someone tonight outside of Duluth."

A judgmental sigh sounds over the phone. "Tell me you're being safe."

"Do I sanitize my strap-on after every session?" I say, wiggling back into the couch. "Sure do. I'm not a monster."

"That is absolutely not what I meant."

I know what she meant. But Frankie has played a surrogate mother role for me my entire life and sometimes forgets that I'm a sexually independent woman in my early thirties, not a dumb, horny teenager. "Just because you've been with like two people in your whole life—"

"Four."

"Whatever. Doesn't mean the rest of us rock that lesbian chastity belt, you know?" I put Frankie on speaker and review the profile of the woman who pinged. "I'm only young once. I'm not looking for anything, and I need to work off this energy. You prefer the gym. I prefer banging it out with some hot woman."

"I'm serious. You really freak me out sometimes. I need to make sure you're safe."

"Yes, yes, I'm safe. Stop worrying." Sometimes I wonder if this is what a healthy relationship looks like for people who have caring moms. Chatting about safety, making sure that I'm not getting harmed, physically or mentally. Although I've accepted our parents are who they are, I can't help my mind fluttering to what a supportive upbringing might have felt like. "Just so you know, I chat with all potential dates to confirm there are no serial killer vibes, then usually meet in a public place to really confirm they're not a serial killer, and *then* I go back to their place, so they'll never know where I live. Besides, I hardly ever use my real name."

"Are you kidding?" Frankie spits out. "You're never going to connect to anyone if you don't use your real name or go on an actual date where you engage in a healthy conversation."

"Are you slut shaming me? Have you ever thought maybe this is what I want?"

"God, you're exhausting," Frankie says. "No, of course I'm not slut shaming."

I know Frankie doesn't get it. Truly. She's with Morgan, her first love, the love of her life. They met as kids. Stayed together throughout high school and then reunited last year for life. Frankie and Morgan are like these weird emperor penguins who mate once, and it's for life.

Me, I'm like a big, hyper cat that hates being caged, and Frankie just doesn't understand that what she and Morgan have, I don't want. Ultimately, Frankie isn't wrong or right. I *am* happy. After leaving New York, the stress of this last decade is already lifting. Is there a part of me that maybe deep down wants to be in a relationship? I've thought about it, and the truth is... no. Relationships suck. I will always choose beer over wine, chips over chocolate, horror over rom-com. That love stuff is meant for someone else.

Besides, I'm not cut out for it, obviously. I've dated (if you can call it that) probably a hundred women since I turned eighteen, and never once felt a connection. I even went down a long internet search to see if I had a personality disorder or was missing a sensitivity chip or *something*, and finally concluded, I just don't do the lovey shit. And that's okay.

"I just want you to be happy," Frankie says, "and I'm not sure if meeting for hookups is it."

"I promise you, tongue blasting a hot blonde makes me happy."

"God, you're insufferable, truly."

I tuck my feet under my legs and go back to scrolling on my phone. "You worry more than Mom."

"Mom doesn't worry."

"Fair point." I laugh, but is it actually funny? Probably not. My and Frankie's childhood was unique. Our parents were never fans of family dinners, steady jobs, or providing that emotionally healthy balanced upbringing that every podcast in the world seems to drone on about. But we were fed, clothed, had beds, and were safe. A lot of people had it much worse.

But did I use Frankie as a crutch? Did I want to make her proud the way some people want to make their mom proud? Did I move to New York the day after I graduated high school to follow Frankie, and move back home to Minnesota a few months after she moved back? Sure did. She's my emotional support person.

Frankie's phone beeps through the speaker. "Just got a notification that the salt delivery is coming tomorrow morning. If they haven't arrived before you and Morgan go to the vendor event, just leave the back door open."

Adding this to my long list of Minnesota things that I still need to get used to—softening water with salt and leaving the freaking door open so random people can traipse through our house. "Listen." I sigh into the phone. "I'm sorry about my first impression with Zoey. It really wasn't my intention to be such an asshole."

"Ah, don't sweat it. Zoey is the nicest human in the world," Frankie says. "I'm sure she's forgotten all about it by now."

What in the actual heck? The pink-and-gold-glittered wall clock shows just after 1:00 p.m., and I still, *still*, cannot shake my interaction with the rudest of the rude Quinn Lee. How is her sister, Frankie, as cool as a banana smoothie, but Quinn is definitely not?

I've worked in the service industry in some capacity for almost twenty years, starting at fourteen in a local grocery store, and have dealt with some real jerks. My former bosses at the grocery store, the husband-and-wife duo, were some of those. But I can normally shake it off. Or at least not dwell on it the way I am now.

Because four hours later, I'm still dwelling. Hard.

The front bell jingles and I walk out from the back. Oh, thank gosh. I smile at one of my regulars, Colby—the woman is around my age or maybe a little older, and she's come in here every Saturday since I opened with her sweet golden retriever, Kona. Colby's smile always hints at sadness, a quiet look of missing something, but other than that I know nothing about her. "Hey," I say and shuffle to the front, my walking boot scraping against the floor.

"Hey, Zoey," she says and pushes her sunglasses to the top of her head.

I swing around to dig a doggie treat from my jar, and crouch down to give it to Kona. I pet her behind the ear as she gobbles it from my palm. Gosh darn Mrs. Pinkerton pushing me to implement a potential no-dog policy because of her snappy Pomeranian. Doing that, I'd miss out on times like this with the sweet ones.

"No crutches, huh?" she says as she looks into the display. "That's got to feel good."

"So good. I feel like my arms can breathe again. For whatever mush happened with my leg muscles, I made up for it in my biceps." I grin and move back behind the case. "You want your usual?"

She nods. And that will mostly be the extent of our interaction. Sometimes I leave wondering more about Colby. Not in a romantic sense, although she's attractive, with her chestnut brown hair and huge hazel eyes that seem to study everything around her. And sure, I know her name based on her credit card. Besides that, she's one of the few townspeople who keep totally to themselves. Sometimes I try to draw her out a little more. But today I'm too distracted.

"Hey, are you doing okay?" she asks, lifting her gaze from the case.

I didn't realize a frown had spread. I attempt to adjust it to a grin but give up. "Honestly, I had an icky interaction with a customer before this, and it escalated."

"You escalated?" She arches a brow. "I can hardly even picture that."

Me either. How *did* it go downhill with Quinn so quickly? I still don't think what happened was my fault. But in the six years since I opened my shop, nothing like that, at least to that extreme, has ever happened. My stomach knots as I replay the moment I told Quinn not to return. "Yeah, it got pretty heated. And I just don't feel good about it."

Colby strokes Kona's ears, and a long silence follows. "When things escalate like that, typically it has nothing to do with the event at hand, and everything to do with outside factors. It's hard to know what someone's experiencing in their daily life. We often get these surface-level interactions and don't understand the underlying issue." She pulls out a credit card for her treats. "I'm sure you'll figure out what to do."

And just like that, Colby has dropped a bit of beautiful advice. She's so right. I have no idea what happened to Quinn this morning, or her lifetime for that matter, and it was probably unfair of me to not be more accommodating.

"Thank you. I think I needed to hear that." I wrap up Colby's raspberry-filled cupcake treat in a single serving box and put a doggie treat in a paper sleeve. "See you next week."

As Colby and Kona make their way to the door, my cell buzzes in my pocket.

> Mom: Hey honey, I had a cancellation with my bridge club, so I can take Noah tonight. Have a good night!

My mom has no idea how much relief this brings me.

> You sure? I really don't mind.

Please say yes, you're still sure. I really need a night to myself to soak in a tub, watch some terrible reality TV show, and not think about work.

> Yep, of course. Also, I'm going to drop by some homemade chicken noodle soup for you later. Going to stop by the church to give some to the priest before heading over.

> And I want to hear all about your cast removal. Freedom!

She follows with so many heart emojis I wonder if it's on accident.

Oh, my mom. She will never not be a mom, no matter how old I am. I smile.

In the office, I flop on the chair, remove my glasses, and rub my eyes with my knuckles. Oh man, what a day. I flip through a stack of mail, when my fingers pause on a pale-yellow card with teal lettering and a small heart in the corner.

My stomach drops. I already know what this is before I peek at the return address. *Josie.*

I know it by the handwriting and the way she loops the Y in my name. I know it by the soft yellow and teal, her favorite colors. I know that if I lift it to my nose, it will carry the faint scent of her rose and jasmine hand lotion.

This is the sixth card I've gotten since January. Josie was always a fan of old-school romantic gestures. Handwritten notes over texts, holding the door open rather than fending for ourselves, planning beautiful wine and cheese picnic dates. The card is absolutely part of her MO.

But why now? Why, two years post-breakup, after Josie moved to Minneapolis, after she shattered my heart, after she broke my spirit and turned me off for a very long time from dating, is she contacting me? I tap the envelope against the corner of the desk and do what I've done with the other ones—toss them in my drawer, unopened, until I'm ready to see what she wants.

Knowing the letters are in my desk tests the limits of my willpower. But when we broke up, I felt so powerless, so hopeless. Maybe this is a way of reclaiming that power? Who knows? Even though Josie doesn't know I'm not reading them, *I know* I'm not reading them, and it somehow makes me feel in control.

Josie was not just a love. Josie was *the* love. The kind people make movies about, others cry over in their books, and Taylor Swift writes about. She was my everything. Until she wasn't. When I got down on one knee was when I realized she had one foot out. The rejection still guts me. I want to find love again, the kind that stands the test of time, but I can't pretend that the ghost of our relationship doesn't still haunt me.

For a year, I lived in this dull space between bouncing between hope she'd return, a bone-crushing sadness, and the fog of denial. I didn't know what to do. When she said she was leaving, when she packed her bags, when she drove off for good, I froze.

It came out of left field. Or so I thought. No warning, no couples therapy, no big fights. A week later when it really hit me that she was gone, I threw up in the bathroom at the bakery.

The worst part of it all, no matter how bad I wanted to, I didn't hate her. I still don't. I can't. I know she wished everything turned out differently. If I hated her, I could read the letters then maybe set them on fire and use the embers to create a specialty s'more. But I don't hate her. Far from it. So, no, I don't open the letters.

I hobble into the back to stack trays and double-check all the ingredients for the prep shift. Flour, eggs, vanilla, nuts... *Ouch*. I've officially pushed my foot to the maximum. I grab a stool and elevate my leg under the stainless-steel counter.

The back door opens, and a warm whoosh of summer air enters. Luna steps in and pushes sunglasses to the top of her pink hair. "Hey! Damn, it's crazy hot out there. My skin's melting off my bones."

"I know," I say and grab my pencil to make notes about the orders. "The air-conditioning can barely keep up."

Luna wraps an apron around herself and crosses the room to wash her hands. "Ended up going to Black Beach today."

I glance up from the notepad. "Oh, how was the tourist situation?"

"Terrible." She grins.

Fair statement. Our town survives on tourist dollars, including my business, but on those rare days off, we all wish the outsiders would disappear for a few hours.

Black Beach used to be one of my favorite spots. Dark-hued sand, lush greenery, rocky cliffs protruding from the earth. Even with tourists scattering every open patch of sand, the place is so peaceful. But it also holds so many, *too many*, memories. Memories of Josie, what it felt like to be loved, and then have that love ripped from me. Sure, I might be lifting from that fog and entertaining the idea of jumping back into the dating pool, but it's still in my mind.

The breakup was painful and messy. And for a long time, the scars kept me from trusting others and turned me cold in a way I don't want to be. Having a high school sweetheart morph into someone I shared my entire twenties with, made me dream of wedding bells and matching rocking chairs when we retired. Is it pathetic that something that ended two years ago still has a faint grip on me? Perhaps. Maybe it's a tiny bit of self-preservation, keeping me anchored to the past before fully jumping into my future.

Of course, I'm over Josie, the person. In reality, even during our final year together, we slipped into too much comfortability. Each of us took the other for granted, and neither of us tried. But some positives emerged from that murky time. Our breakup fundamentally shifted my relationship brain chemistry, and I definitely know what not to do when I step into my next relationship.

Luna rips a paper towel from the holder, meets me where I'm sitting, and glances at the order slip. "Whoa. This is a huge amount of stuff for tomorrow," she says, swiping her tongue across her lip ring. "We're going to be prepping until midnight."

It's a good problem to have. And if this keeps up, which I suspect it will, I'm hiring one more person.

We start prepping. The nightly measuring and stirring dance kicks up, with the electric mixer turning into background noise. Luna turns on Alexa to a pop station while the faint smell of flour and softened butter fills the air.

I scrape off the sugar into a container, measure against the food scale, and add to the mix. Next to the actual decorating, watching the food come alive is my favorite part of this job. I glance at Luna, who's counting out eggs at the counter near the mixer. "Hey, do you remember taking an order for a Quinn Lee on Wednesday?"

She plops the room-temp eggs into a colander one by one. "Quinn Lee? What does she look like?"

What does Quinn Lee look like? I don't want to think about that right now. She's the type of woman that takes someone's breath away. One that you study, wondering if they're a celebrity or were yanked in from a different era and plopped into present day, like a voluptuous, womanly pin-up model, sprung to life. I avoid Luna's gaze. "Red hair and freckles."

Quinn is so much more than red hair and freckles. She reminds me of when I first saw Julia Roberts in *Pretty Woman*, with this sort of red-orange hair, like a how a sunset looks in a wildfire, these bouncing coils bigger than her body that seemed to spring around with total abandonment. And then her eyes... Oh boy. Green, but not just any green. A mix of moss and jade and they sparkled against the sprinkling of freckles. Safe to say Quinn is one of the most beautiful women I've ever seen.

I focus on measuring the vanilla. "You know Morgan who owns the wedding planner business in town? It's her girlfriend's sister."

"Oh yeah, I remember Quinn. She was super funny. I can't even remember what we were chatting about, but I started laughing hard enough where Caleb even noticed. We had some kids in here on a field trip at the same time. It was seriously nuts. Mrs. Pinkerton's dog got loose, and that damn thing was legitimately terrorizing the kids. She really needs to put that thing on a leash." Luna cracks the last egg and tosses the shell into the compost. "Anyway, yeah, she ordered like what, seven, eight dozen Christmas cookies, right?"

My breath stops. "Yes... *Christmas* cookies. Usually green and red."

"Yeah, that's right." Luna turns off the blender and starts whisking baking soda and flour in a side dish. "We even talked about adding a gold glitter bow, but we both agreed the cost of the upgrade wasn't worth it for her event."

Stickiness builds in my throat. "You put *blue* and red on the order form."

Luna stops whisking and cocks her head. "No... no, I wouldn't have done that... That doesn't make sense. Why would I put blue and red?" She races across the room and grabs the order slip. As her eyes skim the paper, she brings her hand to her mouth. "Oh my God... Zoey... With all the Fourth of July parties this year, and the

Jones family had just come in for their gender reveal cake... I was so nervous I'd put pink instead of blue that I said blue over and over in my mind... I think I was on autopilot." Her chin quivers. "I'm so sorry."

I exhale. Dang it. Quinn was right when she told me her order, and rightfully frustrated, and I essentially kicked her out of my shop. A heat creeps into my lower belly and spreads, but I force a smile. No use making Luna feel any worse than she already does. "It's okay."

Luna bites on the inside of her cheek and scans the prep area. "I can stay late tonight and redo her order."

Although I want to say yes to fix this and do something to feel better about kicking Quinn out of my shop, I shake my head. "No, absolutely not," I say. "This was an honest mistake. I'm not having you, or me for that matter, work extra hours. It'll be fine."

I turn back to the pans and line the sheet with parchment paper. My employee did screw up, but I've needed to implement the service-animal-only rule because of Mrs. Pinkerton's dog for years now, and that's on me, not Luna. When that devil-on-wheels disguised in white fur and a pink collar gets loose, it's crazy hectic. No wonder we missed something like this.

Now what? I shift my attention to delicately forming the croissant dough into crescent shapes. Should I call Quinn and apologize?

Although, calling Quinn also doesn't sit right with me, either. The right thing to do is apologize and maybe re-make her order. But even if I want to, it'd take me hours and I still need to keep my leg elevated. After being on shift the whole day, I've pushed my fatigued foot bone to the max.

After all prep is done, and Luna goes home, I stumble up the stairs to my loft above my bakery, and thank the lucky stars, once again, that my crutches are gone. Ten minutes later, I remove my walking boot and clothes and sink into a tub of lavender-scented bubbles and a bucket of Epsom salt. I flick against the iridescent bubbles and let my muscles melt. Gosh, this week has been a lot.

And no matter how much I try to let my mind rest along with my limbs, I cannot get the conversation with Quinn out of my brain, nor the fact that she was justifiably mad at me.

When I tuck myself into bed, the dough scent from my bakery below seeps through the vents. The best part about living above my bakery is that I'm always here if anything is needed. The worst part is that I'm always here. And so, that's how I find myself at midnight back in my shop, elbow deep in flour, butter, and sugar.

SIX

QUINN

I drag the large, heavy tote down from Truck Norris, and Morgan quickly grabs the handle on the opposite side. My pulse is tight in my neck—definitely more from nerves than carrying this tote that weighs four million pounds—and we silently cross the parking lot into the pavilion hosting the Christmas vendor event. Why didn't I ask Morgan this morning if my outfit was okay? Does my outfit give off a hip-farmer vibe who's ready to shake up the Christmas game in this town? Or does it give off the vibe that I have no idea what I'm doing, so I'm playing tree-farmer dress-up? Even though I hate asking for anything, including clothing advice, next time I'm doing it.

Morgan is, of course, dressed to perfection. Crisp, professional blue blouse, white capris, low heels. With her perfectly straight blonde hair and freshly ironed clothes, she perpetually looks sharp and clean. She's the polar opposite of my butch sister with her jeans, T-shirt, and cropped hair. And also opposite of me, which I've lovingly coined *the controlled chaos wardrobe*. In an act of rejuvenation / rebellion / ridiculousness (because I burned a ton of money), before I moved back to Minnesota, I took all of my business suits to the donation center and spent an afternoon reinventing my wardrobe. From that day forward, I declared I'd never adhere to some archaic dress code again. I'm a damn farmer! I can wear whatever I want, whenever I want. Which is why I'm in white denim short overalls and a sparkly red-and-green T-shirt and questioning every decision I've ever made.

The sun is bright, but the humidity broke, and a mineral-laced breeze flows from Lake Superior. I take a deep inhale and catch a whiff of the cookies seeping from the tote. The eight dozen, minus five cookies. Don't judge. They're delicious.

What is *not* delicious... How I acted towards Zoey. I still can't shake our interaction. Last night, I thought about it so much that I cancelled my last-minute hookup in Duluth to wallow. It wasn't like I had Zoey's number and could apologize for being a total shit, and I didn't want to call her business line and leave a voicemail. Even though the interaction was terrible, a huge part of me respects the hell out of the way Zoey stood up for her employee. When she defended Luna, I saw her shaky hands twist in her apron with red staining her cheeks, but she still did it. My former boss would have never stood up for me.

As we step onto the sidewalk, I glance at Morgan, who isn't even breaking a sweat as she lugs this thing with me. She's even in heels, for God's sake. Why didn't I listen to her when she suggested I pack items in several smaller totes, instead of two massive ones? Oh yeah, because I'm ridiculously stubborn. "You know how much I appreciate you being here?"

"You've only thanked me like twenty times," she says with a smile. "A few more and you'll fill a full advent calendar."

Morgan must be tired from last night, and yet she's perfectly peppy and coifed. I don't know how she does it. Right now, Morgan's smack-dab in the middle of her busy season—summer weddings. She didn't get home last night until almost 1:00 a.m. from her clients' wedding. Normally, I'd be fast asleep. But I was still tossing and turning over the Zoey fiasco, and heard Morgan kick off her heels at the door. And yet, this morning, she's the one who grabbed us both coffee from Connie's Coffee and started loading up items into the truck as I tore through the house looking for a missing shoe. Morgan is absolutely cool as a Christmas Holli-dazzle iced berry drink, but my insides are burning up. Today is such a big day, and I cannot screw this up.

"I will hate Frankie forever for not being here right now," I say as the plastic tote clanks against my leg.

Morgan lifts a brow. "Be nice to your sister. She wanted to be here. You know her job..."

"Yeah, yeah, I know." Morgan is way more understanding than me. When Frankie got her dream job last year, Morgan was so supportive and loving, even knowing the amount of travel required for Frankie. Me, I just want my sister around me 24-7. Yes, I know I have co-dependency issues with her. But just because I recognize this, doesn't mean that it magically dissipates. "I saw Frankie more when I was living in New York and she'd fly in for business than I do now."

"She's home almost seventy-five percent of the time," Morgan says as she bumps her hip into the automatic door opener. "I think you're the one who's gone more than you think."

I hate when she's right. I hate when anyone besides me is right.

Inside the pavilion, I'm transported into a winter wonderland. Twinkling white lights hang from the ceilings, large sparkly snowflakes dangle from beams, vendors scurry around to set up long tables and displays of wreaths, ornaments, crafts, and hand-painted plates. Artificial Christmas trees—my competition but also necessary—lace the aisles, beaming with bright lights and bulb ornaments. It even *smells* like Christmas in here, a mixture of sweet pine, spicy cinnamon, and fresh baked goods. I suck in a full, deep, invigorating breath and savor the sensations.

Morgan tugs me over to a large poster taped on the wall. "Table 101 is yours. East corner, by the windows. It's a good spot. You'll get lots of traction."

Have I mentioned how grateful I am that Morgan came with me today? Not only would heaving in this stuff solo be a major pain, but my nerves are eating my insides with all the people I need to charm. For years, Morgan's done things like this—vendor events, networking, meeting with potential clients. Although I love to *think* of myself as the ultimate boss bitch, I'm not sure I am. Running someone else's calendars and meetings is my sweet spot. But doing it for myself to build up my business? I don't know.

Imposter syndrome runs rampant through my head. I have so many ideas of how I want to transform the farm into something special that brings back the Christmas spirit, but can I actually do it? What if people hate it, or don't return the following year, and I've spent my life savings, the small inheritance my grandma gave me, and maxed out a business loan to create something that might not work?

"Right there." Morgan lifts her chin to a long folding table nuzzled in between a homemade, soy-dipped Christmas candles display on the left and hand-painted ornaments on the right. Morgan and I move around each other, digging out items from the tote. We snap the white tablecloth in the air, smooth it against the table, then line the cloth with artificial, but realistic greenery, berries, and birch. In the middle, Morgan sets down a white birch stand, red candles, and a snowflake ornament, a centerpiece she made for a holiday party last year. I stuff business cards into display stands at both ends and lay out fliers announcing we will officially open for business the day after Thanksgiving, a few short months away from today.

A few short months. I swallow what feels like a prickly pinecone lodged in my throat. When I first stepped onto the tree farm property, I nearly fainted. It looked like a junkyard. Decades of broken-down equipment, machinery, hundreds of boxes of old Christmas decorations littered the property. I spent an entire month determining what I could salvage, what I needed to throw, and hired a crew to clean. I learned everything I could on irrigation, planting, creating healthy trees, business licenses, and taxes. The fire hose of information was endless, and I'm still learning every day.

Thankfully, by some Christmas miracle, the trees are healthy. But it's all the other stuff that keeps me awake—like how to capture the joy-filled snowflake and hot chocolate magic for families where children will beg their parents for a second trip out to see Santa, and that families will chat about while opening presents.

We line up Christmas plates of cookies on each end of the table, behind the business cards, so people will have to reach over the cards to grab a cookie. That's Morgan's idea, and once again, she's right. From the corner of my eye, I see Morgan eyeing the cookies. But unlike my sister, who would've dived in fist first without asking, Morgan's waiting for an offer. I hold one out and take another for myself.

"So, Frankie said the meeting with Zoey didn't go as great as we thought it would, huh?" Morgan asks, cracking a small piece off and popping it in her mouth. I don't know where she gets her willpower. I'll chomp on this thing like a sugar-starved toddler and reach for a second.

I pull out a folding chair from under the table and lower myself. My knuckles tighten. I crack them, then stretch out my fingers, trying to shake off the fact that I basically treated Zoey the same way my old boss would've treated me. I was so out of line, and for what? For something that's *blue?* When did I become the type of raging asshole who yells at someone over a color? The cookie I just scarfed down rumbles uncomfortably in my stomach, and I reach for my water.

"Yeah, I screwed that situation up sideways from here to Alaska." I slump back in my chair. "I don't know what is wrong with me. Like, she's a freaking kitten, and I tore into her like she's a pack leader."

Morgan splits off another small piece of cookie and pops it into her mouth. "Don't be too hard on yourself. You've gone through so much change this year and the PTSD from your last job..."

"PTSD?" I chuckle. I can't tell if Morgan is joking or not, but she normally doesn't say insensitive things. "That's for soldiers or people who witness catastrophic events. Not someone who brought in six figures a year and only had to deal with a dickhead boss. I just need to get over it."

A warm hand presses into my arm, and Morgan peers at me. She looks at me for so long without saying anything that the back of my neck starts to itch.

"There will always be people in the world who have it worse. Or better for that matter. Don't discount what you went through. That's not fair." She drops her hand from my arm. "Frankie told me enough stories to make my head spin. Sure, you weren't in combat or saw a grisly murder or something. But it doesn't mean that all the time you spent with your former boss didn't mess with you and rewire you a bit."

My stomach is turning, but I take another bite of cookie, anyway. I don't know... maybe reading a bit or journaling about my time there might help. All I know is, these last ten years, I've changed. The spunkiness, the hopefulness I felt as a child, even with our suboptimal parenting, shifted into massive bouts of irritability and anxiety when I started working in New York. It's like the fire that once ran through me teeters between flickering out or inflaming, and neither one is good.

As much as I'd like to think I'm a special snowflake, I'm not. Isn't this constant feeling—like you've stepped onto a lake you thought was frozen and feel it crack—just what happens when you become responsible for health insurance, rent, and contributing to a 401K? Sure, Frankie remained herself all these years, but Frankie lives out her dream of being a photographer every day. It's not like my childhood dream was to be an executive assistant.

And yet, I feel it in the deepest part of myself, that I'm not the same person I once was. But... slowly, slivers of my old self push through the surface. After years of waking up in the middle of the night, terrified I forgot something, or that my legs wouldn't run, or I was lost in a building, these last few months, I've gotten solid sleep. Might be the fresh air and physical labor, but it's still sleep.

The buttery cookie slides down my throat, and I clap the crumbs from my hand. For my entire life, I've operated like I'm charged by a high-capacity battery. I have boundless energy, which is why farming almost seemed a natural fit. But now, being back in

Minnesota, it's different. For years, jolts of electricity fired in my cells, like I was in a charged hamster wheel, and the harder I ran, the more they zapped me. This rush to prove my parents wrong, that I could actually make it on my own, that I was as gifted as Frankie, fueled me. Then my boss delivered that same message, and I became obsessed with proving myself.

Today, that same rush consumes me, but this time, I'm trying to prove myself *to* myself. I run a palm across the tablecloth and tug the edges. "Hey, are you cool waiting here? I want to check out some of the other vendors. Gotta size up my competition."

"For sure." Morgan hands me a notepad, pen, and a stack of business cards. "Don't forget these."

Saved again.

For the next hour as the other vendors set up, I put on my executive face, lift my shoulders, and shake hands as I stroll the pavilion. A vendor who makes stunning wreaths catches my attention, and we set up a meeting for next week to discuss bringing in her items for my Christmas gift shop. I chat with a man who makes homemade cutting boards, and another with delicate snowflake ornaments. There's even one that takes recycled soup and coffee cans and paints them in winter scenes for pen holders. I love it all. I want it all. My body springs alive as I scribble notes and ideas. The speakers kick on, and the sounds of Billie Holiday and Bing Crosby ring through the space. This is *exactly* what I need. It might be the end of August, but I'm overflowing with the holiday spirit.

I *love* Christmas.

Who would have ever thought I'd get to this point? Joy surrounds me as I visualize these products spread across my gift shop. With Frankie being a photographer, she can take award-winning worthy photos of my place for social media. Morgan is a natural designer, and well, I'm scrappy as hell. Together, we can do this.

I turn the corner and see Morgan chatting with someone and my breath stops. *Zoey.* Oh God, is she a vendor here? It might make sense since she has a bakery that probably goes all out during the holiday season. She's wearing a cute white-and-yellow sundress, her hair is flowy, reaches her mid-back, and is pinned back only on the sides. A walking boot is on one foot, and a sandal on the other. She laughs at something Morgan says and thumbs up her glasses.

God, she's cute. *Ugh.* And yes, I know I'm a hot-blooded woman with a libido the size of the moon. But I really, really screwed this up if Zoey is into casual hookups. I mean, is there ever a more perfect scenario if she's as monogamy allergic as me and lives within ten minutes of my house?

As she and Morgan chat, a tension string weaves in my stomach and tugs. What is she doing here?

More importantly, what the hell do I say?

SEVEN

ZOEY

What in the heck am I doing here? Now that I'm actually in the pavilion at the Christmas vendor event, surrounded by fake trees and snow, and more vendors than I can visit in a day, I'm rethinking all my choices. It took me until 3:00 a.m. this morning to finish the replacement cookies for Quinn, and I did something I haven't done since opening Zoey's Bakery six years ago—I didn't clean up. I left all the dirty pans stacked in the sink with the mixing bowls and utensils on top. My conscience is currently eating away at itself.

I'm keeping all my fingers and toes crossed that the health department doesn't drop by this morning for a surprise inspection. I wrote an apology note to Esther, the morning baker, and promised to make it up to her. But I was *so* tired by the end, and my foot throbbed like I crushed it in a vise trap. Four hours later, I dragged myself out of bed, got ready, and practically tripped over the bags in my eyes on the way here.

But now that I'm here, I'm nervous. A few minutes ago, my gaze had skittered across the room, trying to find Quinn's table, yet praying to all the entities that she got some non-life-threatening sickness and couldn't make it anymore. Because admitting to

Quinn that my employee messed up her order, and apologizing for essentially banning her from the store, feels terrible.

Being raised by two elementary teachers—my mom, kindergarten, my dad, fourth grade—has taught me a lot besides the value of teachers and how deeply underpaid they are. All morning, I could hear my mom's voice in my head, speaking to me like a six-year-old in her classroom: "It's important when we do something wrong to our friends, we say sorry."

So, that's what I did—baked cookies and drove thirty minutes to Duluth to say sorry. Thankfully, the Christmas angels bestowed some pre-holiday luck onto me, and Quinn is nowhere to be found. I'm chatting on neutral ground with Morgan, shuffling several bags in my hand, and counting the moments down where I can politely scoot out of here before Quinn returns to the table.

Morgan points to the bags in my hand. "What do you have there?"

I lift the bags of cookies. "Not sure if Quinn mentioned, but we made a mistake on her cookie order and I brought some replacements." The friendly face of someone who won't bite my head off—no matter how much I may deserve it—allows me to exhale.

"Oh, that's really kind of you." Morgan lifts herself from the table and smooths back her blouse. "I heard there was a little mishap, but I didn't get all the details."

Mmm-hmmmm. Sure. Morgan's a smart, local businesswoman, and absolutely knows how to keep the peace. She lives with Quinn. She's practically married to Quinn's sister. No way she doesn't have the details. But I understand why she's not tangling herself up in the Great Cookie Debacle.

"Are you so excited to not have crutches anymore?" She grabs the boxes from me and stacks them on the table.

"You have no idea. It feels so good to not have a cast. I went through two razors, though." I laugh and glance around the space. Still no Quinn. My initial relief now mixes with disappointment, and I don't know what to do with this conflict inside my body.

Do I actually want to see Quinn? Maybe a little. But why? I'm probably a glutton for punishment. Or maybe I need to clear my conscience. Or maybe I'm drawn to that dusting of freckles that peppers her cheeks... I clear my throat. "Well, I should head back. The staff are managing the shop today, but I still feel squirrelly being far away in case something happens."

Morgan tucks a blonde lock behind her ear. "I think you should stay and enjoy the fair for a bit. Quinn should be back any second. She'll definitely want to thank you for the cookies."

Now I really want to bolt. I brought Quinn an eight-dozen-cookie apology. I didn't do it to get a thank-you, which will undoubtedly take away from the *mostly* altruistic act of making these replacement sweets. I really did intend to do it as an apologetic peace offering, but now that I dropped these off, I feel better. "Oh, um, I think it's best if maybe I just scoot outta here before that happens. I don't think she's really my biggest fan right now."

Morgan pulls out a water bottle from a small cooler and offers me one. "I'm sorry about whatever happened yesterday. She felt really icky when she came back from your shop. I think opening a new business and everything just piled on the stress."

That I can understand. When I started Zoey's Bakery, I left my job as a manager of the bakery at a local grocery store, and I questioned myself every day if I made the right decision. Along with the pressure of being a first-time small business owner, my terrible old bosses spread a rumor around town that I stole their recipes—which I absolutely did not do—and I spent my first year wondering if they were going to sue. Whispers of recipe theft rippled through the town, turning people against me for a while, until the figurative cream rose to the top and people discovered the truth about my old bosses.

"Ah, yep, that first year is *so* hard," I say. "I was running around like a chicken with my head... Actually that's a gross analogy. I'll say it was totally bananas for sure. Pretty sure I didn't even sleep that first month."

"Yeah, and after everything that happened in New York with her job..." Morgan clears her throat and re-straightens a stack of business cards. "Anyway, I just mean she probably wasn't her best self."

My ears perk. Everything that happened in New York? What happened in New York? Great, now I'm curious. New York has always fascinated me. From the Rockefeller Center, Twin Towers Memorial, Times Square, and Broadway, New York is like a spectacularly different world. But now Morgan just added a little Quinn cozy mystery to this already existing fascination, and I want to unravel the plot.

This probably isn't good. I should just slink out of here before Quinn returns, and head back to my controlled life where I stop thinking about customers who I eighty-sixed from my bakery like some drunk-on-power nightclub bouncer. "So, you're saying Quinn's not normally rude and doesn't drop the f-word like swear bombs making the children weep in the corner and staff members cry into their apple pie à la mode?" As I finish the last word, I see Morgan's eyes grow wide. *Cool, cool.* "And... she's right behind me, isn't she?"

"Sure am," a raspy voice says a few inches from my back.

Even though we only met once, I feel like I'd recognize that voice anywhere. It reminds me of a spiced rum velvet cake, and I'd bet good money she can hold a solid tune.

My face is for sure illuminating with about fifty shades of red. How many more cookies do I need to bake to say sorry again? I should take off my walking boot and stick it in my mouth.

Slowly, I turn, and yep, Quinn is right behind me. And not only is she there, she's in white denim short overalls, her bouncy curls boinging in every direction, amber and bourbon freckles warm and pronounced, and my heart does an unexpected flutter. A very, very unexpected flutter.

"That could not have been worse timing." I flash a sheepish grin. "I'm sorry, you didn't actually make any kids cry."

"That's too bad. It's one of my joys in life." She wrinkles her nose with a sparkle in her green eyes and glances at the pink boxes piled next to Morgan. "What's that?"

Morgan lifts herself from the seat and taps her fingers across the back. "Zoey, why don't you take a seat in my spot and take some pressure off your foot? I'm going to go chat with a few people I know."

And just like that, Morgan rips off whatever Band-Aid she had keeping me protected from Quinn and rushes away without another word. I really want to leave. But I also kind of want to stay, and I'm not loving this push and pull in my brain.

"She's doing her Mayor Morgan thing," Quinn says, looping her thumbs in the straps of her overalls and balancing back on her heels.

"What's Mayor Morgan?"

"She literally knows everyone everywhere. It's like she's meeting with her constituents. Morgan always has her shit together and a smile, so you know, she'll win all the votes when she runs for mayor. Which she'll never actually do." Quinn sits behind the table and points at the chair Morgan vacated. "For real, you should sit. Your foot is hurting me, and I'm not the one standing on it."

I really shouldn't. I should spit out my apology and return to the safety of my bakery. But carrying in these boxes and standing on this cement floor is fatiguing my foot in a terrible way.

At least, that's what I'm telling myself as I slide into the seat next to Quinn.

EIGHT

ZOEY

I'm sitting next to Quinn at the Christmas vendor event, elevating my foot, and flip-flopping between scolding myself for not running out of here five minutes earlier when I had the chance to escape the most awkward conversation of my life, and thanking myself for making the trek to see Quinn in these overalls. *Wowza.*

Quinn looks down at the boxes on the floor between us. "What is this? Do you have your own table?"

I twist the rings on my fingers, wishing a Christmas tree would crash to the ground—not break obviously because that'd be terrible, but enough to cause a distraction that I could hobble my way out of here. I open a box, revealing green and red cookies with an edible gold glitter bow. Quinn's eyes grow as wide as the cookies, and she tugs her lips into her mouth.

I don't know her very well, at all, only what Frankie has told me and the one failed interaction at my store, but my guess is that she's not often rendered silent. And something about this makes me smile. "I am so, so, sorry about what happened at my store yesterday." I focus on my fingers, and not my burning cheeks. "I was way out of line and should have never spoken to you like that." I glance up, ready to take whatever punishment I deserve.

"Are you serious right now?" Quinn's green eyes narrow. "I

was a major snatch to you. *Major.* I can't believe you didn't call the bouncers and have me dragged out of there."

I cover my giggle with my hand. *Snatch* is a word I haven't heard since high school.

"Seriously, Zoey," Quinn says as she fans her fingers on my forearm. "What happened in your store was all on me. All. I even signed the order form and still blamed you guys. I am the biggest asshole ever."

A tingle spreads up my arm from the featherlight touch. Her fingertips are warm, and soft, and when she removes them, I kind of want them to return. "But I talked to Luna, and she told me she remembered you ordering green and red cookies, and swore she wrote it down that way, but it was super chaotic in the store that day. She fully owned up to her mistake."

Quinn crosses her legs and flicks at a piece of frayed denim by her knee. "Oh my God, it was really nuts. Is your place always that swamped? There was a huge line, and then a small dog got loose and started barking at everyone. It was like a cookie tornado ransacked that place."

I thumb my glasses back up my nose. "The dog. Ugh. I don't know how to handle that situation. I can't single Mrs. Pinkerton out because I allow dogs in the store, but it happens all the time, and she's so utterly—"

"Clueless."

"I don't want to say that, but..." It's so true. Mrs. Pinkerton is completely clueless to the havoc her Pomeranian wreaks across the store. Why is it that the one time I grow a backbone, it's with Quinn and not with the woman who constantly messes up my store?

A smile passes between us. Quinn shifts her gaze and thumbs the side of the pink box. "I cannot believe you remade these. I thought... I thought you didn't have time."

Involuntarily, I yawn. "Oh, I did it last night after the shop closed."

Quinn's eyebrows scrunch, and she studies my eyes. "Zoey, I

don't know what to say. I'm so sorry you did that, and also, so grateful. I'll stop in tomorrow and pay for these."

"No, no need to come down to the store. It was our error," I say. Although, I definitely wouldn't mind Quinn coming in tomorrow. A full redo of yesterday, where we can have a proper, cordial conversation. "It's totally up to me to fix. Really, it's okay."

A silence stretches between us, but it feels comfortable. The surrounding vendors are adding the final touches to their display, hanging wreaths on screens, dangling ornaments off wooden racks, and peppermint and chocolate scent fills the air from the food vendors. A man next to us lays out carving knives and cutting boards, and I settle back into the chair.

"I can't believe I freaked out so hard over the color blue. *Blue,* for God's sake." Quinn tweezers the edge of the tablecloth with her fingers. "I knew I was taking on a lot starting this business, but I guess I didn't realize how much it was affecting me. I promise, I'm not normally salty like this."

"You might want to tell your sister that," I say, keeping a little twinkle in my voice. "She told me you're always salty."

"Oh my God, I hate her so much. She is seriously going to get it."

Quinn laughs. It's pretty and warm, like hot chocolate with melted marshmallows, and I already want to make her laugh again. And... gosh. Her smile, up close like this, is one of the prettiest I've seen. Full round pink lips, surrounded by freckles dancing on her rosy cheeks. I haven't been attracted to anyone in a long time, but I don't completely live under a rock—I know what attraction feels like, and this is it. I blink my gaze away, quickly. I'm not sure I'm quite ready to feel... this.

With the ice cracked between us, I help Quinn load up the new cookies on an extra platter and we mutually decide that we'll still keep the other plate with the blue and red. She scoots the tote under the table towards me to elevate my leg, talks about the other vendors scattered through the pavilion and how she's dying to bring the lush handmade wreaths into the shop. Before I know it, at least a half hour has passed.

Quinn lifts from the table. "I'll be right back. Don't, you know, stagger away with that heavy boot and all."

I bite back a smile. As she hurries away, I scan the crowd. No Morgan to be found anywhere. And right now, I'm totally okay with that. A few minutes later, Quinn returns with two steaming cups of hot cocoa with a candy cane plopped inside the liquid. "Cheers." She taps her cup against mine and sips.

The warm minted chocolate slides down my throat. *Yum*. One would think with owning a bakery I'd get my fill of sugar, but it has yet to happen. "Did you meet some vendors you might want to work with?"

"So many. I finally feel like everything's coming together." Quinn sets the cup on top of a napkin and slides back in her chair. "I have this huge creative spark, but I've spent so much time getting the farm in a good place that I don't know if I can get the gift shop completely set up in three months."

Yikes. Coming from experience, three months is not a lot of time to get a full shop set up. "What are the plans for the shop? Are you going to buy wholesale, then resell, or make things yourself?"

"Ideally both. I want the wreaths from that woman in the corner." She juts her head to the left. "I'm going to order some hand-painted bulb ornaments and embroidered holiday towels, but I really want to do a lot of it myself. Paint ornaments, burn inscriptions into wood, put glitter on snowflakes, all that good stuff. I'm sort of desperate to capture the warm and cozy magic from back then. Less commerce and more festive. If that makes sense."

"I love everything about this." Christmas captivates me. I'm one of those who live for the season. Tinsel and lights, hovering around the tree jittery with anticipation, opening gifts, and sledding down a hill stuffed into a snowsuit, is pure joy.

"Do you think Morgan will keep using your place as a wedding venue?"

Quinn blows into her cup and takes a short sip. "Yes, I think so.

In July, I stopped all weddings there to get the place ready for Christmas. It's a good income boost, but it's going to take months to prep everything to open the day after Thanksgiving."

"Three months from now to go live, huh?" When I set up my shop, it took six months, and every single day I was in there, painting, prepping, fixing. The three-month deadline makes my chest tighten. "That's a heck of a time crunch."

"I know. Like I'm running around with my tits on fire as it is. And the weddings I've had so far were a ton of work, so I didn't get as far as I needed on the shop. I mean, Morgan and the crew do a lot, but there's permits and sanitation, and last month a couple of asshats from the wedding party went down by where we planted the seedlings. I'm not a violent person, but I legit almost went Chuck Norris on their asses."

I giggle into my steamy hot chocolate. "Chuck Norris? Like the guy from the nineties who made all those karate movies?"

Quinn freezes. Her palm flies to her heart and her mouth drops open like she's just witnessed some monstrosity. "Wait, do you not know any Chuck Norris references?"

I have zero idea what she's talking about. But I can't help but enjoy the sparkle in her eyes. "References? Um, no?"

Now she sets her cup down and turns to face me, with such an incredulous expression I almost start laughing.

"You know like... Chuck Norris sleeps with the lights on. Not because he's afraid of the dark, but because the dark is afraid of Chuck Norris."

That is one of the goofiest things I've ever heard. And that's saying a lot since small children come into my store daily, my parents are elementary school teachers, and my nephew Noah's the self-proclaimed king of dad jokes. "What?" I set the mug on the corner of the table. "I've literally never heard of this."

"You can do it with anything. I even call my truck 'Truck Norris' 'cause it's a beast that won't die, no matter how many poundings it takes." Quinn's shifty in her chair, like energy is spiking directly in her veins, and it's cracking me up. "Like, I don't know, Chuck Norris could bake these cookies with a single look of his heated glare. Or Chuck Norris doesn't have to eat a cookie, they just crumble in his presence. Or Superman wears Chuck Norris pajamas. You know?"

She tilts her hands up sideways in some sort of terrible knife-slice faux karate chop, and I start laughing so hard that the vendors next to us give me a sideways glance. "I don't know if this is painful or funny." My belly spasms as I laugh, hard, and I suck in air to smooth it out. My gosh, how long has it been since I laughed? Sure, I smile all the time, maybe even occasionally giggle. But laughing? It's been way too long. "Okay, I get it now. Like bringing in some movie reference and applying it to real life. At work, when someone does something really awful, we'll say 'you just Rosed his Jack.'"

"You mean from *Titanic*, where she wouldn't just scoot over on the damn floating wood thing so Jack would get on?" Quinn presses her hand into my arm. *Oof.* I don't want her to remove that palm. "That's perfect. You totally just put Baby in the corner."

"Yes!" I pick back up the mug. "How about 'Did you just release the gimp?'"

"Whoa, this took a dark turn fast." Quinn tosses up her hands, chuckling. "Time to reel that back in."

The time flies by. Our conversation morphs into our favorite movies, what we're streaming, and a random shared deep dislike of *The Catcher in the Rye* (*don't judge, it's sold a gazillion copies*). Much like when I laughed, I also couldn't remember the last time I sat and chatted like this with anyone. For the last six years, I've always thrown everything I have into my bakery. My free time, my love, my sweat. The last two years, the rest of my energy went into nursing my broken heart. Even though I'll never tell her, today is proving I need to seriously consider taking my mom's advice and get out more often.

My gaze flickers across the pavilion as folks add the very final touches to their displays. It might be the end of August, but this place is saturated with the Christmas spirit. "I think making ornaments and crafts would be so much fun. I make some every year during the holidays. If I didn't have a bakery, I'd have a craft store."

"Really?" Quinn crosses her legs toward me. "Well, you're welcome to come out anytime you want and make Christmas crafts with me."

"I'm *sooo* in. Seriously, don't offer something like that if you don't mean it. I have an unhealthy obsession with crafts and would probably spend all my off time there if I could." Sitting among the smell of pine and cedar trees while painting ornaments sounds like a perfect day off. Not to mention, I am so curious what the farm looks like now. Last summer, Morgan and Frankie transformed the barn on Quinn's tree farm to be useable for a small wedding venue. The rumors on the street said the place was pretty gnarly before they revamped it all. I wasn't there, but I saw some before and after pictures online. It looked phenomenal.

Quinn has the corner of her lip tucked into her teeth, and if I'm not mistaken, a tiny hint of pink sweeps beneath her freckles. "Is there, ah, is there someone who would miss having you around if you spent all your free time making crafts at my place?"

Huh? "You mean like my family or staff?" And then... *Ohhhhh.* I know what she's asking, and now I feel like my cheeks mirror hers. "Oh, you mean like someone *at home.* Yeah, um, no. Just me. And some very, very sad plants. I don't even have a cat."

It looks like she releases a breath. Wait... is Quinn interested in me? No. What? No. I mean, good Lord, I've been out of the game for a decade, but I think I'm reading into what she's throwing down.

Stop. Man, this is sad. Having a friendly chat with someone for an hour does not mean they're interested.

"Is there anyone for you that might be upset you have someone hanging out so much with you?" My attempt at being smooth fails, and I try not to scrunch my face into a cringe. But I can't take it back. And now I'm not breathing, waiting for the answer.

Quinn reaches for her mug. "Either a hundred of them, or none, depending on how you look at it."

Okay, I am a certifiable dork. We are *so* clearly talking about two different things.

"I don't do the dating thing at all," Quinn says.

So we *are* talking about the same thing. But this revelation twists my gut more than it should, and I'm not totally sure why.

"I have all the time in the world to do what I want, when I want," Quinn says. "No one to answer to."

Surely, when she says she doesn't date "at all," she doesn't mean *at all*, at all. Maybe she had a bad breakup and is nursing a tender heart, but is still searching for Ms. Right. Or maybe she's taking a break. "You don't date at all. Like ever? Or like right now?"

"Ever," Quinn says, pulling the mug to her lips. "I'm a single-serving kind of woman, you know? Maybe two servings if we really click. My longest relationship was two weeks, and honestly—and I will fully admit I'm a total asshole—it's because I had a rare week off work and wanted to spend the time between the sheets. Me and relationships... Nope." She laughs and crosses her forearms to make an X. "What's a terrible combo... Oil and water? Olives and chocolate? That's me and monogamy."

I grin, hiding my disappointment. My deep, deep, delusional disappointment that shouldn't hit me as hard as it's hitting me. "That bad, huh? Although, I make a sweet pickle cupcake, so maybe olives and chocolate wouldn't be terrible."

Quinn scrunches her nose. "Pickle cupcake, huh? I'll give it a try. Just once." A short moment lapses when she shifts and tugs at the edge of the tablecloth. "Are you a single-serving type of person?"

Well, gah. My chest, my head, my ears are flaming pink right now. Is Quinn asking if I'm the type of person who has casual hookups? Is this because she wants to have a casual hookup with me? Nothing like diving into the deep end of a getting-to-know-you conversation while surrounded by Christmas ornaments. And what if I *am* someone who likes casual hookups? Will it just be something we have in common, or will she see if I want to meet later?

I wish my limbs and loins weren't tingling the way they are. It's been three years since I've had sex, minus one sad time during the last year of my and Josie's relationship where it felt like a last-ditch effort to save us. I've never had a one-night stand in all my life. But that night, with Josie, would've been the closest to it, even though she was my partner. And I cried in the shower after.

So, no, I am *definitely* not a single-serving person.

"Nope, but you do you. I'm all about claiming whatever power makes sense for you," I say. Which is true. There is no judgment. I'm simply wired different. But there is a tiny bit of me looking at Quinn's bright smile, beautiful eyes, and sunburst hair that makes me wish I *was* wired a bit more like her. "I'm like one of those weird people who mate once, mate for life."

"Ah!" She smacks her hand against the table. "You are the emperor penguin!"

"The what?"

She shifts towards me with a mega-grin. "That's what I call Morgan and Frankie—emperor penguins. Have you ever heard about them? So technically they don't *always* mate for life, but basically they find their mate and stick with them, and usually return to them season after season."

Ah. I feel like I've heard about these penguins. Not that I would classify myself like this, but I understand what Quinn is getting at. "Yeah, I guess I am, then."

A heavy moment follows this. I wish I knew Quinn better, could read her eyes that flicker downward while her smile remains the same. "Well, good for you. I hope you find that perfect mate someday."

A crackly announcement over the intercom says the doors will open in five minutes. "I should probably head out and let you meet all your new fans."

A flash of panic crosses Quinn's face. "Do you have to go? I don't know where Morgan is." She runs a palm across the tablecloth and smooths it out. "I'm freaking out a little bit doing this on my own. But also, totally cool if you need to jet, because I get it.

The last thing you thought you'd be doing is sitting here with me talking about movies."

This really is the last thing that I thought I'd be doing today, and somehow, it's exactly where I want to be. I saw Morgan walk by a few times, and glance at us, but Quinn's back is to her and didn't notice. And now is a perfect time to call that out.

But there's something about sitting here like this. It's refreshing. Reminds me a little bit of when Josie and I first met, the way we laughed before everything crashed and burned, the way we bonded over the most random thing, like stockpiling the Lucky Charms marshmallows so you could have that one big bowl with double the goodness.

Being with Quinn is easy and light. Everything about my time here today makes me forget, for a moment, about the scars of my past, and makes me think that maybe there is, in fact, a soulmate out there for me.

NINE

QUINN

A knock outside my door snaps my attention away from the book about surviving workplace trauma I've been devouring for the past few days. "You may enter at your own risk. I will take no shit about the state of my room."

I dogear the page, and stuff it under my pillow. Seven weeks ago, at the Christmas in August event in Duluth, Morgan mentioned PTSD, and I thought in true Morgan fashion, she was over-the-top. I'd seen movies on this, but it was all about soldiers who saw combat, or people who'd been in terrible accidents, or really heavy things that I frankly don't want to think about. I genuinely didn't know that PTSD existed on different levels. That, like everything in the world, a spectrum exists, and my New York experience qualifies.

After I berated Zoey at her shop, something clicked in me, and I knew I had to kick my ass into high gear and start getting over what happened. But I'm not quite ready to share the rabbit hole of research I've gone down on the effects of a toxic workplace on mental health. I love my sister, but she's so up in my business, and the last thing I need is her worrying more than she already does.

The other thing that happened since the vendor pavilion? I've thought of Zoey almost every day. So far, I haven't had the courage to do anything more than visit her store a few times a week for some dessert and a quick chat. Her shop is always busy, which honestly is a blessing in disguise, because the thoughts I'm having about her aren't good.

And Zoey made it clear—she's different than me. She's not interested in a hookup-only-type situation, and I will never have a solid, steady relationship. So yeah, these thoughts are making me frustrated in all the ways, and none of them pleasant.

"Christ, it's messy in here," Frankie says as she opens the door and kicks at a pile of bags in the corner.

"Nope. I already said I would take no shit from anyone. You may kindly see yourself out, fuck you very much." I stuff the pillow behind my back and scoot up higher on the bed. "What do you want?"

"I was going to head down to Zoey's and grab some dessert for tonight. Want to come with?" Frankie leans against the door frame and runs her fingers through her dark cropped hair.

The whole cool and casual vibe is not working. I know what Frankie's doing. I'm staying away from Zoey as much for her protection as my own. Zoey has this sweetness, almost a naivete, to her that's rare. Someone who substitutes swear words with other words because her ears are too delicate to handle cussing. The last time I saw her, she even said, "Shut the front door!" with her soft, doe-eyed wonderment, when we realized we have the same cross-body purse in canary yellow. She's gentle, and kind, and caring. I'm saving her from me, even if she doesn't know it.

Zoey's not my type. Like, at all. She's too pure for this world, probably the type of woman who likes gentle sex on a bed with roses sprinkling the ground after having a picnic in the park. I like quick and dirty orgasms, names optional, and moving straight on with my life. Messy and fun. And Zoey is clean and stable. We're built completely different.

So, yes, the thoughts I'm having about her are irrational. But the better I get to know her, the more I think we could be friends. And friends are good. Even though I grew up in this town, there's a reason why I cut ties with everyone and bolted out of here as quickly as I could at eighteen.

Growing up, I never had genuine friendships with anyone, not in the way Frankie did, or I saw in the movies. While Frankie was a sports star, going to state in basketball and brutally taking names in hockey, I was out in a corn field getting wasted with my classmates on cheap 40s and hooking up in cars. During my entire high school experience, I don't think I had a single genuine conversation with anyone. I never talked about feelings or fears or the deep rejection I felt from my parents.

But at the vendor fair, Zoey was like this gentle nymph, coaxing my thoughts from me with her warmth. And I'm not sure I'm ready for someone like her to see all the ugliness inside me.

"So?" Frankie says, tapping the door frame. "Zoey's. Now. Whaddya think?"

"Where's your girlfriend? Go bother her," I say to Frankie. "I don't want to go to Zoey's."

This is such a lie, and Frankie's going to take one look at my face and call me out. I *always* want to go to Zoey's. I think I've hit her place at least a dozen times since we've met. When I see her, something inside me lifts. And every time that happens, I feel a little bit of the old me—the starry-eyed one who fourteen years ago marched to New York with two suitcases filled with hopes and dreams—return.

Frankie crosses her arms and gives me that *look*. The same look she used to give me when I'd dry my tears on the subway and drag myself into our apartment telling her my day was "just fine." *Ugh.* No one can read me the way my sister can.

"First, Morgan has a client meeting so she can't go with. Second, I'm calling massive bullshit on you that you don't want to go to Zoey's. It's like a kid saying they don't want to go to Disneyland, or anyone in the world saying they don't want to go to a

Taylor Swift concert, or a pit bull saying they don't want that piece of bacon or—"

"Got it. Christ, okay." I throw my blankets down and knock over the pillow. I scramble to cover it up, but not before Frankie sees the book. I love my sister. More than anyone in this world. But some things I'm not ready to share.

Her brow furrows as she scans the cover. "You doing okay?"

No. I'm not. I'm lost, and don't know if I made the right decision in buying this Christmas tree farm. I'm scared and maybe a little lonely, and desperate to prove to everyone that I can do this. "Yes, I'm fine, you overbearing mother hen. Come on. Cupcakes are waiting." I toss the blanket back over the pillow, trip over a box of craft items I need to bring to the farm, and stuff my feet into sandals.

"Hey..." Frankie's voice goes soft.

Nope, this is *exactly* what I don't want. Since I was little, Frankie's always been my protector. Strong, quick, will stand up to literally anyone on my behalf, no matter who they are or their size. I loved it back then and still love it now. But some things I need to do on my own. Navigating my deprogramming and relearning my worth is step one.

A hand reaches and grips me, then pulls me into a tight hug.

Frankie and I are huggers. It's who we are, how we show affection, and we probably hug every day. But this one is different. She's trying to transfer a message, and a sliver of me is so close to accepting it.

"Listen to me, okay?" Frankie whispers into the top of my head. "You are amazing, and deserved nothing that happened to you. Got it? I need you to hear me."

I want to bury my head in her shoulder and cry. I want to tell her about how I felt so worthless for so many years that a part of me detached from reality, made me build up a protective persona, and that seeped into everything else in my life. And how stupid it is that some rich old white guy in Manhattan still holds so much power over me. I want to say that combining our upbringing with its underlying message that we were simply tolerated but not celebrated or affirmed, seeped so far into my bones I think it's part of my DNA. And if I don't make the Christmas tree farm work, it will prove all these messages I've received my whole life are true, and I am, in fact, not worth it.

But instead of slicing myself open and throwing my emotional guts on the table for Frankie to coddle me anymore, I squeeze her back, then release. "Come on, cookies are waiting. We're taking Truck Norris, not the motorcycle."

Frankie grins, and thankfully I can tell she won't push me any further. "How can I get Morgan—who never even has a wrinkle— on the back of my bike, but not you?"

"'Cause you do things to Morgan that I don't even want to think about." I shudder with a very dramatic flair. "Gross."

Frankie laughs. "Fair point."

In Truck Norris, Frankie pulls up our favorite podcast, *Love 'Em or Leave 'Em* with Ruby Reanne, as we back out of the driveway and drive down the road to Zoey's Bakery.

"Hey, everyone, welcome to the *Love 'Em or Leave 'Em* podcast, where we do a deep dive into all things relationships. Let's kick this off with an email I received over the weekend. This comes from Maren, who says, 'Hi, Ruby. Last year I left an exhausting and emotionally abusive partner who made it their personal mission to belittle me every day, and I'm finally ready to get back on the dating horse. However, on the few dates I've gone on, I analyze the men in an almost CIA-level of detail, latching on to anything I see as a red flag. Last week I went out for dinner with a really nice man. Everything was great until we looked over the dessert menu. I suggested German chocolate cake and he said he thought coconut was disgusting and was there something else I'd be willing to share. I immediately closed up and still haven't returned his calls. What is wrong with me?'

"First of all, that's just plain good judgment because coconut is delicious and a gift from the gods, and clearly he is totally wrong,"

Ruby Reanne says with a smile in her voice. "Jokes aside, this will take a lot more than what I can offer on this show. Throughout my career, I've seen various levels of emotional abuse and gaslighting. Often it breaks us to a point that we question everything—if we loaded the dishwasher right, if we're as terrible of a driver as they say we are, if we added too much salt to the dinner. These types of put-downs are often what abusers start with, and then it escalates to where we question everything we do, our motivations, our sanity..."

As Ruby continues to talk, I focus on the trees outside flashing by the window, the beginning hues of orange and amber spreading across green leaves. I can't help but relive what happened in the office. Did my boss make me this paranoid, or was that demon always lurking inside of me, hidden, waiting to rise to the surface? I'm buried in this coffin of terror, where every decision I make with my new business might be the one that breaks me. Thank God my aunt and uncle's crew remained at the farm after I took over. But I'm pouring everything I have into creating this gift shop and Christmas experience, and what if it fails? What if I don't do it right and the community hates it, and I ruin this chance for an entirely new life?

By the time we bump down Main Street, I've wound myself tighter than the curls on my head.

Frankie pulls over a block away from Zoey's Bakery and pushes the truck into park. She taps her fingers against the steering wheel and peeks at me through her peripherals. "Talk to me."

I don't want to. Not now, not yet. I'm still processing. And until I figure out all of this on my own, I can't loop in Frankie. "I'm good. I'm good." When she gives me *the look*, I wrinkle my nose and shoo her away. "Calm your tits, all right? I promise I'm good."

A quick exhale escapes before she nods and opens the door. I step onto the cracked sidewalk, shield my eyes against the bright sun, and take a full cleansing breath, pushing away any bad thoughts. I'm about to see Zoey and I refuse to bring this negative energy into her space.

We cross the street and look up at Zoey's Bakery. *What the...?* Frankie tosses me the same concerned look and we both kick up the pace, speed walking. My gut sinks as we get closer. When I jog to reach the front of the store, and peek through the window, it sinks all the way to my toes.

Oh no...

TEN
ZOEY

This is not happening. Someone pinch me with an industrial-size kitchen tong, because this cannot be real life right now. I stare at Ken, the electrician, standing in my empty shop, blink at the fuzzy spots inhabiting my vision, and vaguely hear him say, "I'm so sorry," for the third time in the last twenty minutes as he scribbles on the clipboard.

Ken is the same guy who graduated with my dad, brings his granddaughters in every Saturday for strawberry cake pops, whose kind eyes crinkle all the way to his gray temples when he smiles. And right now I want to strangle him.

Well, not him, exactly, because I'm not a complete sociopathic killer, but the situation.

He finishes jotting down a note on his clipboard and glances at me. Oh no. I *know* that look. I've seen this look before. Heck, I've even delivered this look when I had to fire an employee a few years ago. I twist the bottom of my apron. *Don't say it, don't say it... Please don't say it.*

"Two weeks' closure, minimum."

Minimum? *Minimum!* In the six years I've been open, I've never even taken a full week off. I finally adjusted to taking partial

Sundays and Mondays off, but really, that's to catch up on all the paperwork that I miss over the week.

I think I'm going to cry. No... I'm positive I'm going to cry. My lip trembles and I'm sure my cheeks have turned a ferocious shade of red. Ken's eyes go wide. He lobs his hand up like I'm going to fall while inching backwards, and he's ready to catch me. If I don't pull it together, my glasses will fog, I'll be a complete mess, and the entire community will know that I bawled in the middle of my store.

This morning could not have been any worse, starting with being jolted awake by a frantic 5:00 a.m. phone call from my morning baker, followed by an emergency call to the electrician, and one to my mom for moral support.

My place is ruined. Zoey's Bakery as we know it will cease to exist for the next few weeks because of... chipmunks.

Freaking, stupid, horrible chipmunks.

Somehow, those cat-sized rats got underneath my bakery crawl space, chewed through some wire, and did some other damage that I tried really, really tried hard to pay attention to when Ken told me, but all I could focus on was that the electric affects everything in my fridge, in my freezer, and if I don't get this stuff out of here in the next hour, I will lose it all.

And now... I'm closed for two weeks. *Minimum.*

Putting a sign in my door this morning saying I was closed for unforeseen circumstances was terrible enough when I thought this would last a day. I really thought I could just call someone and have this fixed, and we'd be back up and running in a few hours.

"Oh gosh. Two weeks? Is there anything we can do?" *Don't cry. Don't cry.*

He stuffs the pen back in his breast pocket and shakes his head. "No, unfortunately not. These little buggers got ya good. Honestly, two weeks is best-case scenario because the inspector still has to sign off after it's all fixed."

My belly twists so hard I feel like I'm going to be sick. I have customers and weddings and birthday parties and anniversaries and so many commitments to so many people, and they will absolutely hate me if I can't fulfill their orders. People's special days will be ruined, and there's nothing I can do about it. I bite at the inside of my cheek and take a breath. "Well, um, I guess, thank you for letting me know." My feeble attempt to keep my voice cheerful fails. "Here, let me pack you up some cookies for the road."

"Oh, you don't have to do that," he says, but his eyes are already scanning the case.

I move from the kitchen to the shop and flinch when I see Frankie and Quinn outside, cupping their eyes against the window to look inside. Quinn scans the space, and when she sees me, she stumbles back a foot. Through some unexpected, warm flutters in my stomach, I give her a weak wave and she waves back.

Seeing Quinn is probably the only decent thing about today. Ever since the Christmas vendor event, I've thought about her a lot. Probably excessively, if I'm being honest. But that day, I saw Quinn transform from feisty and blunt, to blushing and fidgety when people approached the table. Throughout that day—and yes, I ended up staying the whole day—her hard shell exterior cracked, and I got a glimpse of the gooey inside. And I really liked what I saw.

And then she started visiting my shop, several days a week, and each time she pops in, my pulse surges. When she's here, we chat effortlessly and brainstorm things like me selling cookies (*green and red!* She'd laugh) when she opens for business. And every time she leaves, a part of me wishes she'd stayed longer.

I just have to keep reminding myself that Quinn's desires in life are different than mine. As long as I do that, I won't get hurt.

I pack up a large box of cookies and cupcakes, and hand it to the electrician. Through the storefront windows, I see Quinn wrap both hands around Frankie's upper arm and physically try to drag her sister down the sidewalk. But Frankie is standing solid, her hands shoved in her pockets, with a grin. I can only imagine the avalanche of swear words flying from Quinn's mouth right now.

Ken rests the box in his arms and gives me one more sympathetic glance. "I'll let you know the moment the replacement parts arrive. Who knows? Maybe it'll be quicker than what we think."

I appreciate the white lie, but I know things like this move at the speed of a sloth. I grab the paperwork from him and unlock the front doors to let him out.

The warm sun hits me, and I squint into the morning light. Winter is creeping around the corner, ready to swap the fall leaves with chilly air and frosty breath, and I want to soak in the last bit of warmth. Sadly, because of a gang of hairy rodent monsters, now is not the time. "Hey, guys," I say to Quinn and Frankie with a quiet smile, swallowing back the fierce urge to cry.

"Hey," Quinn says with a scrunched brow. "Everything okay? Your sign says you're closed?"

My traitorous lip trembles. My bakery—*closed*. All those people disappointed, all those days ruined, all my staff left wondering when they can return to work. This is terrible.

"Whoa. Did that guy do something?" Frankie narrows her eyes down the street at the electrician, her muscular arms crossing across her chest. "Do him and I need to have words?"

This makes me crack a smile, which thankfully halts the sniffles. "No, no, he's nice. Please don't hurt him."

"Good." Quinn lets out a breath, tucking a red coil behind her ear. "Frankie's the muscle, but I can do a solid verbal beatdown if needed."

I can't help it. Tears fill in my eyes behind my glasses.

"Oh no, I swear I'm just kidding. I won't give this guy a verbal anything." Quinn steps forward and rests a hand on my shoulder. "Are you okay?"

"Stupid freaking chipmunks! Chipmunks of all the things," I say, and swipe at a tear. My glasses fog up behind the lenses, and I remove them to fan my face. Quinn and Frankie flash a sister-code-only look at each other, but I can easily translate. They think I've lost my mind. "A rabid band of chipmunks got under the crawl space of this building and cut through some wires, and now most of the electricity in here won't work. My industrial freezer and fridge are shot."

"Oh my God, no," Quinn says and removes her hand from my shoulder. I kind of want her to put it back. "Holy shit, that sucks so bad. Is there anything we can do?"

"Not unless you know someone who owns an industrial fridge or freezer." I cannot believe all of my stuff—pounds of butter, dough, pastry sheets, eggs, fruit, and more—will be destroyed. My heartbeat thuds against chest, and sticky sweat prickles against my neck. *What in the ever-loving heck am I going to do?*

A slow smile passes over Quinn. Why is she smiling? This isn't funny. My baby, my home, my everything, is in crisis. She shoots Frankie a glance with an arched eyebrow, and Frankie gives her a quick nod.

"Just so happens I *do* know someone who owns an industrial fridge and freezer," Quinn says and checks her watch. "How much time do we have to save your stuff?"

ELEVEN
ZOEY

For the next hour, Quinn, Frankie, and I fly around my bakery. While Frankie runs to the grocery store to grab bags of ice and buy out the entire stock of Styrofoam coolers, Quinn and I dash to the kitchen and start packaging items. We hardly speak as I zip through plastic-wrapping and Quinn boxes items like our life depends on it.

"Okay, all the eggs are in one space. Do you want me to add the frozen pastries on top of them, or the frosting?" Quinn calls out as she stacks items in a cooler and Frankie runs to the gas station for more ice.

"Let's do the pastries, then put the frosting in the second tub," I call out over my shoulder. "Do you see the stacks of pie crusts?"

"Yep! Got them."

Shoving my work, my livelihood into boxes and coolers, pops beads of sweat across my hairline. "The wedding this Saturday in Duluth is massive. What am I going to do? A quadruple-tiered cake and I have to bake it in layers..." If I had more time, I'd bawl. But right now, I'm on a rescue mission. The tears can wait.

The wedding couple's day will be totally ruined. Yes, yes, the wedding is not only about the cake, but I'll bet the cake is one of the top-ten most important parts of the day. I fan the bottom of my shirt, trying to remove the stickiness, but the air-conditioning is out and it's pointless. "And Phoebe has her baby shower cupcakes for Sunday, and we have so many birthday cakes... I can't let these people down."

It's so flippin' hot in here. I rip off my shirt to my tank top and toss it on the counter behind me. Did Quinn just give me a look? The kind that flashes once up and down with a pop of red warming her neck? Maybe. But I don't have the luxury to think any deeper because I'm literally going to ruin the days of so many people. "What will they do? They can't get replacements now. Do you think I can go to their houses and bake there? Gosh, what the heck am I even saying? I can't do that. And I have to make so many calls and—"

"We got this, okay?" Quinn reaches for my hand, and I swear she must have some magical CBD balm laced in her palms, because my pounding heart evens out almost instantly. "Let's just do things one at a time. I have permits for food prep and a kitchen station, but I don't have the stove that you probably need. How about you do all the prep at my place, and then bring it back here to bake, if the ovens work?"

I exhale. By some grace of the great cupcake spirit, the electricity to one oven and a few kitchen lights remained unharmed during the chipmunks' temporary hostile takeover, and Ken never told me I couldn't use those specific ovens.

Quinn unravels her hair from her ponytail and twists it back up into a floppy bun. "Do you have the orders and information on your laptop?"

I nod.

"Perfect." Quinn dumps ice in the bottom of a cooler. "Just bring your laptop to my place. We'll contact all the people on the list and let them know that you're closed, but they're still a priority. Maybe you can offer a delivery service?"

How is Quinn being so calm and efficient? I mean, I understand this isn't her business and she does not have the level of emotional attachment to my bakery that I do, but she is so organized and level-headed that it feels like she's my manager. It's exactly what I need right now for my thudding pulse to not jump right out of my skin.

My breath slowly stabilizes. I can make deliveries. Most everything is local, minus the wedding, which I would've had to deliver anyway. "Okay, yes, that might work."

Quinn stacks frozen pastry sheets in the cooler as I drag items out from the freezer. "Do you have deliveries coming in this week? Supplies or products, maybe?"

I push my palm into my forehead. "Ugh. The deliveries. Yes, of course I do. Weekly." Maybe for once I'll get lucky and the driver will forget my entire order, not just hazelnuts.

"Okay, we'll contact them, too." Quinn snaps the lid shut and fans her face. "So, first thing, we'll move the perishable items. Then we'll call the people who have orders this week because word will get out quickly. Then, the deliveries and your staff. Do you need to call insurance?"

My insides revert to burning. I *cannot* believe this is happening. I grab one of the ice cubes and hold it against my neck, the sharp coolness tingling my skin.

"Don't worry." Quinn cuffs her T-shirt sleeves to her shoulder then returns to fanning her face. "We got this."

Do we? Do I? The amount of information and things I have to do is bubbling up and over. I feel off-balance, but when I peek over the coolers at Quinn, her green sparkling eyes hold me in place, centering me. "How are you so calm?"

"Well, I mean, this isn't my shop, so I can be more objective. But also, this is what I did in New York." She waves to the stack of coolers. "Organized shit and kept things on a schedule."

"You did?" I stack the cooler next to the others on the floor and take one last look at my empty fridge. "I'm so curious about your time in New York."

"I'll tell you anything you want to know." Quinn attaches the lid to the cooler and takes a final scan of the kitchen. "But first, let's secure these items."

The heavy alleyway fire door swings open, bringing with it fresh, heated air from outside. "Wow, you two made awesome time," Frankie says, stepping into the kitchen. "Is there anything left to pack?"

"Nope, I think we got it all," I say. "We should stuff my car as much as possible since I have air-conditioning, and then put the rest of it in the back of your truck?"

"Sounds good," Frankie says as she lifts two coolers while Quinn and I grab one.

We move lightning fast to load the cars, and ten minutes later, I'm flying down the highway toward Quinn's farm near Maple Creek. I make a quick call to my four staff members to give them an update after telling them not to come in this morning, then crack open the window and take in several full breaths of the fresh, warm autumn air until my nostrils sting with the wind. *What in the actual frick?* I still cannot get over that this happened. But now that the immediate crisis is over, the knot that had been cinching my gut all day releases.

"Hey, Siri, call Mom," I say to my phone, and it rings through my car speakers.

"Honey! I've been worried sick. Do you have an update for me?" my mom says through the speaker. "I'm so sorry I couldn't be there with you."

Knowing my mother, this fiasco probably shadowed the joy of her two-day shopping trip to the Mall of America with some of her friends. When I called her this morning in a panic, she told me she'd leave the hotel that moment and be back in Spring Harbors in a few hours to help me. Of course, I told her absolutely not, but also requested that she not call me until I had things under control. I'm kind of surprised she honored my wishes.

"Thank you for not calling and interrupting," I say and cross lanes to pass a semi. I love my mother so much, but next to the Minnesota Vikings, making hotdish, and going to church bazaars, her favorite pastime is worrying about her kids and Noah. "Quick update. Going to be out of commission for a few weeks—"

"Oh no! A few weeks?" she says with the faint sound of shoppers chatting in the background. "What are you going to do with the shop?"

I put on my blinker and follow Quinn's truck off the highway and onto a bumpy county road. "Right now, I'm moving all the chilled stuff to Quinn's Christmas tree farm because she has a fridge and freezer, then we'll figure everything else out later."

A pause follows. "Quinn, huh?"

Oh no. The smile in her voice is undeniable, and I cannot deal with it right now. I made the tiniest mistake last week of mentioning Quinn *twice*, and my mom latched on to Quinn's name like a bulldog with a bone. I had to break it to her that Quinn and I are just friends—if you could even classify it as such—and will never be any more than friends.

When she pressed me, I'd clammed up, and she backed off. Thankfully. I didn't want to explain that Quinn and I want fundamentally different things from a relationship. Quinn is unapologetic in who she is, and what she wants from women. Honestly, I wish more women were up-front and just owned that part of themselves. The heartache I went through with Josie was enough. I'm not setting myself up for that kind of pain again. No matter how cute and tempting Quinn may be, knowing what she wants versus what I want is like a relationship warning label: ENTER AT YOUR OWN RISK. My heart is fragile enough—I'm not risking breaking it again.

"Yes, Quinn," I finally say. "She and Frankie helped me pack everything up. Anyway, I'm turning into her place now, but wanted to let you know that I'm fine and I'll call you later."

Maybe not the entire truth, as I have at least another half mile, but I don't have the energy to field any potential invasive questions. We say goodbye and I grip the steering wheel as I crunch over the gravel leading down the winding road into Quinn's property. Burnt oranges and reds pop from the trees through the lush greenery. I follow the truck through one more turn, bump over some potholes, then pull in next to the women in front of the massive gray wood barn with chipped siding.

Once I kill the engine, I fly out of the car. Me, Frankie, and Quinn move items from vehicles into the barn, and set them on a stainless-steel table in the kitchen area in the far back corner. Hurrying, I kick a rock out of the way but stumble on the path.

On my second trip back to the car, I'm nearly sprinting. If any of these items thaw, they're unusable. I need to salvage anything I can.

Quinn stops me as I pass her. "Hey, how about Frankie and I bring these in, and you start stacking the fridge and freezer? I know your walking boot is off and all, but this property has so many dips and rocks, and I'd hate for you to trip and fall and sue me."

I'm tempted to say I'll be fine, but I've only had my boot off for a week, and I'm still getting used to using my foot full force. If I break it again, I'm going to bury myself in a mountain of almond flour and never return.

Frankie and Quinn are serious workhorses. Quinn might not be as strong as Frankie—not sure who is—but she's as quick and lifts almost as much. Inside the small kitchen area, I pop open the nearly empty freezer and refrigerator, minus a case of water and a case of Chardonnay.

"Don't judge," Quinn calls out over her shoulder, her messy bun slipping to the side. "It was left over from a wedding party in May."

"No judgment here," I say, removing it and setting it on the empty wooden bench next to me. "I'm just wondering when we can dive into it."

Quinn checks her watch with a grin. "Well, it's technically after noon, so I say anytime."

She bolts back through the open barn doors. I pop the top off the Styrofoam cooler and try not to gag when it squeaks against the bottom. Ugh, that sound makes me cringe. I stack the items like my life depends on it—which it feels like it actually does—when Quinn joins at my side and hands me products.

"Last one," Frankie says as she crosses the barn floor. "Is everything holding up okay?"

"Yes, thank gosh." Everything that Quinn's handing me still feels cool to the touch, and the tightness in my chest is evaporating. "I think we'll be okay."

"I mean, really, would anyone know?" Quinn says, handing me eggs. "I ate a box of mac and cheese yesterday that I didn't know expired six months ago and I'm alive to tell the tale."

"Gross." I groan, adding the final egg carton to the bottom shelf. "If someone got sick because of me, I would never forgive myself."

Frankie opens the cooler stuffed with butter and stacks them in the fridge. "Never ever take food advice from Quinn. She likes ketchup on her noodles."

Quinn nudges Frankie with her elbow, then reaches around her for the fruit compote. "I spice it up with Cajun seasoning, though, so it's practically gourmet."

Double gross. I'm not sure if they're joking or not so I don't say anything. The last thing I want to do is come off as a food snob—which I very much am—and insult the woman who just saved my heinie.

We scramble at a breakneck speed to get everything into the fridge and freezer, and when I finally close the doors with the most satisfying click of my life, I nearly collapse. Frankie crosses the almost bare room and returns with three folding chairs, Quinn tears into a case of bottled water, and I plant my palms on the cool stainless-steel table and close my eyes.

Once Frankie unfolds the chairs, we all flop down, polish off bottles of water, and sit in silence.

My gaze travels the space. Last year, Morgan and Frankie fixed this barn up to host a wedding. The barn is rustic and bare besides white lights wrapped from the beams. The floors are in good condition and the windows look new. Boxes and totes line the wall. There's one simple cash register sitting on a wooden mantle in the corner alongside dozens of mason jars, and stacks of folding chairs and tables rest in racks in the corner.

The place is an empty palette. Clean, unaffected. If given the right time and tools, Quinn could absolutely bring back that Christmas magic. It might be mid-October, but I could use some Christmas magic in my life after this disastrous day.

Frankie leans back in the chair and fans her shirt. "Now that we're breathing again, what are the next steps?"

"Wait, let me grab a notebook." Quinn scurries to the corner and returns, flipping to a page and poising a pen. "So, I think you should put something out on social media letting the community know that you're closed for the next few weeks for unforeseen issues. Did you tell your employees?"

I twist the top back on the bottle and set it next to me. "Yes, I called them this morning."

"Okay," Quinn says, "so then we have to cancel the deliveries for the next few weeks, contact the parties that you have prescheduled orders..."

As Quinn scribbles down everything we need to do, I discover that she may look and sound like a red-headed tornado storming through the town, but she's actually hyper-efficient and organized, at least with this stuff. "You're really good at this."

The chair beneath Frankie squeaks against the floor when she lifts herself. She paces back and forth, and it takes a moment to realize she's not upset, just bored with sitting. "This is Quinn's expertise. I got the ADHD in the family, so my brain fires on all cylinders, but Quinn thinks in bullet points."

Quinn taps the pen on the outside of the notebook. "Well, you also got the muscles and I'm stuck with the freckles."

I will never say this out loud, but the freckles win. Not that Frankie isn't attractive—she really is. Short cropped hair, dimples, a really nice smile, muscles that make me want to get myself to the gym. But Quinn is just so... I shake my head. I need to stop thinking about how pretty Quinn is. I think I'm just looking for a distraction from this mountain of chaos, and she is a lovely, lovely, distraction.

Frankie's phone rings and she steps outside. A breeze picks up from outside the large open barn doors and fills the space with the faint smell of burning wood. I finish the second water bottle and twist the cap back on. "I really appreciate you doing this. It was such good timing that you were at my shop this morning. Or, I guess unlucky timing for you, but good for me. I couldn't have done this without you."

Quinn pulls the notebook to her chest. "It's no problem. I needed a break from all the Christmas stuff today, so this is a perfect interruption."

My gosh, what in the heck am I going to do? My business just got shut down, I have a ton of orders that I need to fulfill, I need to call a million people... My breath locks in my throat again.

When I opened Zoey's Bakery years ago, my parents begged me to take on a partner, but I refused. I wanted, *needed*, to do this on my own and have control over all aspects—its success and fail- ures. To be the boss I wished I'd had, to bring joy to the community in the way I wanted to, without double-checking with someone else. And honestly, I thought Josie would quit working at the vet hospital and join me at the bakery. But now, facing this colossal poop-storm on my own is too much.

I toss my glasses on the table and rest my head into my hands. My thumbs dig into my temples, and I try hard to breathe through the tension.

"Are you okay?" Quinn asks. Her raspy voice is just above a whisper, but echoes in the open space.

Am I? I'm so glad that I'm not doing this alone and that Quinn and Frankie helped me. And I'm really lucky it wasn't a fire or something more catastrophic. But I'm not okay. I've needed a break for a while, but not like this. Not by letting everyone down who counts on me. "Yes, it's just... a lot. I have so many calls and things to do. I'm worried about my staff and I need to pay them, but not sure with what. It's just a lot."

Quinn pulls her chair next to me, so much so that our legs are nearly touching. I feel this tingle, almost like static electricity, like if I moved any closer, I'd get a little shock. It's comforting being this close. Something about Quinn makes me feel like things are going to be okay, and right now, I need to believe everything will be okay.

"I totally get it. And you're a really nice boss. I've never worked for anyone so worried about their employees before." She bites the corner of her lip. I'm drawn, just for a moment, to her mouth, then tear my gaze away. "But hopefully insurance covers all that. We can look into this and make a few calls."

Several moments pass, and I can't help thinking *why*. Why is Quinn—who I've only known for a couple of months—giving up an entire day to help me out, without seemingly asking for something in return. This is not the way my life typically plays out. Yes, I have an amazing family who'd do almost anything for anyone, but my mom and dad are so busy with their jobs and helping my sister and Noah that I never ask. My employees are my employees, which is different, and I don't have a ton of friends that I spend time with that I feel like I could call. And here I am, with Quinn and Frankie, who just did it. "Why are you helping me with all of this?"

"Why not?" Quinn shrugs.

It's so simple, so quick. Just two tiny words but they carry the weight of something much stronger than six letters. It gives me a glimpse into the type of person Quinn is, and for the hundredth time today, I'm grateful I met her.

If this had happened a few years ago, would Josie have helped? Probably. Josie's a nice, decent person. But I always had to ask, for everything. During our relationship, I chased her, begged for her to give me the things I needed from our relationship. But, in the end, she was the one who said I didn't communicate. Maybe she was right. After years of saying what I needed, fatigue poisoned me and turned me cold. I so desperately needed Josie to intrinsically know me well enough to know what I needed without me giving her a map.

And here... Quinn just did it. Without being asked.

A shadow emerges from the door. "Hey, do you guys need any more help?" Frankie asks, tapping her fingers against the door frame.

I've taken up hours of their time that even if I needed more help, there's no way I'd ask. "No, not at all. Can I offer you cupcakes for life? You have no idea how much I appreciate your help."

"Ah, this was actually pretty fun." Frankie stuffs the phone back in her pocket. "Are you okay bringing Quinn home? Morgan wants me to meet her for a late lunch in Duluth."

Right now, I would bring Quinn to the moon if Frankie wanted. Not that Quinn owed me anything at all, she doesn't, but I sat with her the entire day at her Christmas vendor event, so there's a touch less guilt involved. But Frankie's just a customer, helping from the goodness of her heart. "Of course, happy to. Seriously, thank you. Once I get back up and running, I promise I'll make it up to you."

"What? Stop, Zoey. This is not a big deal," Frankie says. "You saved me from going to the gym, it's a beautiful day out, my sister was nice to me for once—"

"Hey!" Quinn throws a water bottle cap toward her sister.

"We are all good. I promise." Frankie grabs her keys from her pocket and twirls them around her finger. "Catch you guys later."

Now that we've taken a break and I'm not running at marathon level speed, I unwrap the shirt I tied around my waist earlier and tug it over my head. The adrenaline of saving thousands of dollars' worth of my products lifts, and I'm hit with decision paralysis of what the heck I'm supposed to do next. All of my products are in Quinn's gift shop kitchen, but then what? I come here every day? At night? Get keys to the property? I didn't think all of this through. My focus was on saving the items, not what happens next.

I readjust my ponytail and glance at Quinn, who's still scribbling in the notebook. "Hey, I'm thinking we should exchange numbers. I'll figure out a time that works in your schedule for me to grab the items and move them to a more permanent, well semi-permanent, home."

Quinn stops writing and clicks the pen against the notepad. She has this smile that's hard to decode, but it makes me feel warm and reassured. "Happy to give you my number, but how about we figure out a solid plan together."

My trapped breath releases. She has no idea how much relief this gives me that I'm not in this alone. I nod and scoot my chair closer.

She flips back a page in the notebook. "I think we need to start with phone calls. Are you comfortable with me looking at your insurance paperwork, while you call the customers with pending orders?"

A million things exist that I need to do, but right now, I need to offset all this negativity. And I know the perfect way to do it. A slow smile spreads. I cross my fingers and hope Quinn will join me in a small adventure. "How about we have a bit of fun first?"

Quinn's brow hikes and the corner of her lip twitches into a grin. She closes her notebook and tucks the pen in the spiral binding. "I am *always* up for some fun."

"Good." I lift myself from the chair and grab my purse. "Because I know exactly where I want to go."

TWELVE
QUINN

Okay, so this is *really* fun. Probably the most fun I've had since moving back to Minnesota. After Zoey and I scrubbed out a kids' wagon that a bridal party had used for a wedding photo prop, we loaded it into the back seat of Zoey's car and drove back to the bakery. It took less than a half hour to package everything in the display case and then we took off with a wagon full of chocolate and raspberry croissants, cookies, macaroons, cakes, and cupcakes.

First, we drove to the animal shelter and dropped off several boxes for the volunteers and workers. Then we went to the salon where Zoey gets her hair done, and one of the local grocery stores (not the one Zoey worked at years ago because apparently there's a juicy story Zoey needs to tell me about later when they accused her of stealing recipes). And now we're strolling up and down the sidewalks with the sun beaming on us, stopping at each store on Main Street and handing them out like Mrs. Claus herself.

At the hardware store, Zoey opens the door, and I drag in the wagon behind me.

"Hey, Erica!" Zoey says to the woman behind the counter.

"Zoey, what the heck happened to your store?" Erica says, tugging off her garden gloves. "I went there over lunch and saw the closed sign."

"Electrical problems, can you believe it?" Zoey tosses up her hands. "Gonna be a few weeks before we open."

I feel so freaking bad for Zoey. If an unexpected closure happened at my farm, I'm not sure if I'd be able to handle it. And Zoey had seemed frazzled, of course, to the point I thought a swear word was close to slipping from that pretty mouth of hers, but she pulled herself together. And not only did she overcome this huge setback today, she gifted the town with her baked goods rather than dealing with insurance and logistics.

The more I learn about Zoey, the more time I spend with her, the more I like her. Things like giving up a rare day off to sit with me at the Christmas event—even though I'd chewed her out the day prior—shows me her heart. And now, when this chipmunk catastrophe happens, the first action she takes is to brighten others' days with her baked goods.

Who *is* this woman? And... why is she single?

I step forward with a small box and hold it open to Erica, the same drill I've done for the past ten stores. "But may we offer you a box of cookies for you and the crew, compliments of Zoey? Although, to be perfectly honest, I've been taking partial credit for the last hour."

Zoey flashes a smile at me. "You can take full credit. There's no way I could've done this without you today."

Everything in me warms. This interaction, this entire day, these last few weeks. I feel a blush sweep beneath my freckles.

"Thank you! Yum." Erica snatches the cookie box. "How's the tree farm coming along, Quinn? You haven't been in here for tools lately. Ya musta found yourself a new store, or getting the hang of things."

Being back in Spring Harbors, I'm constantly reminded of how things are so different than New York. Yes, I grew up here, but as a kid, I either didn't know or didn't care about the community's interconnectedness. At first, it felt suffocating. Like the town plants spies everywhere, ready to tell my parents anything to make them even more disappointed in me than they are already. But now I realize it's how the community rallies and supports each other.

"Nope, I'm not cheating on you," I say back to Erica. "I've just finally hit my groove. Although, I need to come back later this week for a wood-burning tool if you have it." Sure, I could get some of these items, often cheaper, online, but there's something so gratifying about spending my money locally.

Something else deeply gratifying? Spending my day with Zoey. *Oof.* It's been a very, very long time since I've had a friend like this, and I think this is exactly what my soul needs.

Not to mention she's cute. She's so damn cute that even through the chaos and sweaty foreheads and rushing to save her products, she continually catches my eye. And when she stripped down to that white tank in her kitchen, flashing me more skin than she probably meant, everything in me revved.

Yes, I'm a feral woman in my sexual prime, but anyone would flush with jolts of electricity when around Zoey. Sadly, *so very* sadly, I cannot look at Zoey that way. It's not respectful, and the last thing I'd ever want to do is objectify her. She was so upfront and honest about wanting a life mate. And I respect that. I do. So, from here on out, I need to constantly remind myself to not be drawn to her mouth, or smooth skin, or the slope of her neck, and look at her only as a friend.

Zoey tucks a fallen strand of hair behind her ear and glances at Erica. "Is Amanda still on maternity leave?"

I swear Zoey is just like Morgan. She seems to know everyone in town, who's getting married, having babies, who just had surgery. She has this sort of quiet softness. People gravitate towards her like she's a warm hot tub during a snowstorm.

But, for once, I actually do remember that Erica's daughter—and employee—Amanda had a baby. A "guess the due date" calendar was at the front of the store, where you could drop in dollars on the predicted birth date. Half the pot went to mom, half to the winner. Was it an illegal gambling ring? Yep, kind of. But even a few of the sheriffs joined in on the fun.

Erica crunches into a chocolate cookie and dusts the crumbs from her fingertips. "Yep, Amanda's going to stay on maternity leave for a few more months. She loves being at home with that little peanut. I bought baby Berkley a pair of denim overalls, but Amanda said I have to wait until Berkley's at least potty trained before I can put her behind the registers."

We chat for a few more moments, then step back out onto the sidewalk. The nearly empty wagon squeaks and bobs against the bumps in the sidewalk, and Zoey and I take turns dragging it behind us. Although I've had enough sugar to wipe out an entire army of Sugar Plum Fairies, my belly rumbles. "Last few cookies," I say. "Who's the lucky winner?"

Zoey stops right outside of the bakery door and steps underneath the pink-and-white awning. Shade falls across her face and she yawns into her sleeve. It's pretty obvious the activities from today have finally caught up with her.

"I think we've done all the good deeds I can handle for today," she says, blowing bangs away from her face. "Maybe I just toss the rest of the cookies."

"Blasphemy!" I throw my hands on my chest like I'm warding off a heart attack. "I'll take them home for Frankie."

"Perfect." She digs out keys from her purse and jingles them into the lock. "My foot is throbbing. I might have overdone it."

"Oh shit, I totally forgot about your foot." I grit my teeth and scan her ankle. She's in tennis shoes, thankfully, but it's hard to see if there's swelling. "Do you think you should elevate it?"

She nods and opens the door. A waft of doughy and sticky air meets us, and I follow her inside. This is a time where I could leave. Call Frankie to come get me since she and Morgan should be back from Duluth now, or see if there's an Uber available. But being around someone like Zoey feels pretty damn good, and even with the full, chaotic day, energy fills me. It's almost dinner time, and I'm not ready to call it quits, yet. And with the way Zoey is not hesitating at the entry with me and instead saunters through her place with me at her heels, I have a sneaking suspicion she feels the same.

"God, I hope my home isn't muggy," Zoey says, and we cross the waiting area room to the swinging kitchen doors. "Just my luck we have a heat wave in October."

"Where do you live?" I ask.

She points up to the ceiling. "Right above here is my bedroom."

I'm not sure why a tiny zip springs through me with the word *bedroom* and knowing where Zoey sleeps. It's like a little insight into her that I'm not sure she shares with other customers. Which I think means we are, officially, in a solid friend-zone. I'm part of an inner circle and helpless to stop my goofy smile. I made a friend. A *real* friend. "No way. You live in the loft?"

"Yep." Zoey escorts me into the kitchen. We pass by the station where we wrapped items this morning, and she tosses her bag on the counter. "Hey, do you want me to bring you home?"

My stomach drops. No, I don't want her to bring me home. I want to stay here and ask her everything about her life. Cats or dogs? Beer or wine? Water or pop? Fruit or veggies? I want to know about past relationships and embarrassing stories and her celebrity crushes.

Today was everything I needed. I'm more imbedded into the community than before, I made a friend, and the last thing I want to do is go back to my place, alone. "Do you want me to leave?"

A long silence stretches, and I wonder if she's thinking the same as me. Maybe, in a strange sort of way, even as awful as things were, she also needed today. She nibbles the side of her lip. She has such a pretty mouth, and I can't help but let my gaze fall. Soft pink with a cupid-bow shape, and maybe I shouldn't notice it, but I do.

"No, I don't," she says.

And... a flutter bounces inside me.

But I'm sure this tingling physiological reaction is just a friends thing. The spark of having someone I connect with, outside the bedroom. Just because it's been a while since I got laid, I cannot confuse what's happening on my insides with what's happening outside. *I. Cannot. Confuse. This.*

Zoey opens the door to a small office off the kitchen and I step inside. As far as having an office about the size of a broom closet, it's rather cozy. A couple of plants, a pink-and-white lamp on a dark wood desk, some scattered water bottles, a framed picture of her and a few folks outside of the bakery, and two chairs. She rolls a chair my way and slumps into the one at her desk with a very heavy sigh. "What a day." She plucks off her glasses and pinches the bridge of her nose. "Now that the fun part is over, there's so much to do. I'm not even sure where to start."

I ease into the chair and am keenly aware of how small the space is. If I scooted just a foot closer, we'd be touching. "Didn't I tell you I specialize in this? I'm on it. And I kind of love it."

"Seriously, what job did you have in New York?" She puts her glasses back on and rolls back at least a foot.

Message received. I push myself back to give her more space.

"I'm so curious what your life looked like there," she says.

I can't imagine she *really* wants to hear about my time in New York. She probably wants to hear about the New Year's Eve ball drop in Times Square, or Central Park, or about random run-ins I may have had with celebrities, which only happened once. Scarlett Johansson. *Swoon.* But she was so totally normal, had no paparazzi following her or band of fans, that I only realized who she was a block later.

No chance Zoey wants to hear about the terrible coffee in the breakroom, me crying in the bathroom after my boss yelled at me, sitting on the subway next to men who take up too much space, or listening to our neighbors banging it out after a fight. "You don't really want to know about my time there."

She looks at me with so much sincerity I can tell she really does want to know. She props her elbow on the table, rests her chin in her palm, and something inside me clicks. Yes, Frankie and Morgan are interested in what I do. They always check in to talk about the details of my day, convinced me to finally leave my terrible job after one too many sobbing phone calls, ask me on the regular about updates on the farm.

But outside of them, I haven't had this—someone who wants to know anything about me outside of the bedroom. Sure, I choose women who are as equally allergic to commitment as I am, but still, this fills me with a warmth that I wasn't sure that I needed. But now that I have it, it feels really fucking nice.

"Yes, I absolutely want to know," Zoey says, readjusting her foot to elevate it on a box. "Like what does day-to-day look like there? Do people eat breakfast and go to the store, and stop for Sunday visits with family like we do? At the office, do you sprint from one room to the next like they show in the movies? I want to know it all."

A grin fills my face. A much goofier one than I intend, but here it is, ransacking my cheeks with no regard to reason. "I have an idea. I know I've eaten like ten cupcakes today, but how about we order pizza, go through the stuff we need to do for your shop, and I'll tell you all about New York."

"Perfect," Zoey says, lifting her head from resting on her palm. "Pepperoni good?"

"Yep, and anchovies."

She scrunches her face so hard that her glasses almost fall off. "No. You? Really? That's fish. Fish on pizza? Sounds truly terrible."

"It *is* fish, but really it's more like a salt bomb." I lick my lips with a dramatic flair. "It just splits that tongue right open and deposits the goodness. Heavenly, I tell ya. You cannot knock it until you try it."

She giggles, but her eyes drop, just for the briefest of moments, to my mouth and the movement halts me.

Nope. I am not doing this. I'm not ruining the first friendship I've made in Minnesota, the first friendship I've made in forever, by messing it up with sex. I've never mixed the two and don't plan to start now. Sure, I tried to date. But either the dates were so conversationally stimulating that the sex was boring, or the sex was so hot that I didn't care about the conversation. It probably makes me sound like a terrible person, but I can't help it. Closeness, intimacy, all of that makes me queasy. Not queasy in some melodramatic way, but genuinely physically ill. I don't know how to act around a woman that I both really like and am sexually attracted to. Do I flirt? Be myself? By the time the evening ends, I've worked myself into a total tizzy.

It's not that I don't like the women I sleep with. Mostly, I do. I just don't want to combine emotional and physical intimacy. It's one or the other and never both. I've never had what Morgan and Frankie have. I've never been so in love that it took years to get over, or so in love with a past partner that I reconnected as an adult like Frankie and Morgan. I've never had that "person," the one that I want to walk down the sidewalk with and hold hands with and snuggle up with a cat on a couch and watch movie marathons. That type of love is not in the cards for someone like me.

I'm a little fucked-up. I know this. So no, I'm not giving Zoey the same whisper of gaze she just gave me. Zoey's an innocent. Someone too pure for this world. And I'm not.

"How about this," I say and cross my legs. "We'll get anchovies on the side, and you try one little bite. And if you hate it, I'll do something."

Her mouth twists. "Hmm. You'll do *something*? I mean, we're talking about fish. On perfectly good pepperoni. I think I need you to be more specific."

Ugh. If that cute little teasing tone doesn't do the tiniest thing to my insides. "Specific? I'm fresh out of ideas."

Several long moments pass before the corner of her lips tugs into a playful grin. "You have to Cusack me outside my window."

I have less than zero idea what she is talking about. "*Cusack* you? What does that mean?"

She pushes herself back from the table and crosses her arms. Her blue eyes are dancing underneath the light in the office, sparkles of cobalt and aqua mixing in a beautiful hue. "You're telling me you call your vehicle 'Truck Norris,' but don't know the

Cusack reference?" She laughs, a pretty, airy laugh. "So there's that movie *Say Anything...* from the eighties, right? And John Cusack holds the boom box high above his head and blasts 'In Your Eyes' outside of Ione Skye's window, and it's like the most romantic movie scene of all time."

This is all vaguely familiar, probably off some social media reel I saw, but based on Zoey's grin, I'm sure as hell going to google this later.

"So," she says, crossing her arms in a solid, definitive motion, "if the anchovies are terrible, you have to Cusack me."

I love everything about this. Even if I don't know what it is exactly. But right now, to keep that smile going, I might agree to just about anything. "I don't even know where I would find a boom box."

Zoey rolls her eyes. "We don't have to get super technical. You can use your cellphone."

I reach over to shake her hand. "Deal." And if I am not mistaken, she holds on a moment longer than I do.

"Okay, I'm going to go grab my phone up front and order." She lifts herself and limps towards the door.

Ugh, I should have noticed that today's activities pushed her too hard. I would've delivered the treats on my own and let her rest if I had noticed. From here on out, until I leave tonight, I'm making it my mission to get Zoey to relax as much as possible. "I'm going to jot down some notes. Do you have a few extra pens?"

She steps outside of the room and points at the desk. "Yep, in the drawer. I think I have an extra notebook in one of the drawers, too."

After she leaves, I roll the chair to her desk and dig through a few drawers looking for pens and a notebook. When I reach the bottom drawer, my breath catches in my throat. In front of me lie unopened, soft yellow and blue envelopes with Zoey's name written across in beautiful penmanship. The return address says *Josie Bakersfield*. I don't know who that is, but the loopy letters, the heart in the corner, the way the envelopes are all resting in the drawer like a memory box, makes me feel like I stumbled upon an underwear drawer. But not in a good way. I'm invading something, and I'm way too curious, and I should not be this curious for a friend.

Footsteps approach. I grab the notebook and slam the door.

"They'll be here in about twenty minutes," Zoey says and grabs her keys from the desk. "Want to go to my place?"

I do. Too much. Which is a problem I'll deal with on my own. But something about seeing those envelopes is so unsettling that I almost don't want to go anymore. I swallow back my thoughts and hold out my arm. "Yep... After you."

THIRTEEN
ZOEY

I've had no one to my place—besides my mom and sister, who obviously do not count—since Josie. Literally for two years, not a single person has entered my space. And so that is clearly the *only* explanation as to why my hands tremble as I open the door to my apartment. "Oh, thank God, the lights work," I say. "I was worried that the chipmunks destroyed the electrical to my apartment as well."

Quinn follows behind me and pauses at the door, quiet. I feel like I've gotten to know her, and quiet is not a typical baseline. She's looking at my place, scanning the open floor kitchen, the living room, the hardwood floors, and the hall. "This is one hundred percent nothing, and I mean *nothing*, like what I was expecting."

I grin at this. I'm not shocked by this reaction. I'm Zoey, the bakery owner who loves pink, white, and gold, and pretty cupcakes. But I'm also Zoey, who loves dark horror movies and will periodically slip into a serious grunge-era stage with my music, owns black skull underwear, and back in my twenties, lived for raves in Minneapolis and Chicago. In fact, that was one thing Josie and I used to do when we were in our early twenties—save up money and drive to Chicago, the Twin Cities, even Seattle once on a road trip. We'd visit all the underground raves we could squeeze into a weekend with thumping music, strobing lights, and bass that rattled our bones.

Quinn's eyes continue to travel my entire space. Dark saturated colors fill every inch of this space—rich dark reds and forest greens, black leather furniture, plants, and deep cherry wood floors.

"This feels like a smoky whiskey bar in Lower Manhattan," Quinn says as she closes the door.

"Is that a compliment?" It feels like a compliment. Comparing anything of mine to anything in New York City feels like I upped my cool factor. We both kick off our shoes at the door. I really need to sit before my foot swells from here to Jupiter. I grab two sparkling sodas from the fridge and direct Quinn to the couch.

"Yes, it's definitely a compliment." Quinn sinks back and tucks a leg underneath her butt. "But I have so many questions."

I love that she's curious about me. After living here my whole life, everyone in this town already knows the full details of my life. Even when Josie and I broke up, news traveled so fast that by the next day, fifty percent of my customers asked me if I was okay, and the other fifty percent gave me that sad droopy smile showing me they knew, but were too polite to say anything.

But there's something liberating about Quinn not knowing everything about me. That—besides what Frankie and Morgan may tell her—is unfiltered. "What does your place look like?"

Quinn cracks open the soda and a mist sprays the air. "Well, the house was my grandma Peaches's, but she left it to me and Frankie. Not sure if you knew that? It's a rambler built in the seventies, huge yard, garage, shed, all the things. And we're really lucky."

This is a fact. Owning a home around this area is relatively affordable, at least compared to New York or some of the larger cities. Teachers, people who work at the hardware store, blue-collar workers, have home ownership in the realm of possibility.

"In New York, the home-ownership dream was shot," Quinn

continues. "The best we had was a rent-controlled apartment since we lived there for close to fifteen years. So, I totally get my privilege."

I let out a quick snort. "Okay, it's established that you are one lucky duck. So..."

"So, my bedroom has a faded yellow-and-orange carnation wallpaper border and mauve-colored walls. It's so outdated," Quinn says. "And honestly, if Morgan didn't live with us, it'd probably still have the same original avocado carpet and orange countertops."

I stuff a pillow under my leg on the coffee table. "Those colors are making a comeback."

"Sure, but variations of them. Not straight-up pea green and puke orange. But before Morgan moved in, she ripped everything out and had hardwood floors installed and painted the walls in the kitchen and living room all eggshell and white. She likes super light colors. We have a ton of plants. Looks like we stepped into a Bombay or West Elm or something. It's so completely different than my and Frankie's apartment in New York, with our shitty couch and bean bags. It's like we could never quite move into adulting."

I like hearing about Quinn's life. When Josie and I lived together, our place looked similar to what Quinn is describing— light colors, festive atmosphere, bright—which has its place of course. That's how Josie wanted it decorated, and I was fine with whatever, at least I thought I was. But when she left, I needed to change everything, to gut my place, myself, remove the reminders of her. I needed to be my own person and go back to who I was before I met her.

Sometimes I think I'm still trying to do that. The desire to have people like me, the fear that people are mad at me, has been there since I was a kid. I don't know if that will ever go away. But with Josie, everything I did was to make her happy. I went where she wanted to go, ate what she wanted, watched what she wanted. For a decade I did this. To the point where I wasn't sure if I liked the same things she liked, or if I just lost myself.

The breakup was so hard. But I think losing myself and relearning who I am is harder.

I shake out my ponytail, puff the bangs out of my face, then wrap it back up on top of my head. "Okay, I want to hear all about New York. Did you really work on Wall Street? Does it look like how the movies show it?"

"You've seen the movie *Fargo*, right? Like it's so freakishly accurate to how Minnesotans are, but also not at all." Quinn slides lower into the couch. "It's the same concept. So, yes, I worked on 'Wall Street,' but technically it was just in the Financial District and not the *physical* Wall Street. That's just what people call it. But yeah, I'd work intense hours, wore a business suit every day, rode the subway, speed walked in my tennis shoes, and changed into dress shoes in the lobby."

This does sound like the movies. A high-powered career woman weaving her way through the city, making business calls. I picture Quinn marching down the sidewalk among cab drivers honking and yelling, with headphones gripped to her ears, a cell phone in one hand, and a latte in the other hand. "What did you do there?"

Quinn flicks at the top of her sparkling water can. "I started as an assistant at an investment firm and then worked my way up to executive assistant. I did that for the last ten years."

Raspberry bubbles flow down my throat. "Executive assistant? Honestly, I don't even know what that means." I really hope I'm not being too pushy, but I'm so curious. Who is Quinn? There's something about her, beneath those sparkling jade eyes and pillowy soft lips, that I'm desperate to unravel.

She tucks a curl behind her ear. "Basically, I reviewed the VP's emails, made sure he got to meetings on time, scheduled meetings and outings on his behalf, those kinds of things."

The lightbulbs go off. Besides the fact that Quinn is not emotionally involved in my store, all day I couldn't understand how she remained so calm and organized. "Ah. It's all becoming very clear. That's why you're so good at organizing."

Quinn pulls a coaster across the coffee table and sets down the can. "Yeah, I guess. I mean, I *thought* I was good at my job, but my boss thought I was terrible."

A look passes on her face. Not quite sadness, not quite self-deprecation. I can't place my finger on it, but I wish the look wasn't there, and I want to take it away. "What do you mean? You said you worked with him for a decade but thought you weren't good at your job?"

"Yep." She tugs a pillow into her lap and wraps her arms around it. "My boss was really, really hard on me. For years I thought he was pushing me to be better, which is why he was so tough. But I had so much anxiety, this constant cloud of fear that I was screwing up. And he raised his voice, a lot."

I wince. Never, ever would I raise my voice to one of my employees unless I'm celebrating them. "Oh gosh, that sucks. And the yelling? Sometimes I hear people talk about how females can't be strong leaders because we're too emotional. But then there's a man with no control over his temper, which they don't see *that* as emotional."

"True," Quinn says, and a long silence follows. "But I did screw up a lot. Or maybe not. Honestly, I don't know. Like he'd tell me to schedule a meeting, and I would. And then something would happen, and he'd yell at me, claiming he never wanted a meeting. Or he'd give me an assignment, and I swear I'd take every instruction down almost verbatim, and then he'd say that he never said it. I tried to get him to put things in writing, or send emails, but he'd just say that was why he hired me, so he didn't have to do shit like that." Quinn tightens her hug around the pillow. "It was constant. He wanted his calendar color-coded one way, and I'd do it, and he would freak out that he didn't like it and say I'd wasted time. Every day I'd walk in and brace myself."

An environment like that would completely stress me out. I can't imagine the anxiety I'd feel every day thinking the person I worked for hated me. I stuff the pillow under my leg to elevate it higher, then glance at her. "Why didn't you quit?"

She blows out a breath. "That's the thing. I think if my boss was *always* terrible like that, then I would've quit. But sometimes he was super nice and complimentary, and I thought I was excelling. I'd let my guard down the tiniest bit and then *bam!* He'd yell at me in the hall or snap at me in a board meeting. I walked on constant eggshells, felt this dark energy brewing right below the surface. And then after a while, I started thinking how lucky I was to work here, you know? He'd say that to me too, all the time—that I should be grateful he keeps me around because no one else would put up with me. And... I believed it. I made pretty good money and even though I clearly sucked at my job, he kept me on staff."

Heat rises to my chest. "So, he one hundred percent gaslit you."

My heart sinks as she keeps telling me her story, each word weighing me down. She's staring at her fingers, not me, her voice deflated, as she talks more about her former boss. I flash back to the day I first met Quinn, when she came into the bakery and was adamant she didn't screw up the order. I did the same darn thing to her she'd experienced for years. No wonder she snapped the way she did.

"I've been a boss for six years. Before that I managed the grocery store. I've fired two employees, and I've never felt so awful in my life," I say. "My guess is that you were phenomenal at your job, and he knew he was a big, terrible jerk and was scared you'd realize that. So, he beat you down, so you'd never leave. Because trust me, if you were *actually* that bad, he would've fired you right away."

Something in her softens, and a pink sweeps her cheeks. I think she needed to hear this. My arms are twitchy. I have this urge to lean over and give her a hug, but thankfully, a knock rapping against my door stops me from any uninvited touching.

"Oh, pizza, yes! I'm so hungry." My foot might be achy, but I practically sprint to the door. When I return with the pizza box and a pile of napkins, I dig in with total abandon and crunch into the chewy dough. I spy the anchovies and giggle at the anticipation on Quinn's face. "Am I really doing this?"

Her red curls bounce as she vigorously nods. "Yes, you are."

Okay, here it goes. I give it a quick sniff test. Not... terrible. Saliva grows in the back of my throat. Fish on pizza. First meal with Quinn and she's already getting me to try things I didn't think I would ever do. Here we go. One... two... three. I take a hefty bite of the chewy salty fish and nearly gag. "Nope. Oh my gosh, heck no. Gross! How do you like that?"

Quinn laughs and sprinkles anchovies on her slice. "No way, really? I'll gladly double up. If you see my veins start to pop or anything from the salt intake, will you let the paramedics know?" She swallows a bite and glances up at me with a playful grin. "Does this mean I have to Cusack you now?"

"Yes, you do. A bet's a bet." I swipe the napkin across my mouth. "But you'll have to come up with the song yourself. Which is a ton of pressure because how do you beat 'In Your Eyes'?"

Quinn chuckles and shrugs. As we polish off the pizza, we talk about what it is like owning a business, especially the first year, and all the things that no one ever talks about like workers' comp insurance, licenses, and permits. By the time we're done eating, we've settled into the couch. Comfortable. So comfortable that I'm almost uncomfortable. Quinn has this way about her, something unique and freeing. Almost like I could say anything, and she wouldn't even bat one of her beautiful eyes. Very quickly, the shock of having anyone up to my place besides Josie fades, and morphs into feeling like Quinn has been here a hundred times before.

We crack open more sodas, I tease her about polishing off the entire side of anchovies (still so gross), and we fall into talking about our different experiences growing up here. Sure, it's a small town, and it feels like everyone knows everyone, but I didn't know Quinn as a kid, and I'm consumed by figuring out all the details.

"Did you ever hear about what happened at the grocery store I worked at?" I ask.

"No, not really," Quinn says, leaning her elbow against the back of the couch. "Something about stealing recipes, maybe?"

"Grr. That's so annoying. I didn't *steal* any recipes. At my old place we had chocolate, vanilla, and marble cakes. That was it. At my bakery now we have lavender macaroons and salted caramel croissants, and pistachio cupcakes with a Kahlúa drizzle." I really don't want to be a snob, but my stuff is simply better and more creative than the grocery store's. "The owners were sort of skeezy, you know? Not nearly as bad as what happened to you in New York, but they didn't treat us fairly, refused to honor time-and-a-half wages for overtime, fostered an overall unkind atmosphere. So, what did they do to get back at me after I left to start my bakery? They started a *prayer chain* for me."

Quinn nearly spits out her drink. "What? What are you talking about?"

"The owner's wife is in a prayer circle at the church with a bunch of ladies. So she had them pray for me to absolve me from lying and stealing. And it became a whole thing. And of course, this got back to my mom, who then told me." I roll my eyes. Sure, the story is amusing now, but at the time I wanted to move away to a foreign town where no one knew me. "But yes, quick heads-up. The easiest way to gossip about someone is to pray for them."

Quinn has her hand over her mouth covering her extra-wide smile, but I wish she'd drop it. Her smile is so easy, so full, one that lights up a room. And it stirs something in me, something warm and gooey, but the feeling quickly dissipates. I think I'm tired and emotional. It's been a heck of a day.

I keep going back to our conversation at the Christmas vendor event, where Quinn said she doesn't date. How can someone like Quinn, who's so magnetic, so easy to talk to, so funny and energetic, not date? Did someone break her heart? Has she just not met the right one?

"Can I ask you a question?" I say, reaching for a napkin to take off the grease from my fingers.

Quinn nods. "Of course."

I continue staring at my napkin, now wiping phantom grease. "When we were at the vendor fair, and you said you were a single-serving kind of person, did you mean that? I mean, is that just your preference, or do you really not date. Like ever."

The corner of Quinn's mouth lifts into a quiet grin. "I've never had a relationship in my life. It's just, I don't know, not something for me. I don't long for it, or yearn for it, or feel sad that I don't have it."

I'm quiet, watching her facial expressions, seeing if there's something underneath there that she's hiding. But so far, nothing. She's not shifty, not looking down, not looking like she's avoiding.

"You know how there are some women who want to be moms, and some that don't? And the ones that don't try to explain to the ones that do that they really, really don't want to be a mother. But the other women just can't understand it because it's so imbedded into their biology to be a mom. That's me when I explain this to people." She taps her rings against the side of the soda can, with a gentle *tink*. "Sex to me is a means to an end. A release. A way to get off so I can just get back to my life."

Oh. Wow. And, ouch. She probably doesn't mean for it to sound callous, but it kind of does. Although, I need to keep remembering that I'm framing my reaction to my wants and needs, not hers.

"I've never once cared about any of the women I've been with. I know that's really harsh to say, but it's true. And the women I'm with, they're the same. We know nothing exists between us. We're both in it for the same thing, so it's uncomplicated and easy. Unlike relationships."

I don't know why all of this hurts me. She's opening up, she's being kind, and yet, I can feel this murky pang blooming inside of me and I wish it would go away. "Wow. Thank you for sharing that with me." What else am I supposed to say? Congratulations for being free and sexually open and everything I'm not? Congratulations on your robust sex life when I haven't slept with anyone for years?

Quinn sets the can down on a coaster and leans back into the couch. "So, same question back to you. Are you really an emperor penguin, or have you ever just let loose and spent a weekend doing naughty things with someone you weren't dating."

"I really am a penguin, I guess." I ball up the napkin and toss it on the table. "I've slept with two women in my life, and I proposed to one of them."

Quinn's mouth drops open. "No. Freaking. Way."

Her reaction makes me chuckle. It's like I said I have a closet full of lifelike dolls that I tuck in at night. "What can I say? I'm a one-woman woman. You can tattoo *boring* right on my forehead."

"No, don't do that," Quinn says. "You're not boring and I'm not a ho and that's that."

There's a finality in her tone, one that lifts me, one I think I needed to hear.

She opens her mouth to say something, but then closes it and keeps her gaze on her fingers. As she twists the trio of rings on her finger, she takes a quick, sharp breath. "I have to confess something."

There's a sheepishness in her tone that gives me pause.

"I wasn't snooping, I swear. But when I dug in your desk for notebooks, I saw a stack of pretty cards in there with hearts on them." Quinn cocks her head. "Do you have a secret admirer?"

Oh boy. This is not the confession I was expecting to hear. How do I explain everything about Josie? Why those cards are there, why I don't toss them, what happened with us. I twist the ring on my finger and take a deep breath. "Not so much a secret... and not really an admirer. They're from my ex-girlfriend."

Quinn pulls her lips into her mouth. "The one you proposed to?"

I nod.

She doesn't ask any follow-up questions, and it's so hard to know what to offer. Does she need to hear the details of how my heart broke when Josie left? Broke and shattered, and how I convinced myself I'd never be whole again, and that it has taken me until this year to open up my heart to the possibility of someone else? "I haven't read the letters."

A small line forms between her brows. "Why not?"

I shrug. "I don't know. The breakup was so painful that I'm not sure anything in there is what I need or should hear." I swipe my tongue against the inside of my mouth. "We were together for ten years, and I thought she was the one. I was convinced she was the one, obviously."

I can't help but flash back to that day. Gooseberry Falls. The rush of the waterfall behind us. The rich greenery. The lump in my throat, the shakiness of my fingers, the weight of the ring in my jeans. Josie had been off for a while, but I thought it was stress. She was a vet tech, working with injured animals all day and... I thought it was stress. And when I got down on a knee, and she started bawling... I knew. It wasn't tears of joy.

She never even saw the ring. We drove home in the most excruciating, awkward silence ever in existence, and she moved out a week later.

"So why not throw the letters away?" Quinn asks.

I think about this a lot. Why *not* just throw them away? "I guess I'm not ready."

Quinn's face turns warm. She shifts, studying my face. "Are you over her?"

This answer is much more complicated than what I can give right now. I've let Josie, the person, go. I had no choice when she left. I'm ready to move on, ready to find the one, ready to find a soulmate. But I'd be lying if I said I let the relationship go. To this day, parts of it still haunt me.

Quinn's leaning in, her eyes wide and expectant, and I can tell she really wants to know. And I can't tell if it's because there's a small tug between us, or because we're friends, or if she's just curious.

Finally, I sigh and say the truth: "Honestly, I'm not sure."

FOURTEEN
QUINN

The bed squeaks underneath me as I roll over and flop to my side. A couple weeks ago, after the fiasco at Zoey's, we ended up staying up until midnight reviewing her paperwork, contacting insurance, calling her clients and special orders, and coming up with a plan. We brought her industrial cake mixer—which was so heavy I thought I'd crack a limb—to the barn among some other tools and containers. Zoey will use my space to prep, then bring the items back to her bakery to bake in the one oven that was unaffected by the electrical mishap. Since she isn't doing daily orders for the shop, she'll schedule times for the people to come pick up the items at the bakery.

I write a quick note in my journal. A little manifestation of how I want things to be, and a little bit of patting myself on the back for the things that I've accomplished. After reading one book on PTSD, I read another, and another. Journaling, being in nature, being creative, are all things helping me overcome what I went through at my last job. And every day, I feel myself lift and morph into who I want to be.

A knock on the door sounds. "I'm dead, go away." I shove the journal to the side.

"You know, there are morning people, and night people. But

you are like a never o'clock person," Frankie says as she enters, uninvited as usual, with a grin.

"Wow. Did it take you all morning to come up with that little zinger?" I chuck a pillow at Frankie, and of course she grabs it midair. If she did that to me, my reflexes would be too slow to dodge. It'd hit me in the face.

She lobs the pillow to the edge of my bed. "Morgan and I want to check out that new bar in Duluth, the Pine Street Tap House or something? Wondering if you and Zoey want to come with."

My sister is the least subtle human in the world. Her voice lifts too high when saying Zoey's name. But, as much as I can read her, she can also read my face like no one else. I lie back down and throw my arm over my eyes. "I don't know... I'm not even sure if Zoey goes out. Is that the place with open mic nights?"

"Yeah. There's a band playing there next Friday. Might be fun?" Frankie says, shrugging. "I'll be DD so you can all get shit-faced and I can take advantage of my girlfriend."

"You're disgusting," I say as I peek out from under my arm with a scowl. "Our walls are too thin, and I cannot possibly put my noise-canceling headphones on any higher. I'm sleeping in the basement that night."

"Even better." Frankie bounces her brows. "For real, just ask Zoey if she wants to come with. But if you really don't want to, we can just go us three."

Frankie's voice drops at that last part. Not that I am a third wheel. Or maybe I am. I've always just been there, like Frankie's extra limb. We've always lived together, we've always been together, we do so much together that I'm surprised Morgan hasn't disowned us both. But I can tell how bad she wants me to come with and bring Zoey. And even though I've spent what feels like every waking minute with Zoey, it feels like it's not enough. Extending that time with her makes me damn near giddy—which is exactly why I shouldn't do it.

"I just, I don't know if it's a good idea to bring Zoey." I flip the pillow under my head and wiggle into a comfortable spot. "But maybe I'll go."

A moment passes as Frankie studies my face. I hate when she does this and I try to blank my mind so she can't see what's happening inside. She leans against the doorframe and crosses her arms. "Why, Quinn? Why is it not a good idea? I see you two texting and that shit-eating grin that grows when you're on the phone with her. You've been with her like every hour of every day. I can hear you giggling when she calls..."

Why is this not a good idea? Because I'm two steps away from being a certified fuckboi, and Zoey deserves much more than what I am, than what I can offer. Although, interestingly enough, I haven't checked my dating app for several weeks. And since the moment I met Zoey, I haven't had any hookups. But still...

Besides, it is very clear that not only is Zoey the one-relationship wonder, the marrying kind, she is also not over her ex. The way Zoey stared at her hands, her voice cracking while telling me about how she proposed, was so raw I felt it in my heart. That her ex has sent her a stack of love letters that Zoey hasn't tossed, is so telling. Even if I evolved enough as a human to join the adult party in wanting a relationship, I'd be a consolation prize. And even though I may still be struggling with my self-worth, I know that I am more than that.

"Frankie." My voice goes dark, and emotion stirs in me. I'm not sure who I am half the time. A business owner? A thirty-two-year-old with the emotional intelligence of a twelve-year-old? Sometimes I feel like I'm never going to figure out myself. "Do you ever think that I'm just not cut out for a relationship? Like maybe I'm the type of person who shouldn't have one? I see you and Morgan, and you have everything. You just *know* each other. But I don't think that's in the cards for me. I can't even think of a time that I saw a woman for longer than a week."

Frankie steps into the bedroom and lies down next to me, sharing the pillow. "First, what me and Morgan have, not everyone does. We met when we were ten years old, you know? I've had a lifetime to get to know her." She nestles her shoulder to mine. "You know there's a spectrum of people, right? Aromantic, poly, demi, people who really just do not want a relationship, the list goes on. And if you were one of those, great. I'll support you in any way. But deep down, I think your path is different."

My eyes catch on a yellowed spot on the ceiling, and I stare at that to keep from tearing up. "But what *is* my path?"

Frankie shrugs. "Only you know that. But we weren't exactly given the best foundation or modeled emotionally intelligent behavior from Mom and Dad. It's no wonder this stuff isn't crystal clear."

She's not wrong. Our parents are fine. There's a baseline of bad parenting, and our parents are one step up from that. Frankie and I were never a priority, ever. It's like we were both "oopsies" and our parents just sort of dealt with it. Or rather, let us deal with each other on our own. Frankie's the one who basically raised me as our parents were always too busy doing anything but parenting. They aren't mean people. Just... uninvolved. Uncaring.

My lip trembles and I clamp it between my teeth. "I just don't know what I have to offer, you know?"

Frankie shoots up and stares at me. "Are you serious? Quinn, you're one of the most driven people I've ever met. You're smart, and funny, and kind, and giving."

"And moody and scattered and can't commit to shit," I add.

"*And* a good person," Frankie says. "Look what you did with Zoey when her electricity went out. Helping her all day with her food, letting her use your place so she can fulfill those orders, helping her call all her customers."

I appreciate what Frankie is saying, but isn't this just what people do for other people? I'm no Mother Teresa for giving up my day. And yet, Frankie's words warm my insides. I rest my head against her shoulder.

"You really are a good person. Someone who is worthy." Frankie taps the side of her head against mine. "I'd tell you that you're beautiful, too, but I think I've inflated your ego enough that you're going to float out of here."

I grind my elbow into her shoulder. "So, basically, I'd be like you. Got it."

Frankie pokes me in the side and slides out of bed. "I gotta run." She stops at the doorway, and taps the side of the frame. "You're good, Quinn. With *everything*. Your decisions, your path, who you are. You're good."

I lie back down and let her words cover me like a blanket.

Maybe I am good. Helping Zoey, though, proves nothing. I like being around her because she makes me feel like a better person. She brightens my world. And isn't that kind of selfish? I don't know. Maybe I'm overthinking all this.

A message pings on my phone. I roll over and check it.

> Zoey:
>
> Going to stop by Connie's Coffee before coming out to the farm. Can I bring you the vanilla chai or hazelnut latte or something else?
>
> And definitely not the gingerbread latte.

Everything in me warms. Zoey remembers the two drinks I tried and loved, and that one that I really didn't, and why this makes me as happy as it does, I don't know. Zoey is sweet and kind and exactly the type of woman I run from. Thus, I need to stop all this warming up nonsense over a basic text.

I type a quick response, and rush to get ready. Today, Zoey has no special orders so she offered to make Christmas ornaments with me to sell in the shop. And I can use all the help I can get. I have no idea why I thought setting up a shop would be easy. It's not. I'm decorating, moving, setting up tables, taking down tables, having display shelves built, buying supplies. A never-ending cycle of build and prep. But the magic of Christmas is close, peeking around the corner, and I'm sure I can pull this off.

I think.

When I roll Truck Norris up the gravel road, I hop out, zip up my light fall sweatshirt, and roam the grounds. Sometimes I still can't believe that this property is *mine*. There's a stillness here as I walk the property—stepping on twigs, the grass mushing beneath my work boots, the smell of pine and cedar filling my nose. In New York, there was no stillness. I was in a constant state of hyper-hustle. But out here, as I stroll the lush grounds and check the irrigation systems, I imagine the kids on the back of a tractor trailer sitting on hay, couples strolling through the property that sparkles with white lights and colorful wreaths, and a giant bonfire in the corner. A noise catches my attention, and a deer skitters across the field. I take a moment to just breathe. Let so much go. *Appreciate.*

I can see the Santa and the hayrides. The hot cocoa and the gift shop. I want it magical, sparkly, joyful. And that feeling washes over me before the tension rises. Less than two months away, and I'm still so far behind.

A car rolls to a stop and Zoey pops out, her long hair in a loose ponytail, her bangs swiping her forehead. She's in ripped jeans and a long-sleeve T-shirt. And I hate, hate, hate that my breath hitches. I need to sit with these feelings for a bit because the very last thing I want to do is hurt someone like Zoey. To use her because I'm lonely, to lose this friendship because I'll do something dumb.

"I have the best surprise for you!" Zoey says as she bends over into her backseat. I also hate that my gaze dips to her ass. I shouldn't be sexualizing her at all. But she has a really, really nice ass, and even though I *try* not to look, I do.

I shouldn't.

"Did you put Jodie Foster in the back seat for me? *Honey*," I say. "This is really too much."

"Sorry, no Jodie Foster, and sadly, Sarah Paulson and Kristen Stewart were also booked." Zoey hands me a coffee. "But I do have a box of Christmas craft items we can look at. My mom said we could take anything we wanted."

"Oh..." I reach over and help her lift out a huge tote. "I love inspiration." And I need as much as I can get. There's a fine balance between filling a store with functional and decorative, affordable and high-end, store-bought and handmade items. Right now, I have plenty of store-bought stuff, but need to up the handmade. Besides, I have nearly depleted my funds. Not that I want to think about that now.

We lug the tote inside and line things up on the table. My heartbeat kicks up a notch as I check out everything from glitter to paints, blank canvas ornaments, unpainted snowmen, and snowflakes. We organize all the products on the workstation, and step back to look at the inventory. "Are you sure you want to stay and help me? You probably have way better things to do." *Please say you'll stay.*

"Are you kidding? I live for arts and crafts," Zoey says, then takes a sip of her coffee. "Besides, I think you might be stuck with me a little longer. If you'll have me."

My heart nearly skyrockets. I try not to smile. "I'll always have you." I hope that didn't come out as desperate as it sounded. "But why? What's up?"

"Electrician called," she says, stuffing paint brushes into a mason jar. "It's going to be at least two more weeks before I can open back up."

Two more weeks? I get to spend the next two weeks with Zoey? My belly certifiably flips. I feel terrible for her, but so happy for me. I really need to wipe my smile off my face, but I can't. "Oh shit. That sucks. Did they say why?"

"I don't know." She unwraps the plastic wrap from around the acrylic paints. "Something about when it's rodent related, the state needs to send in additional health inspections, and there's a backlog. I tried to pay attention but zoned out on the terminology."

Zoey smiles. I swear the more I learn about her, the less I know. She's so very nice, probably the nicest person I've ever met. But I realize she never wants anyone to feel bad. This is maybe an admirable trait, maybe not, but it makes it tricky to determine if she's choking back sobs, or if she's genuinely okay. "Damn. That's a blow, huh? I'm so sorry."

The wind picks up, gusting into the space from the cracked window, and a lock of hair swipes across her cheeks. I want to tuck it for her, let my fingertips linger just a moment on that soft-looking skin, but she reaches out and tucks it behind her ear. "It really is okay. I didn't realize how much I needed a break. Running my own business for all these years, I never stepped away. Even when Josie and I split, I didn't take a day off. For the first time in six years, I'm taking some downtime, and it's giving me the opportunity to, I guess, re-evaluate a lot of things."

She peeks at me from those huge blue eyes behind her glasses, and I want to dig more. Re-evaluate her business? Her former relationship? I swallow... *Me?* No. I internally shake my head. This whole close-proximity thing is messing with my brain cells. "And then you use your downtime to help me out."

"But I love this stuff." She waves to the workbench. "This feels like a vacation."

I want to hug her, but I keep my hands to myself. We roll up our sleeves, literally, and get to work. We crank Alexa high, open water bottles, and dig into the cases of plain ornaments, stencils, glitter spray paint, and acrylic. Will these items turn into a huge moneymaker? Most likely not. But for each Christmas tree ornament I paint, my gut unclenches a little.

Not surprisingly, Zoey is an incredible artist. Where I'm using stencils to work out the details, she freehand draws trees and stars. I take things outside to spray-paint, she adds glitter details to globes, we brainstorm what to do with the cases and cases of mason jars I found in a shed. Hours pass, and we go back and forth between chatting like we've been pent-up for years, and having long bouts of comfortable silence.

What does she do when she goes home at night? Does she have women she chats with? Based on the conversation that we had about Josie, I assume she's not really dating, but is there someone else? I haven't chatted with anyone on the apps since I met Zoey. Something about it doesn't feel right. That chase I looked for before, that need to get laid and temporarily filling something inside me, disappeared after I met Zoey.

Maybe this is what it's like having a real, true friend.

In between adding another snowflake to the outside of a mason jar, she glances at me. *Dammit.* She totally caught me staring.

"Are you okay?" she asks.

I don't know why I'm nervous. We're friends. Friends go out and do things all the time. Zoey is the first friend I have made in years, and I don't want to screw it up. I don't want to keep watching the way her mouth twists as she concentrates, or the way her glasses slip and she pushes them up with the back of her hand, or the way the slope of her pale neck looks as soft as an angel-wing feather. My hands are so clammy, I'm in danger of the paintbrush slipping right through them to the floor.

"Yep, I'm good," I say. *Come on. Just ask her.* Worst-case scenario she'll say no. I swallow. "Actually... do you have plans next Friday night?"

FIFTEEN
ZOEY

"Munchkin!" I kiss my nephew, Noah, on the top of his scraggly blond head, grab a handful of Goldfish crackers from his bowl, and pop some into my mouth. "How was school today?"

"Look what I did!" He rummages through his backpack and pulls out a scrunched-up paper of... something.

I cock my head. Some sort of multicolored tissue paper is glued on cardstock with some random drawings, and I think a blob of glue, but I'm not sure. "I love it! It's beautiful. Tell me what it is."

"It's an igloo and a Christmas tree and fall leaves and an ocean." He rotates the paper, and points a chubby finger to the corner. "Oh, and a spaceship but I didn't have time to finish that yet."

"Ah, yep. I totally see it now. I love it! Great job." I give him another squeeze. "Is Grandma putting it on the fridge?"

"Mom said Grandma would have to arm wrestle her for it." He crunches into a Goldfish and kicks his legs under the table. "Don't tell Mom, but I think Grandma can beat her."

Mom probably can beat my sister. My sister, Carrie, is one of the toughest people I know. As an ER nurse, she sees and manages things I can't even fathom. I love my sister, but we are not particularly close. Although, it has everything to do with her schedule, and our ten-year age gap, rather than us as people. But she works long hours, overtime, and random schedules.

Noah returns to drawing. Within a few moments, I can tell he's in his zone, so I step away and look for my mom. My gosh, what I would give to be a first-grader again. The thrill of learning something new every day, spending hours drawing and creating, and not worrying about employee wages and electronic maintenance costs.

These last few weeks, I've spent every single day with Quinn at her farm, and it's so freeing. This week alone, we've made almost a hundred ornaments, from hand-painted bulbs to glittery snowflakes, from little gingerbread men to reindeers. Leaving my bakery is good for me. Once I discovered that insurance would cover lost wages for my staff and me, plus the lease payment for the month, I could breathe. After six years, I'm letting go, temporarily at least.

It's also allowed me to really process everything that happened with me and Josie. She sent another card yesterday, and I stuffed it in the drawer. Up until recently, I didn't open them because I was nervous what they'd say. What if she was trying to get back together with me? Even though I know in my heart we're not right for each other, what if I folded and did something unhealthy for both of us? The temptation to fall back into a comfortable life, with someone who once held my entire heart and soul in her hands, has hovered below the surface these last two years.

But now, something's shifted. Now, even though I'm not ready to throw them, I'm not opening them because it doesn't seem right. I'm no longer *scared*, no longer worried that Josie will say some gentle words and I will catapult two years back. Now I'm not opening them because it doesn't feel right.

And I know why. *Quinn.* As much as I'm fighting it, I'm developing feelings for her that are deeper than friendship, and it's terrifying. At night when I come home after spending the day with her and lie in my bed, I stare at the ceiling and think of Quinn and fight with what's brewing inside.

So, I keep these letters. Maybe it's keeping a string attaching me to the past. A safety net, where I'm comfortable, holding me back from completely jumping into the future.

"Mom?" I call out as I step into the garage. *What the heck...* "What are you wearing?"

My mom wears some funky outfits. She is a kindergarten teacher after all. But usually it's apples on sweaters, alphabet sweatshirts, or lots of bows. But today she's wearing a backwards baseball cap, dark half-moon lines under her eyes, and a Twins jersey.

"Spirit week at school." She taps the brim of her hat. "I'm a baseball player, obviously."

"Obviously." I grin and look over her shoulder as she sifts through a mound of boxes. "What are you doing?"

"I remembered that I have more supplies that you can take with you to Quinn's." She slides a tote from the shelf towards her, peeks in, and frowns. "I know it's here somewhere."

"This is really nice of you," I say. "Are you sure you don't want to use this for the classroom, though?"

She shakes her head. "No, there's not enough of everything. And if one kid doesn't get something that someone else gets, tears will happen. Besides, the rules are different for the type of supplies I can bring in." She tugs a heavy tote from the bottom shelf and grins. "Ah. Here it is. Yep. Christmas trees and miniature Santas."

The box contains wooden Christmas trees that are begging to be painted, but also embroidered towels, paints, cotton balls, glitter. It's the Christmas jackpot. I cannot wait to show Quinn. "These are great! Quinn's going to love it."

My mom tosses me a way too big of a grin. Oh no. Heck nope. I *know* this look. I don't want to engage in this look. Heat warms my face.

"So, you've been spending a lot of time with her lately."

That I have. In all actuality, I've been spending almost ten hours a day with Quinn. Somehow, even after we've wrapped everything up for the evening, I end up staying. And when I have orders to fill, I prep at her place, and she drives with me back to my shop to bake and wait for the client. Even though she has a ton of work to do at her place, she always seems happy to join me.

"It's really fun, you know," I say. "What else am I going to do with a month off?"

Mom doesn't say anything, and now I totally avoid her gaze. Of course, I could be doing a lot of things. Go on a trip, take a small vacation, volunteer at the school. And yes, I love doing all the crafts with Quinn. But really, I love spending time with Quinn and learning all about her in bite-size pieces. These last several weeks, I've discovered that she's never listened to Nirvana (*is she serious?*), that she loves her steak medium rare, hates apples, and has a full back tattoo of angel wings. Every single piece brings me closer to her.

And, *oof.* I am *so* attracted to her. There, I said it. And gosh, a part of me wishes I was as sexually empowered and open as Quinn. I want to push this side of me away, the side that emotionally attaches with sex, that dreams of a honeymoon with a single kiss. For one night, maybe I could let myself be free. But as soon as that thought enters my head, I ignore it. My heart will break. I know this. And it's not worth losing my friendship with Quinn—and crying into my pillow after—for one night of heaven.

I help Mom drag the tote off the shelf and to the corner. "Besides, I think Quinn really needs the help. Her shop, farm, everything is opening the day after Thanksgiving, and she's not even near ready. She has some inventory, but I don't think it's enough. We need more people, but it's not like she can hire out." Quinn and I chatted about the lack of inventory. Being an owner myself, I understand the delicate balance of spending money upfront to fill a store but not knowing what will resonate with customers and not wanting to lose everything.

Mom taps her finger on top of the workbench. "So, what I'm hearing is that she needs people who love crafting." A slow grin spreads.

Oh no, I really, *really* know that look. "Mom..."

She waves me away. "I have an idea. I'm going to make a few phone calls, okay?"

"Should I be worried?" I ask, but it's useless. Once Mom sets her mind on something, nothing stops her. "I've got to run. I'm going out tonight with Morgan, Frankie, and Quinn."

"Really? That's great. I can't even remember the last time you talked about going out." My mom lifts the other side of the tote and walks to the car with me. "I'd really love to meet Quinn. Hopefully, sooner than later."

I pack everything in the car, give Noah and my mom a hug, then rush back to my place to get ready. We're not leaving for a few hours yet, but it'll be nice getting more dolled up than normal. The flutters in my belly kick in, but a muted gray cloud hovers over the excitement. Through my shower, curling my hair, searching my closet, something is eating away at me.

Yellow-and-teal envelopes.

I need to cut something in my past, and now is the time. Praying my neighbors don't see me, I rush down the back-alley stairs from my loft to the bakery in my slippers and pajamas and rush into my office. I grab the letters from Josie and run back upstairs.

At my kitchen table, I take a deep breath and tear into the first one.

SIXTEEN
QUINN

Glue is a spectacular substance. It can hold so many things together, from paper, to wood, to stones. And skin. *Ugh*. I worked until the last minute trying to put together a SANTA THIS WAY wooden sign with an arrow, and right now, I'm pretty sure I got more glue on me than the actual wood. As my conditioner sets, I'm scrubbing my fingers in the shower like I'm performing an exorcism, and *finally*, the last of it balls off my skin and runs down the drain.

A heavy knock sounds outside of the door. I already know who it is based on the annoyed fists. "Dude. I just got done with a workout and need a shower," Frankie yells through the door. "If you use up all the hot water, I'm going to wipe my sweat all over your pillow."

"You are so disgusting," I yell out while rinsing my hair. We seriously need to invest in a bigger hot-water heater. "Okay, okay, just one more minute!"

I hop out of the shower, stub my toe, and knock over the hair dryer with a crack. *Shit*. I attach the pieces back together, gather my stuff to get ready in my bedroom, and try to breathe out the nerves.

Nerves. Okay, fine. I'll admit it to myself—but absolutely no one else, no matter how many times Morgan and Frankie ask. Yes, I'm nervous for tonight. It's not a date. My mind knows it's not a date, but fails to send this message to the rest of me. This evening, I ransacked my closet for an hour and must've tried on twenty different outfits, swung by the drugstore for new makeup, and could barely choke down dinner because my belly is all twisted. Even my limbs are shaky.

However, the limbs shaking might very well be because of everything I've done this week. The less than a month countdown until the shop opens the day after Thanksgiving ticks away like a time bomb. Between keeping up on posting about the farm activities on social media, and unpacking merch, and overseeing the crew working the grounds, building racks, and shelves, I am tired.

After Zoey and I assembled the third artificial Christmas tree today to decorate inside the barn, my skin was raw and beat-up from all the scratches. I've checked and rechecked the list my aunt and uncle left me, but I just know I'm missing something. And if I don't figure it out, I'll ruin the opening day. For more than a decade, they failed to capture the Christmas spirit the way the community wanted. So, who knows if the list they left is everything I need to do.

And what if no one comes? What if the entire community has already purchased their artificial tree, or still drives a few hours away to the nearest tree farm, or they hate it and everything fails? I plant my hands on the counter, take a deep breath, and try to reassure myself everything will be fine.

A ping pops up on my screen and my belly does a flip at Zoey's name.

Not a date. Not a date.

I have something to tell you when you get here.

Ummmm. How should I read into that? It sounds so ominous, like when a boss says, "Can you come into my office." Before I figure out a response, another message pops up.

Oh! That sounded so suspicious. It's good (I think!)

And it's like she knows me already. I send her a raised-eyebrow emoji response and pull out an arsenal of hair products to tame my mane. Knowing I will be here forever trying to get my curls to pop, I put in my AirPods and turn on the *Love 'Em or Leave 'Em* podcast to be entertained by Ruby Reanne's relationship wisdom.

"Hello, all my friends. A listener wrote this question last week and I knew it was perfect to spark some conversation with my audience. Sometimes I thank my lucky stars that me and my wife, Amelia, have been together for so long, because diving into the dating pool with all that uncertainty and angst and hesitations... Yikes. I'm not sure I'm cut out for that. I digress. Here we go—"

I flip my hair to the other side to diffuse. Dang it. The AirPod slipped out. I adjust it and hit play.

"'Hi, Ruby. There's a woman in my graduate school night class who I've grown close to this entire semester. She's smart and funny, and after one minor hiccup, we hit it off. We study together, have done two group projects together, and we've found ourselves more often than not sharing a pizza in the corridor and talking about personal stuff instead of schoolwork.

"'I'll be honest. I was a bit of a loner in high school, and have only dated maybe a handful of people. So, I cannot tell if she likes me as a fellow student, as a friend, or as more. I want to ask her out, but am as equally scared of the rejection as I am of losing our fun time together. My question is: How can I tell if someone likes me as more than a friend?'"

The blow dryer is too loud. I click it off, lean against the counter, and listen for the response.

"This is tricky. Like, hello, vulnerability! Right? It's scary when you don't know where you stand. But I can help give you some clues," Ruby says. "When you walk into the classroom, does she consistently seek you out? After class, does it look like she's lingering or maybe making an excuse to talk? That might be one indicator. Another one is physical touch or at least sending some body cues. Does she touch your arm, or back, or hand, and has it happened a few times? She might be just a super friendly person, or it may be just for you. Pay attention if she does that with everyone, or if it seems like she's singling you out."

Physical touch. I do this with Zoey, and she does this with me. Does that mean... I shake my head and turn back to the mirror to put on some makeup. I'll diffuse after this segment.

"And this might be super hard, but you could just ask her. If that is too intimidating, you could say something like, 'I always wanted a girlfriend with your sense of humor,' and see what she says. If she says something like, 'Oh God, no, you'd never want to date someone like me,' as opposed to 'And I've always wanted a boyfriend like you,' then this may open the door for more conversation. Good luck to you! Please write back in and let me know how it goes."

I shut the podcast off. Ms. Ruby Reanne is making me think too hard right now, and I don't want to think. I go back to prepping. An hour later, after I've scrunched my hair until it reaches the stars, I tug on my shoes and run out to the car. Frankie and Morgan are in the front seat, I'm in the back, and I'm trying to settle my insides as we roll down Main Street to Zoey's.

Not a date, not a date.

All of this would be so much easier if Zoey wasn't as smart, kind, sweet, or beautiful. Like if any of those could fall off the list, I'm sure my brain would interpret this message and shoot it to my cells in a way more efficient manner.

Frankie pulls down the alleyway and puts the car in park. "Do you want to call Zoey and let her know we're here?"

My hand is already on the door. "Nah. I'll just run up and get her." I don't know why I feel like I need this bit of alone time with her, but I do. Even though I was with her all day, I can't get enough.

I run up the stairs and knock on the door, shifting my weight between my feet. A moment passes and when it cracks open, my breath stops.

Oh, dear Christ.

In front of me stands Zoey, in an off-the-shoulder loose white top, her beautiful, bare midriff peeking out with a *very* surprising navel ring, and a ruffled skirt grazing her upper thigh. Chestnut waves cascade from her shoulders to her mid-back, and it takes all my strength in me not to fist those locks in my hand. Underneath the dipping magenta-and-golden horizon, her aquamarine blue eyes sparkle and... *Shit.* She is so goddamn beautiful.

"Oh my God, you look amazing!" she says, breaking me from my trance.

Me? Did I take extra care in my ripped jeans and tank with a chunky knit sweater and the best bra I own? Yes. And applying makeup and making my hair bounce as high as my boobs? Yes, I did. But I'm not even holding a candle to Zoey. Everything in me springs to life, but I'm quieting this. I refuse to let my momentary dry spell and raging hormones ruin what Zoey and I have.

"What? Get out. You look beautiful! Look at us scrubbing the farm off us and showing up like ladies," I joke. "Ready?"

Zoey bobs down the stairs with me. Do I open the door? Is that weird? I don't want her to think of this as a date, even though it feels like it. And she looks so womanly and beautiful... I'm over-thinking this. She crosses the car to the other side and slides in.

"Hey!" Zoey says as she fastens her seat belt. "Thanks for picking me up."

"Of course," Frankie says as she pulls out of the alley and turns right. "Thanks for coming with."

"Morgan," Zoey says, leaning forward in her seat. "I chatted with Angie yesterday about the wedding cake. She changed the colors from pale pink to lavender."

Morgan turns in her seat, a frown line popping up between her brows. "Again? Does that mean she's going to call next week needing a new flower arrangement? We're so close to the wedding date. I don't think we can pull that off..."

As Morgan and Zoey chat about the upcoming wedding they're both hired for, I can't help but sit back in the seat and absorb this moment. Zoey's bare leg is close to mine, she's grinning, and oh my God, she smells so good. Some sort of warm amber and jasmine. I'm so glad we are in a closed car because maybe the scent will seep into my clothes and I can sniff it tonight in the privacy of my room.

Once we head on the highway toward Duluth, Zoey turns to me with a grin. "So, I talked with my mom today and she gave me some more craft items we can use for your shop."

Seriously, this woman is a personal Michaels store. "I don't even understand how she has so much... stuff."

"Trust me. It's like she grew up in the Depression, but not really. Scarcity mentality. She throws nothing away. But... that's not what I was going to tell you," Zoey says, tugging at the seat belt strap. "She has an idea, but I'm only going to tell you if you promise to be totally honest with me if this is overbearing, or not what you want, or is just... too much."

Well, now I'm so intrigued that I'll say just about anything. "I promise to tell you the whole truth, and nothing but the truth, so help me Santa Claus, okay? Lesbian Scout's Honor."

Zoey's chest lifts in an inhale. "My mom made a bunch of calls today. Church group. Parents of the kids in her class. Other teachers. And, um... how do you feel about having forty or so people out to your place on Sunday?"

My mouth drops. Morgan turns to stare at me, Frankie eyes me in the rearview mirror. I move my gaze back to Zoey. "Um, what? For, what? I'm not even open for business. I don't even have signs made."

Zoey grabs my hand, and I'm immediately disarmed. Her skin is soft, smooth, and her grip firm. "No, no, not to buy anything. They want to make Christmas crafts. For free. Volunteer. Once my mom made a few calls, more people made more calls, and well, now we have all those people who want to come out. I can bring cookies, and the church ladies mentioned doing a potluck. Honestly, I think all you'd have to provide is bottled water and chairs."

As Zoey continues, she says how her mom's students are so excited and the church ladies are always looking for a place to get together and chat outside of the church basement. Everyone's giddy at the idea of spending an afternoon at a real Christmas tree farm making ornaments and trinkets for my shop.

I don't know what to say. I'm stunned quiet, my heart filling, expanding, overflowing. "But why? No one knows me. Your mom doesn't even know me... They just want to come make stuff that I can sell in my shop? I don't understand."

Zoey's hand is still holding mine, sending a warm current through my veins, and I hope she never drops it.

"People around here love helping each other," Zoey says, giving my hand a squeeze, then pulling back. "Truly. If you're good with it, I'll let my mom know."

Good with it? I'm overwhelmed by the generosity. My anxiety is melting. It still seems surreal. Like a ball will drop, or there's a catch, or something will happen. But with Zoey's grin, knowing she will be there, my insides warm.

This might be a magical Christmas after all.

SEVENTEEN

QUINN

Once we get to the bar, we navigate to the table. Morgan and Frankie not-so-subtly excuse themselves to get us a round of drinks, even though I'm sure this place has a full waitstaff. The place is beautiful, much prettier than I thought, with warm lighting, a mirrored back wall, big cedar booths, black tables, and a huge dance floor. Music is playing, but the band hasn't taken stage yet.

"So, I'm thinking tomorrow I'll prep cookies at your place, maybe right away in the morning, but then bake them that night when I go home so they'll be fresh for Sunday morning," Zoey says, tossing her hair over her shoulder.

I still can't get over that forty random people will be volunteering their time. *For me.* My mind is blown. "I need to help you, obviously. Pay for supplies. Something. I feel so, I don't know, guilty."

Her multiple silver bangles clank together as she waves me away. "Absolutely not. I've used your kitchen for weeks and have not paid you anything. This is just what we do around here."

Morgan and Frankie return with our cocktails, and we all lift our glasses in cheers. As Zoey peppers Frankie with questions about her job at the magazine, and how much she loves the new winter product line, I sink back in the chair. Yes, I'm engaging, laughing, sprinkling in a story about how peaceful it is when Frankie is gone in New York for business because Morgan is much nicer than her. Frankie scowls but laughs and tosses a balled-up napkin at me.

But really, I'm observing everything about Zoey. The way she grins, that beautiful, beautiful mouth curving up, popping up the smallest laugh lines that reach her eyes behind her glasses. The way her cheeks suck in when she sips through the straw and highlights those sweet apple cheekbones. The way she smiles at everyone, and scoots her chair left and right like a pinball machine so people can walk around her as they weave through the crowd.

God, she's just so... perfect. *Oof.* This is terrible.

Yes, yes, I want to sleep with Zoey. Anyone could look at her and want the same thing. Zoey is *stunning.* But it's not just that. Images of me cuddling and hugging her, rubbing her sore feet, staying in bed watching movies, making her breakfast, all flash in my mind. And this is a problem. A big, big problem because I know my track record, I know what I want, what I've always wanted, and this is not it.

The band takes the stage and within three heavy drumbeats, Zoey leaps from her chair and grabs my hand. "Is this a nineties tribute band? Oh my gosh, I freaking love this song! Come on!"

There is no one on the dance floor. *No one.* I'm not one to be self-conscious about things like this, but getting my sober butt onto a dance floor in front of a room full of strangers is a little much even for me.

But there's no way I'll tell Zoey no. Her eyes are dancing, her body is jumping, and her energy is infectious.

Thankfully, the crowd quickly fills in around us as the band pumps out Nirvana, Smashing Pumpkins, and Pearl Jam, although Zoey had to tell me each of the groups as the music played. As the space around us gets tighter, and we get closer, the energy shifts, becomes alive.

Soon, drumbeats match my heartbeats, and Zoey and I are practically hugging each other. Her long hair sways along with her body, grazing my arm. Her scent reaches me, makes me hazy, does something tingly to my insides. I'm a goner. God, she's incredible.

When I peek at Frankie and Morgan, to make sure they didn't feel like I ditched them, it becomes very, very obvious that tonight was never about them. They're smiling, but I should've known. Frankie rarely drinks and Morgan is a wine and fine dining kind of person. These two are not the type who visit bars to listen to a live band.

I really love my sister and her girlfriend.

"I freaking love this song!" Zoey yells next to me, for no less than the fifth time in a row. She is laughing, dancing, encouraging me to loosen up, and it works. Soon, I'm jumping along with her. Her shirt lifts from her belly as she raises her arms, and I hold back from drooling at that pierced belly button. I try not to let the rosy cheeks and the warm air and how good she smells affect me, but it does.

She's touching me a lot. Like *a lot, a lot*, and I love it so goddamn much. But I'm definitely thinking more things than she's thinking. She's acting like any friend would act to another friend... Grabbing a hand, bouncing into me at every single new song that comes up, hugging me. I'm seeing a new side to her—fun, free-spirited, open. It's like she's let all her guards down, released whatever baggage she's been holding, and is opening up. It's wonderful and also terrible, and confusing. I simultaneously want more and less.

We never even sit down. For the rest of the night, we dance. Frankie and Morgan bring us water then swiftly return to the seats. We scream when they do a grunge rearrangement of "...Baby One More Time." And Zoey grabs my hand, reels me out, and brings me back in for a quick, giggling spin.

Zoey's skin glows in the lights. Her forehead glistens with a soft coat of sweat, and hair mats against her face. Seeing this sweet, pure person morph into someone who's almost head banging at a song, makes me feel like she let me read her diary. Like I'm part of the inner circle, accepted, and I absolutely love it. Zoey trusts me enough to see beyond the baker persona, the woman who thinks "darn" is a swear word, the innocent, and shows me the other parts of her.

I'm wincing that she might hurt her foot again, but the smiles and laughs show me she doesn't care. She's letting go. Her hair swings along with her hips. She whips off her top, down to her white tank, fully embracing tonight like she's at a rave.

I can't help it. The moisture sticking to her chest, the dancing, the pink flushed skin. I'm sucked into the Zoey world, and I don't want to leave.

When midnight rolls around, Frankie bounces out to the dance floor. "You ready to go? Morgan needs to get up early, and no one likes a cranky Morgan."

Zoey wraps her hair up into a bun and fans her face. "Sure. I should get to bed, too. I don't even remember the last time I stayed up this late."

As we weave our way through the crowd, Zoey lazily links her arm in mine, and I'm trying so, so, so hard not to read into the movement. She was clear with me. Not only is she looking for a commitment, she's not over her ex. And that's okay. She didn't lie, she didn't shove it under the rug. She doesn't know I'm having all these feelings, and having her arm linked in mine is giving me damn near diabolical thoughts.

Oh shit. Yep. It's so clear to me. I have feelings. Actual, full, reach-into-my-gut feelings for Zoey. Feelings that say maybe, this could be something. Feelings that say I think what I wanted before might have shifted. Maybe I could have a special someone, settle down, allow myself to love and be loved. *Oh Christ*. Did I mention this is bad?

The car ride home is more eventful than the car ride there. Zoey's animated and chatty. We had exactly one drink each, and she's jabbering like she threw back shots of tequila. "Okay, for real, anyone else here just dying when they played 'Smells Like Teen Spirit'? Like, come on. I was definitely born in the wrong era."

Frankie glances at us. "Was it better than 'Tonight, Tonight' from the Smashing Pumpkins? All they needed was to drop in Amy Winehouse and I'd be done for it."

Morgan and I toss a smile to each other. These two can chat about their musical tastes. Me, I just want to soak up everything about tonight. The way Zoey looks. The way she makes me feel. The way she makes me think about possibilities that I never thought were possible before.

As Frankie rolls to a stop, Zoey puts one hand on my knee and one on the door. "Thank you, guys. Seriously. I had no idea how badly I needed a night out," she says.

"When was the last time you went out to a bar like this?" Frankie asks.

Zoey makes a dramatic gesture at looking at her watch. "Six, maybe seven years?" She laughs. "I know, I know. Before you say anything, I was just too focused on the bakery and well... I blinked and am practically middle-aged."

"Oh my God, stop. You so aren't." When she opens her door, I do the same. "I'm going to walk you up."

"Wow. Such a gentleman." Zoey grins. God, she has such a great smile. "Frankie, Morgan. Thank you so much for inviting me. I feel like the popular girls invited me to the party, and it was the most fun I've had in forever."

Morgan pats Zoey's hand that's resting across the seat. "Anytime, Zoey. I mean that. We could all use a little more fun."

Frankie grins at Zoey. "This was great. Let's plan something again soon." She glances at me. "Take your time, Quinn. I'll be making out with my girlfriend."

When she wiggles her eyebrows, I groan.

Once Zoey and I step out in the alley, our steps become slower. The night is cool. A trail of goosebumps skitters across my skin, and I cross my arms over myself.

"I think my cheeks are burning from smiling so much," Zoey says as she digs out her keys from her cross-body bag. "You have no idea how much tonight meant to me. How much... this all means to me."

Her eyes dip on that part, and I feel the words to my core. I know what she's saying. Our friendship, our time together, our... whatever this is. What is this? To me, it's more than friends. I don't go to bed thinking about friends and wake up this excited to see friends. I don't spend an evening getting close so I can smell her hair and my skin sparking when she touches me and zinging with electricity every time she grabs my hand with *friends*.

I've never been more than friends with someone. And it's not what I want. I don't think. No, I'm pretty sure. Maybe. Do I?

Her keys are in the lock, but she doesn't twist. She's just standing there, and even though there's a chill in the air, and I can see goosebumps flush up her skin, I turn warm. Everything in me heats. My eyes dip to her mouth and back to her eyes. She's looking at me, and I think she's looking at me in that way, but hell... I don't know. And I hate, hate, hate not knowing. This is my wheelhouse. I'm a master at this. But yet, this all feels so totally different than any other time I've been alone like this with a woman.

"I propose we add a new playlist to Alexa tomorrow," I say, but I don't want to talk. I want to stop looking at those lips and taste them. I want to swipe my thumb on that powdery soft cheek, and tug on her bottom lip, and feel how she responds.

Her gaze drops to my mouth and stares for two seconds too long. It's all I need. I'm scared and this is stupid, but right now, I don't care. I don't wait, I don't ask, I don't think. I don't *want* to think. My hand grips the back of her neck. I pull her into me, and brush my lips against hers.

She doesn't even hesitate. Not for a second. She presses her mouth back into mine, her perfect, sweet, beautiful mouth, with a much firmer kiss than I ever thought would come from someone as sweet as Zoey.

Hands grip my hips, and she pushes me against her, and my pulse thuds hard against my throat. She moves against my lips, parts me with her tongue, and swipes gently. I want more. I want it all. My hands move to her sides, my thumbs graze her stomach, my chest rises. And... Shit. *Shit!* What am I doing?

I tear myself away. Her head flinches and her eyes dash between mine.

"I'm... Oh God. I didn't..." I say, but I'm flustered and my mind is watery. I'm underwater, in a daze. My pulse is thudding so hard against my chest, but my brain moves in slow motion. "I'm so sorry. Oh Christ, please don't..." Please don't what? What do I want to say? Please don't let me ruin our friendship by doing something stupid. Please don't fall in love. Please don't *not* fall in love. Jesus, I'm spinning.

"Ack!" Zoey throws her arms around me, her peppy energy bounces from the bricks outside her building. "This was so much fun! Okay, tomorrow. Nineties music only. Maybe some Gaga, too, 'cause, well, she's the queen obviously."

My lips are warm and red and still tingling from the kiss, and Zoey is acting like nothing just happened. She's acting like her knees didn't buckle the way mine did, that the light hitting her isn't hitting me, like we didn't just share a phenomenal kiss. What in the hell is happening?

She cracks open the door. "Thank you for tonight. Gosh, we have to do this again. I'll check the band schedule and see the next time they'll be in town."

Okay, well, this meant nothing to her. Just a nightcap. And I should be relieved. Why am I not relieved? I push away the urge to cry and instead flash a wide smile. "Definitely. Okay, tomorrow, Gaga. I hear you and I raise you a Chappell Roan."

Zoey steps inside her loft and flicks on the light.

And everything inside of me drops. Like a lightning bolt has cut through me, splitting me in half, making me crash to the ground. Sprawled across Zoey's table are the letters from her ex. Whatever kept her from reading the letters before changed. *She read them.* She read them, and didn't say a single thing about it. And whatever it was clearly made her happy. *This* brought out this energy-filled side of her tonight.

My throat feels tight.

For the first time in my life, I understand what some women in my past felt when I thought I was clear that I only wanted to hook up, but they wanted more. The sadness, the hurt in their eyes, the ickiness they said they felt. I never understood it, because I always thought we were on the same page. I never lied about who I am or what I want.

But now, I get it. I want to cry. Instead, I smile at Zoey. It's not her fault. I didn't know that under her kitten facade, a tiger lurked. That's on me, not her. She's been honest with me since the beginning. And she knows how I am. Maybe she thought by kissing me back she could sow some sort of wild kissing oat, since I told her about my inability to feel intimacy with physicality. That it would be no big deal, that I'd be into it, that I was the safe one she could experiment with. She couldn't have known that she unlocked something in me that I didn't know existed.

I spin on my heels. "Good night," I say and turn before I can look at her again.

This should comfort me. Why am I so upset? I should be relieved. Maybe we're cut from the same cloth, and she didn't realize this about herself. And how cool would it be to have a sex buddy that lives so close, that I can call anytime I want. I should be damn near elated. But as the stairs creak beneath my feet, every step down, my heart sinks further and further.

This is why I don't do emotions, or love, or anything. It's too hard. Zoey told me from the beginning that she wasn't over her ex. She didn't lie or withhold. I've slept with plenty of rebounds. Hell, that's almost my go-to. The fresher the rebound, the quicker the fuck, the knowledge they were never over their ex was my infinite get-out-of-jail-free card. Rebounds let me off the hook. No guilt, no shame, everyone's happy.

But this time, it's different. Everything feels terrible. By the time I hit the bottom step, I burst into tears.

EIGHTEEN

ZOEY

Oh my gosh... that just happened. I swipe my finger against my lip, and yep. One hundred percent I am not hallucinating, that really just happened.

Quinn kissed me. And not just a kiss. We are talking an earth-shattering, my-knees-are-still-quaking, pretty-sure-my-breath-has-left-my-body-and-flown-halfway-to-Chicago *kiss*. I close the door and lean against the wall. My pulse pounds so hard in my head I think I might get dizzy. Should I open the door back up? Invite her upstairs? It's been two years since I had sex, since I kissed, since I did literally anything. Oh God, I want to. But it's not smart. She will never want what I want.

And yet, maybe I can try the casual thing, if it means being casual with Quinn? I crack open the door, cross all my fingers and toes, and hope so hard Quinn's standing there. But she's not. She's left. I'm as disappointed as I am relieved. Because who am I kidding? I can't do the casual thing. Look at me right now. Only one kiss, and *bam*. I'm stuffing my fingers in my pocket to keep from calling her.

My body buzzes with warmth. *Gah!* Quinn and I just freaking kissed!

What a whirlwind of a night. I lean my forehead against the

door and wait for my heartbeat to calm. Okay, I like Quinn. I really like her, and I know I've liked her for a while, and now, I believe this shows that she likes me, too. But I can't be a one-night-stand person. I just can't. I want more. With her.

So, now that I've established that, what the heck do I do?

Josie's letters still lie scattered across my table from earlier. I gather them into a pile and toss them in the trash. The letters are friendly and kind, just like Josie. But also filled with regret. The messages ranged from her being sorry that things ended the way they did, to regret that she moved down to Minneapolis, to her missing my friendship. But really, at the core, I think she just misses me and is hoping to reconnect when I'm ready. And as much as I can appreciate this, since I was in the same spot last year, reconnecting is not something I need or want.

Josie was always a big fan of hearts and sweet cards, but some of the cards were just funny. She works at a veterinarian clinic, and at least two of the cards were pictures of cats sleeping in awkward positions. It's clear Josie is going through something, but really, it's not my business.

It's nearing 1:00 a.m. and I've officially checked my phone a million times to see if Quinn sent a message.

She hasn't.

Bright sun illuminates my room and I blink against the blinds. I tuck the pillow in my arms and roll over to look at the clock. *Wowza.* My eyes are crusty, a low-grade headache pounds against my head, and my mouth is as dry as a week-old croissant. It's almost like I had more than one drink. But this hangover feeling is about the emotions of the night and getting only six hours of sleep —not the alcohol consumption.

In the shower, I replay feeling Quinn's mouth on me. My gosh, she is such a good kisser. Firm, controlled, yet also soft and luscious. But am I really ready for what this may mean? And what is she thinking?

I know we need to have a conversation, but how would that look? Like, "Hey, Quinn, I'm really falling for you, and it would kind of kill me if you saw other people, and I really want to have sex with you, but also, I really don't because then I'll really fall for you and you don't mix sex and feelings, and I wish you did, and please see my first point that I'm too scared to fall for you because my last relationship really gutted me, but here we are."

That will land like a bag of wet flour.

As I roll into town, I crack the window open to let in the mineral scent drifting off Lake Superior and wisps of fall into my car. It's chillier today, low 60s, the type of weather I like. The browns, ambers, and oranges of the leaves fly past my window. After I grab a coffee, I step out onto the sidewalk and see Colby and her dog, Kona.

"Colby!" I wave and walk toward her.

Colby's normally saddish smile lifts a bit, and she moves toward me. "Hey, Zoey. Enjoying the last of the warm weather before it's ripped away?"

"You know it." I squat and rub Kona's head and fur. "Hi, girl. I've missed you. I'll have a huge pile of doggie treats to give you when I open back up."

Colby switches the leash from one hand into the other. "Do you know the date you'll reopen? I think the whole town is going through withdrawals."

"That is really nice to hear." Yes, I do want to open back up. Obviously. I need to earn a living, I miss my staff members, I miss the customers. But also, when I open back up, that means I'll no longer see Quinn every day, and I don't want that, either. "Actually, next week we should be good to go as long as the inspector signs off on the fix. I'm not sure how much I'll have for sale those first few days. I didn't want to put in too big of a supply order if I'm not able to use it."

Colby runs her hand around Kona's fur. "What have you been doing with your time? Hopefully, taking a break, catching up on sleep?"

What have I been doing? Falling headfirst for my friend. Watching my heart tiptoe outside of my body, praying it won't get trampled. "Actually, did you hear about the Christmas tree farm in Maple Creek? A friend of mine, Quinn Lee, bought the farm and is revamping it. She's opening it back up for Christmas, so I've been out there helping set up, making all sorts of Christmas crafts."

Falling for her...

"Oh, that's great," Colby says. "No, I don't think I knew about that tree farm opening back up."

This doesn't surprise me. Although the entire town knows about the tree farm, Colby, I think, gets her town gossip only from me. I've heard no one else ever talk about Colby, and she's always alone. For all I know, she lives in an entirely different town and only comes here on Saturdays.

My phone buzzes in my pocket. *Mom.* I better get it. I glance back at Colby. "Hey, so sorry, I have to head out. I'll post on social media the opening date the moment I know." I rub the top of Kona's head. "Good to see you."

"You too," Colby says and strolls back down the sidewalk.

Back in the car, I put the phone on speaker and dial my mom. "Hey, sorry, I missed the call. What's up?"

"Hey, honey. Quick update. There's about ten more people coming tomorrow to the tree farm. Noah and I will swing by early and help you two set things up."

"Oh, okay, cool." I slow to a roll at the stoplights. "Did you find those old wagons that Dad talked about?"

"Yes, we did. He found even more items out at Grandma's. That's really why I'm calling. We have a ton of stuff Quinn can just use or have, but you know me... overbearing to my last dying breath. Just let me know if you think she'll be overwhelmed, and will you please let her know I won't be offended if she doesn't use it."

"Yep, I will." I pull onto the highway. "Thanks—"

"And I'm really calling to see how everything went last night."

I knew it. My mom's sparkle in her voice is too bright. She wants to get me married and give her more grandkids ASAP, and when Josie and I broke up, she was almost as hurt as I was.

But I don't know how to explain it. Comfortable, warm, perfect, and the best kiss I think I've ever had in my life. But I'm not going to tell that to my mom, who will absolutely plant mistletoe all around the barn and force me and Quinn to stand under it.

But does Quinn have feelings? Yes, she reached in and kissed me. But she's also just like that. She told me that, more than once, and I believe her. Kissing me doesn't mean she has feelings for me. From how she describes it, she hasn't ever had feelings. It would be pretty egotistical of me to think I hold some mystical power and could flip someone like Quinn into the relationship type. "What? So sorry, you're breaking up."

"I can hear you just fine," my mom says with a laugh. "Okay, okay. I'll back off and spare you the whole 'you're not getting any younger' speech. But what I will tell you is that you are brilliant, and amazing, and deserve so much happiness. And ever since you and Quinn met, I've noticed some extra sprinkles on your cookies. I just want to see you happy."

A wave of emotion hits me. "Did you just use a cookie analogy? Sprinkles on my cookies?"

"It sounded better than 'spring in your step,'" she says. "Okay, *fine*. I'll stop meddling. If I don't hear from you, I'll see you tomorrow at ten."

I click off the phone, and as I drive into the property, I grin at a few of the wooden signs Quinn and I worked on this week that are lining the pathway to the barn: Anyone seen Rudolph?, Santa's open for business, and Merry and bright right this way.

I roll to a stop and glance out the window. Quinn's hauling hay from a pile and adding it to the back of a trailer. She's wearing overalls and a flannel, with her hair plopped on top of her head. She might even be cuter than she was last night, which is hard to beat. She tugs her work gloves and waves at me.

"Your signs look great," I say as I get out of the car.

"Oh, good. Thanks. Do you think they're spaced out enough? I want to add one more, maybe the 'ho ho ho' one or the 'Santa's workshop this way' one, but also don't want to use up all the good signs and not have any once people park."

Last night Quinn's lips were on me, and today we're back to normal, as if she didn't completely rock my world. And before anyone says anything, yes, I know. She's following my lead.

I freaked out, okay? Completely and utterly freaked out and didn't know what to say at the time because the kiss was so dang good, and Quinn is just so pretty, and she makes me laugh, and I wanted to ask her to come into my place, and...

So yes, I panicked but wanted to show Quinn I wasn't panicking, that I can handle something casual. Which I know, I can't. But I'm not losing my friendship with her, so I will match her casualness, toe to toe.

Maybe this is good. We can ignore what happened. I'll just chalk last night up to a life experience and replay the feeling of her mouth on mine when I need a little pick-me-up. "I think the placement is just fine," I say, "but maybe only one more and save the rest for outside?"

"Cool." She hops off the trailer and moves toward the other side of the barn. And something is so very wrong. I can tell.

Ugh. How do people have casual hookups? I think I'm envious. Do they not have these twists and turns in their gut, feel like someone is stealing the air from their lungs, not think about the person afterward?

"Getting the hayride set up, I see?" Such a dumb question. But what I want to say, I can't.

"Yep. I want to do a sign like 'Caution: owned and operated by the elves. Cannot be held responsible.' Something that's funny, but also if a kid falls off the back and breaks an arm, I won't be sued." She swipes rogue hay strips off her overalls.

"That's smart. I think that sign should cover it." I can't help it. My gaze falls to her mouth, and I want to do it again. I want to rush into her arms and tell her how scared I am, but she unlocked a piece of me, and I'm ready to explore. I bite on the corner of my lip. The kiss from last night lingers in the air like wet smoke, and I can't breathe.

"I had so much fun last night," I finally say. "I didn't realize how much I needed a night out. It was... perfect. Everything was perfect." There. I said as much as I can say, laid down as much as I can possibly lay down, and hold my breath for her reaction.

Quinn digs her boots into a rock before she takes a deep breath and looks at me. "I am so sorry about last night. The kiss and everything. Like, holy shit, that is not me." She stuffs her hands in her pockets and balances on her heels. "Actually, it *is* me. My MO, and it really wasn't cool to do to you."

Wait, what? "I don't know what you mean. I'm not mad that it happened. I just... I'm in a weird place with everything..." I tug on the corner of my lip. This is *so hard*. Yes, I have feelings for Quinn, but also, I'm terrified. The ghost of my past relationship is still there, hovering. And I haven't had this sinking sensation that's so wonderful and scary in so many years.

Quinn flops on the stack of hay and tugs on a straw. She doesn't speak for so long that I think the conversation is over. Through the ray of light beaming through the trees, she squints at me with a flash of regret.

Regret. Oh no. Regret is not good.

"I'm so grateful for our friendship, Zoey," she starts, bowing a strand of straw in her fingers. "Everything you've done out here this month and the time we've spent together means so much to me. I haven't told you this, but I've never had a friend before. Like a real one. I know that sounds pretty pathetic, but it's true. Not like this, not like what I have with you. And I'm scared I royally screwed it up." She crisscrosses her legs. "If I somehow gave you the wrong impression last night, will you please just forgive me? I wasn't thinking and I really acted out in the moment. I wouldn't want to do anything that would hurt us."

Everything Quinn is saying is kind, and I'm hearing her, but the back of my eyes sting, hot with unshed tears. "Why, um." I swallow, heat filling my cheeks. "Why do you think it would hurt us?" This is me, putting myself out there as much as I can. Dipping my toes into barely frozen water, checking to see how much the ice will crack and splinter around me.

Maybe we can take a chance. Maybe this is something that could work. But if it doesn't, then this friendship, which means a lot to me, is ruined. But I cannot do one-night stands. Intimacy and sex are as intertwined as the roots on the cedar tree I'm staring at, and I need to be in sync like this with someone I sleep with.

Quinn pops her elbows on her knees and leans her chin into her fists. "Zoey, you are, like, too good for this world. And... I'm not. I've grown a lot this last year, but I'm not there yet. And this isn't about my job or other things. This is *me*, who I am as a person with relationships, with everything." Quinn's exhale is long and shaky. "I have sex, you know? I fuck and that's it. That's all it ever is. And I'm so sorry, that probably sounds crude to you, but I need you to know who I am, so none of this, us, is romanticized, okay? I really, really care about you too much to let my need to get laid mess with what we have building here."

My breath catches in my throat, and I try to grasp at nonexistent air. She is delivering the message as kind as she can, but it still hurts. Quinn bravely just drew a boundary line, even though I can tell it's tearing her up. The last thing I want to do is to make her feel bad about herself, just because we have different views.

So I rush to her, drop to my knees, and pull Quinn in for a hug. A deep hug, full from my soul, and she presses against me, gripping me, relaxing against me. "Thank you so much for being so honest with me." I hate that my voice verges on cracking. "I'm so happy we're friends."

This is what I say. And it's not untrue. But a minute later, I excuse myself to use the bathroom, and cry into my hands.

NINETEEN
QUINN

A car door slams and my heartbeat kicks up. I take one last quick look at the inside of the barn. It's not opening day, far from it, but having fifty people out here for the first time pushes my need for perfection to the top.

Newspaper and disposable tablecloths cover long banquet tables, folding chairs scatter the room, a station of wood pallets and signs rests in the corner. Every single craft item I own fills the tables—mason jars with paintbrushes, water, paper towels, glue, glitter, and everything in between. Zoey said the church ladies were bringing items with them, too, thank God, because I don't think I have enough supplies to keep them all occupied.

Even though I set everything up last night, I got here by seven this morning. Honestly, I should've brought a sleeping bag and pillow here yesterday, because it was useless going home and staring at my ceiling until I returned. Which is exactly what I did—stared at that yellowed spot on my ceiling, replaying the conversation with Zoey from yesterday, until my heavy eyelids finally closed.

After Zoey prepped the cookies yesterday, she made a really terrible excuse about needing to leave early to bake and run errands. It was painfully obvious after our chat that she forced herself to stay as long as she could, which was half the time as usual.

I saw her tear-streaked face after we talked, but didn't say anything. What could I say? She knows who I am. I told her in the beginning. But yesterday, I had to hammer in the message. She needs to know what will happen if we take this any further. It wouldn't be fair, otherwise. Inside, I held a sliver of hope that she'd tell me to shut up, that she didn't care, that she was ready to try because I was worth it, and we'd figure it out together.

But she didn't. And although she hugged me, and thanked me for opening up, the sting of rejection still burrowed deep. But also, I can't blame her. Not only are we fundamentally different, but she's also still so hurt over her ex that she's rightfully cautious.

And Zoey still hasn't told me that she read Josie's letters. Not that she's obligated to, but I want her to. I want her to open up to me, to share everything in her head, to let me in more. These thoughts torment me, poke me at night, poison me through the day.

But why do I want her to do that? Because I think, for her, I can change. I already have changed so many parts of myself this last year. I've discovered a new piece of myself, one that wants cuddles on the couch and to laugh about music, and sample cookies before moving into a bedroom. But can I sustain that? Can I really be the exclusive, committed person she wants?

Even if I can, am I assuming that Zoey is thinking the same thing as me with just one kiss? She knows I'm open and free, and maybe she was using the opportunity to test out a kiss on someone who told her physical things mean nothing. I probably would've done the same thing. So, what if I just sat down, communicated all of this, and she said, "I want to be with you." And then, per every single encounter I've ever had with a woman, I clam up, shut down, and can't do it. Then, friendship gone.

God, I'm overthinking all of this.

The sound of gravel crunching beneath tires breaks my thoughts—thank Christ. I rewrap my hair on top of my head and run to the door.

"Hey!" Zoey waves from her car with a box tucked in her arm, the wisps from her ponytail flying in the breeze. A woman, maybe mid-fifties or so, steps out of the passenger seat with an arsenal of canvas bags, as a cute little blond boy leaps from the back seat.

This must be Zoey's mom and Noah. I scoot over to them, smiling. Yes, I'm glad they're here, but I'm really glad Zoey is here. After the conversation yesterday, I couldn't help but think she'd bail on me. "Hey, let me help. What can I grab?"

Zoey hands me a grocery bag, then points to her family. "Zoey, meet Debbie, my mom, and Noah, the best kid in the entire world. And I know a lot of kids." She gives Noah a tousle on the hair, and he buries his head into her hip.

"Oh, Quinn." Debbie drops the bags to the ground, opens her arms up wide, and rushes to me like I'm a child returning from deployment. "Finally, we get to meet! I've heard so much about you and this place. I cannot wait to see everything you've done."

The warmth already fills me. Zoey gets her hugging skills from her mother, clearly. Frankie hugs me all the time, but I don't remember the last time my mother hugged me. Years, probably?

I squeeze Debbie back and release, and chuckle at Zoey's cringing face. "Same. I'm so happy you all are here. Thank you so much for helping me... I'm still overwhelmed by everyone's generosity."

Debbie shoos away the comment. "Spending a fall day on this gorgeous property making crafts with my friends. I need to be thanking you." Debbie picks up her canvas bags and scans the property. "Quinn, this property is absolutely beautiful. These trees, this land... Stunning, really."

Yep. I am beaming. Wide and bright, and I don't even care. "Thank you. It was a ton of effort, lots of scratches and bruises, and even more tears, but everything is finally coming together." I glance at Noah, who is still snuggled into Zoey's side. "And, Noah. Do you have any idea how much your auntie Zoey talks about you?" I ask, lowering myself to meet him closer to eye level. "She says you are the best artist in the whole family."

"Yep, I am!" He lifts his head, his smile spreading across his chubby cheeks. "Zoey said Santa is coming here. Is he here today?"

I peek at Zoey, who just shrugs, but there's a soft twinkle in her eyes. She's watching me, watching this interaction, and she looks a bit nervous. Not sure if it's because she thinks her family will do something embarrassing—which wouldn't bother me anyway—or if this is something more. Nope... doing it again. *Overthinking*. If I keep doing this, I'm checking myself in for a lobotomy.

"No Santa today," I say to Noah. "But we're trying to make this place really special for him so he'll visit."

Noah moves his body away from Zoey's hip, and is now *really* grinning. "I know Santa likes milk and cookies and reindeer and presents, so I'm going to paint all those things for him."

If I could just bottle up this child's wonder in one of my mason jars and release it on Christmas, my heart would be full. "I think that is a perfect plan."

Zoey taps the bag in her arm. "This is getting heavy. I'm going to head inside. Noah, grab that plate of cookies and come with me. Quinn, can you help my mom bring in the crockpots and show her where the plug-ins are?"

"Absolutely," I say, and follow Debbie to the car. She pops open the trunk and a gust of hearty smoked meat hits me. Not only does Debbie have a few crockpots, I'm pretty sure she's emptied the grocery store. I see buns, bags of chips, a cooler, fruit salad, paper plates, and... *No way*. "Did you make Minnesota sushi?"

Debbie's grin rivals Noah's. "Of course I did. When was the last time you've been to a potluck? We'd have a mutiny on our hands if I didn't."

The last time I was at a potluck, I was probably in diapers. My mouth is salivating at the dill pickles wrapped in cream cheese and deli ham. I wonder if I can sneak one before the rest of the crew arrives.

"I am so happy to talk to you, *finally*," Debbie says as she loads up my outstretched arms. "Ever since you and Zoey met, she's been Chatty Cathy about her time with you. I haven't heard her so excited since we finally gave in and bought her a custom skateboard when she was twelve."

Not only does my heartbeat speed up, but I also have so many questions. Skateboard? Zoey? What other little details is she hiding? Every morsel I uncover about her makes me want to dig for more intel. "Oh, really?"

"Oh yeah. She calls me at nights on the way home from being here with you. And well, I just think whatever you two have is something really special. It's the happiest I've seen Zoey in a long time, and just warms my mama heart, you know?" She grabs a crockpot, and we stroll towards the barn. "I'm just glad she met someone so special to her."

I am swooning at this information overload, and bite back the urge to learn more. I smile at Debbie, but a small pinch grows in my chest. Zoey is special to me, too. So much so that I can't do anything that will harm what we have. For today, I need to stop thinking about all things Zoey and focus on the craft bonanza about to occur.

Inside the barn, Debbie stops in the doorway and drags her gaze across the space. "Quinn. Oh my gosh, this is beautiful!" She steps further inside, sets her crockpot on a table, and rests her hands on her hips, doing a full turn. "I really can't believe it. You've done such a fantastic job."

The place is coming together, finally. And thank God, too, because we are at t-minus three weeks before opening day on Thanksgiving weekend. Besides severe lack of inventory—which will hopefully get supplemented today along with the shipments of wreaths, cloths, and candles coming in next week—I can almost see the holiday spirit fill the place. The huge, artificial trees in the corners of the barn drip with light, Santa's photo op station is nearly complete with the large wooden chair and painted signs, and the display stand is built and ready to get filled.

"Thank you." I'm beaming so hard it's embarrassing. I plug the crockpots in at the prep station and reach for some serving bowls for the chips. "I could not have done all of this without Zoey's help."

"Oh gosh, stop. You totally could have. I've never seen anyone move so fast in all my life," Zoey calls from where she's sitting by Noah at a craft table.

"Well, you two are certainly capturing the magic of Christmas," Debbie says. "And that is something to be really proud of."

It's official. I am asking Debbie to adopt me.

Within a few hours, the space fills quickly with kids from Debbie's school, parents, grandparents, and the church ladies. The children scatter among two tables, most painting small wooden ornaments of Santa Claus. Debbie assumes a teacher stance and bounces between tables, helping kids, wiping hands, and filling up paint stations.

The church ladies are almost louder than the children, and it cracks me up. One, with the help of her husband and few other folks, even lugged in this insanely fancy sewing machine that auto-sews a Christmas message on dishtowels. Another small group is in the corner, ironing embroidery stencils on dish rags, and others are either painting ornaments or putting together foam snowmen with top hats.

As the chatter sounds below, and Alexa booms holiday music, Zoey and I are on ladders on the opposite edges of the room, wrapping the last string of lights across the beams.

"Higher?" Zoey calls out to her mom, who dashes to each corner of the room to check the angle.

Debbie cups her hands around her mouth. "Yes, a few inches, no, lower... There! Perfect."

"Thank you!" I call out and carefully lower myself from the rungs. The very last thing I need is to pull a Zoey and crack my foot before opening night. When I reach the bottom, I clap my hands off and allow my gaze to fall over the room.

This... is life. People chatting, BBQ and sloppy joe scents swirling in the air, Christmas music, the children proudly putting their ornaments on the drying table. The church ladies stack towels and rags in a corner, some hang things on a tree, others decorate the display case. My heart is so full I think it's gonna burst.

It feels like a family. An actual family. Support, community, the type of environment people talk about, probably what Frankie felt like on her sports team, but I've never had this. It feels full. Wonderful.

My chin trembles. I can't believe I almost risked this all by kissing Zoey.

"You doing okay?" Zoey says as she steps to me and hands me a bottle of water.

"I am. I just... I'm shocked all these people came here." My voice cracks and I suck in my cheeks. When she lays a warm hand on my back, filled with some sort of power that transfers healing messages to me, I sigh. Before she got here today, I thought I screwed everything up with her. But right now, as I lean back into her touch, I'm so grateful that the kiss didn't ruin anything. And I vow that I will never do anything stupid like that again. This, right here, is enough.

We lean against the back wall, shoulder to shoulder, and watch the scene.

"I can't believe this is my last day here with you," Zoey says, twisting the cap back on her water. "I'm having visions of figuring out how I can create a craft station at my bakery so you can be there with me during the day. Or maybe make Zoey's a chain, and I'll open a second location in your shed."

"I fully support both those ideas. Give me a week to develop the business plan, and we'll go to the bank together." Even though I'm grinning, my gut is dropping, twisting low and sad inside me. Something about this feels so final. Will we stay friends? It's easy to build a relationship when you are together ten to twelve hours a day. But I can't help this aching sense in my stomach that this chapter is closing.

Might not be a Christmas miracle after all.

TWENTY

QUINN

I slip into the fluffiest, bubbliest, warmest bath of my life. Fat iridescent suds surround me. I flick at a few before I rest my eyes and sigh. What a week. After the festivities at the barn last weekend, and Zoey returning to work, I spent the next five days cleaning from the event, pricing all the items the kids and church ladies made, and setting up the shop. Zoey's dad found these amazing antique wagons at Zoey's grandmother's place which are perfect to hold the nonbreakable bulbs I ordered from a vendor. Then yesterday, Frankie spent all day building the Santa photo op station, complete with MERRY CHRISTMAS signs, a red-drape background, and oversized holiday gifts and plastic candy canes.

And I spent every single day thinking of Zoey and missing her so much that it hurts. In a surprising and delightful turn of events, Zoey and I still chat every single day, often multiple times. When she has downtime between customers, or late at night, or even getting ready for the day, we're talking. And still, when we hang up, I miss her immediately.

I dip a washcloth into the warm water and set it on my forehead and eyes. The two-week countdown is on, and my nerves are gnawing at me. The precut trees will be delivered next Friday, the shop is close to completion, and I have the entire temporary crew hired and their W-2 paperwork filled out.

And yet, something is missing.

I'm sharing these things with Zoey as a friend. But I want to share them with her as more than a friend. My feelings for her have only intensified in her absence, not lightened, and everything that I ran from, everything I thought I didn't want, the life I thought wasn't for me, I realize it is. I am falling for Zoey. In the hardest way. And I need to tell her.

I think. I don't know. Ugh, why isn't this easy? And what does "more than friends" look like? Marriage? That's her goal, and I still don't think it's mine. And she shouldn't settle. Anyone who says it's easy, or to just open up, or to communicate with Zoey, has clearly never had this. Not only is the deep impending doom of rejection hanging over my head—which I've never had before and feels absolutely terrible—if I tell her how I feel, and she doesn't feel the same, I'll have ruined it all. So no, it's not that easy to just pick up the phone and confess everything and hope for the best.

My phone rings and I glance at it. *Zoey*. Any other person in the world, I'd send to voicemail. But I could be doing almost anything and want to hear her voice. "Hey," I say, grateful for waterproof phones. I tap the speaker then lower myself back into the water.

"What are you doing?" she asks.

Thinking about you. "I'm in the tub."

"Are you singing 'Kiss' by Prince?" she asks, and I hear pots banging in the background.

"Um... no, why?"

The pots stop banging. "If you don't catch this reference, I'm out. Seriously. Our friendship will cease to exist from this point forward. *Pretty Woman?* Bathtub scene."

"Please don't leave me," I say through a giggle. "But I have no idea what you're talking about."

"Hopeless." The banging stops and is replaced with shuffling. "You have that gorgeous hair just like Julia Roberts in that movie.

And in that scene, she was singing off-key in a bubble bath... You know what? Never mind. I'm adding this to our movie-night list."

A few weeks ago, Zoey and I created a movie-night wish list. Along with summer day trip, best burger search, and concert wish lists. "Want to get together tomorrow and start tackling that movie list?" I ask. "I'll be really nice and let you choose first, even though I won our rock, paper, scissors war fair and square."

"That's super generous of you considering you cheated," she says with what I know is her teasing half smirk, half grin from when she's giving me shit. "Actually, I can't tomorrow night. I have plans. How about Sunday?"

My ears perk up. Plans? What plans? With someone? Maybe family, but if so, why not say? Zoey is never cagey about the details of her life, from what she had for breakfast to customer stories, but she's never mentioned *plans*. "Plans?" I try to add a smile to my tone, but fail. "Anything fun?"

"I'm not sure fun is the right word, but I'll let you know. I'm, uh, I'm actually meeting Josie for dinner, if you can believe it."

I nearly drop my phone into the mound of bubbles. What are the chances that there is another person, like maybe a cousin or aunt or something named Josie? Even surrounded by heated suds, my neck tightens. "No way, really?" I squeak, then clear my throat.

This is not what I want to ask. I want to ask if they're getting back together, and if she thinks she'll kiss Josie, and if it goes well, will they go back to Zoey's loft? Will they laugh and hold hands, and will Zoey hug her the way she hugs me? I can't handle everything tearing through me right now, ripping me from the inside. I don't want Zoey to have dinner with Josie. I want her to have dinner with me. *Dammit.* I push my wet thumb against my forehead. If I lost my chance with Zoey because of being too scared to admit my feelings, I will never forgive myself. But if I confess now, it will absolutely be seen as a manipulation tactic. And honestly, if I dig deep enough, which I hate doing, it would be a manipulation tactic. And I refuse to do it.

I want to ask more. Did Josie ask her, or did Zoey ask Josie? Is this a getting-back-together kind of thing, or a friends thing, or what? And *why*? Why after two years is Zoey meeting with Josie? Maybe they own property together and need to chat about a sale. Maybe there is a death in the family and Josie is here for a funeral. Maybe Josie wants Zoey back.

Fuck. Josie wants Zoey back.

I lift myself a few inches from the water and inhale a breath. "Where are you two going to go? Somewhere fun?"

The sound of Zoey sipping something comes through the phone. "Orchard's."

Orchard's. This does not give me the intel I need to properly discern if this is a date. The place is right off of Main Street, more upscale than a diner, but not as upscale as some of the tourist places. It's not dark and overly romantic, but it's also not family friendly and they do have a full wine list. Ugh. Nope, I'm gleaning nothing.

"Nice," I say. Am I coming off as casual? Carefree? Unaffected? I think so. Even though I'm anything but. God dammit. Zoey's going on a date with her ex. "At least you'll get some good pie out of it."

Zoey giggles. "True. But I swear after working at the bakery all these years, the last thing I want to do is go somewhere else to have treats. Well, that aren't mine. I'm too critical and don't want to judge these nice people."

I slide a little lower and the water sloshes around me. My heart is hurting, my shoulders are stiff. Everything that is not supposed to happen in a luxurious bath is happening. "So, do you know what she wants?" I really shouldn't ask, but I can't help it. "Do you think she wants to get back together?"

"Who knows?" she says with what sounds a little like a chuckle, but it's not enough to read into.

Zoey still hasn't mentioned that she read the letters. The image of those lovely yellow-and-blue envelopes scattered across her table the night we shared that kiss is burned in my brain. Zoey is always honest, and I know it's illogical and not fair, but I feel like she kept this from me.

Don't do it. Don't do it. "Did you ever end up reading those letters she sent you?" I hate myself the tiniest bit right now.

"I did," she says softly. A moment passes. "They were... nice."

Well, God dammit, what does that mean? I hate this. I hate, hate, hate all of this. I'm too hot in this tub. I'm sweating and going to overheat and pass out and I need air. "Oh yeah?"

"Yeah. I think she was just going through some things and needed a familiar person. The letters started with how much she regretted breaking up, wanting to talk again, but the last several were more of just life messages," Zoey says. "Honestly, I think she's lonely. She moved to Minneapolis and doesn't really know anyone, and I think she just needed a friend."

I feel marginally better. *Marginally.*

"Hey, I gotta run," Zoey says. "So, pizza and movies on Sunday?"

"Only if you try anchovies again."

"You still owe me the Cusack moment from forever ago!" She laughs. "Call you later. I have to finish washing these pans."

When she hangs up, I slide all the way in the tub, only leaving out my mouth and nose. Cool, so Zoey is meeting up with her ex. Is this the first time she's seen her since they broke up? What if they get back together? What if the spark between them is dormant and they touch once and it flames alive and kills any chance that we might have?

Do I want a chance? Yes. I think so. Am I willing to put all this scary shit behind me to take a chance and risk our friendship? I don't know.

The tub ceases to relax me, and a few minutes later, I'm so worked up that I hop out, throw on a robe, and traipse down to the kitchen.

Morgan is at the kitchen table with her laptop and multiple papers, focusing hard on her screen. When Frankie is back in New York for work, like she is now, Morgan spends all her hours working on her event-planning business, so she has more free time when Frankie is home. She'll probably be in this same position until 2:00 a.m. She pauses mid-type and peeks up. "Hey, you hungry? I have leftovers from dinner if you want them."

"No," I grumble. I'm not hungry, I'm terrified. Zoey and Josie are going to get back together and there's nothing I can do about it. I open a cabinet door, looking for something, I don't even know what, and slam it shut. Open another, slam it. Another, slam.

A gentle hand touches my arm.

"How about if we give these doors a little bit of a break," Morgan says and closes the cabinet. "They're old and fragile and I really don't want them to shatter before we do the kitchen remodel."

I tug on the knot around my robe. "I just want some fucking chamomile tea."

Morgan lifts her eyebrow, opens the cabinet I had just slammed shut, and reaches behind the coffee beans for a box of tea.

I exhale a puff through my nose and press a palm into my head. "*Sorry*."

She points to the barstool. I dutifully sit as she puts water in the tea kettle and flicks the stove on. I lay my head down on the cool countertop. A few minutes later, I lift my head as she slides a mug my way.

"Two weeks until opening day," she says, dunking the tea bag in her own mug. "It's a lot of pressure."

It's *so* much pressure. Not only are my life savings, plus a hefty business loan, sunk into my farm, so are all of my hopes and dreams. If this fails, I don't know what I will do. "It is," I finally say.

Morgan pulls out the stool next to me and sits. "Being an entrepreneur is extremely difficult. Doing this alone as a single woman, without a business or life partner, is terrifying. I get it. I think people underestimate the difficulty in undertaking something like this."

I squeeze a dollop of honey in my tea and stir. Maybe I haven't given myself the credit I deserve. So many times, I thought, well, my aunt and uncle left great instructions, and well, I have my sister and Morgan, who guide me, and well, I have Zoey, who helped for a month.

But I did do it, and I *should* be proud of myself. But I'm not giving myself that luxury until I see if it's successful. "What if no one shows up?"

"They will," Morgan says, blowing into her mug and taking a short sip. "It's like the Christmas field of dreams. Build it and they will come."

She says this like I know what the hell she is talking about. "What?"

Morgan grins. "Really? The movie *Field of Dreams*. The baseball movie. You know, the famous line: *If you build it, they will come.*"

And just like that, I bury my head in my hands and start crying.

A solid moment or two passes before Morgan tugs me in for a stiff hug. She is not a hugger at all, at least not with me, but she's Frankie's proxy while my sister is gone. So here I am, letting the tears flow, drip down my cheek onto her shoulder. I stay like this, a minute, maybe two, maybe three, but I'm letting it all out. The stress of this last decade, this last year, these last few months. My insecurity that I'm not enough, I'm not worthy, that I'll get hurt. Broken. *Destroyed.*

"This is not about the farm, is it."

Morgan's not asking. Of course this isn't about the farm. I know this, she knows this, but I don't know if I'm ready to say anything. I lift my head and swipe the back of my hand under my chin to catch them. When I catch my breath, I lean back on the stool.

Morgan dunks the tea bag a few more times, then sets it in a discard bowl. "When your sister came back here last year, she threw my world upside down." She taps her ring on the edge of the mug. "I thought I knew my path. My purpose. I was so focused on saving my company, and being strong, and never falling apart, and hiding my feelings. My God, did I hide my feelings from Frankie. For *years*."

Their situation differs from mine. They couldn't have been as scared as me. Morgan and Frankie share a past. They knew each other, and what love and deep feelings feel like. All of this is so new to me—the feelings, the yearning, the sensation of my heart always on the verge of splitting and nothing has even happened yet. Everything is new and terrifying and exciting, and I don't know what to do.

"Quinn," Morgan says and meets my gaze. "I almost let Frankie go. I was so close, I practically pushed her out of here. But my God, I'm so glad that we fought for each other. Fought for our right to be happy, together."

The warm tea slides down my throat and soothes my belly. "But weren't you scared?"

"Are you kidding me? I was *terrified*." Morgan slides back on her stool. "I'd already experienced heartbreak with Frankie. True, gut-level heartbreak. The kind that makes you timid and tense and makes you question everything, makes you question if it's worth ever trying anything again because the pain was so raw, and real, and you're not sure you can go through it again."

My chin trembles again, and I quickly sip the tea. This is what I'm talking about. I don't know if I'm strong enough to put myself through that. What if I'm terrible at relationships and clam up and don't know how to act and destroy everything. Losing her friendship feels as gut-wrenching as not telling her how I feel. "I don't know what to do."

"It's Zoey, right?" Morgan asks.

I arch my brow.

"Sorry. Of course." Morgan crosses her arms and takes a breath. "Well, you obviously have feelings for her. And from everything I see, she does, too. She practically lights up like the star on a Christmas tree every time you walk in the room."

My chest lifts. "She does?"

"Do you not see that? I mean, I've known Zoey for at least a decade, and even though we aren't like close friends or anything, I've certainly worked with her enough over the years to get insight into her personality. Her baseline is always friendly, always nice, always giving. But with you, everything is elevated—her smile, her laugh, her mood. *Everything*. It's clear you amplify her happiness."

Tea or not, my insides warm at this. Morgan is not the type of woman to blow smoke up my ass to make me feel better. If she is saying this about Zoey, she must mean it. But tomorrow, after she sees Josie, everything might change. And I'm totally helpless to stop it from happening. In fact, I need it to happen. I need Zoey to compare, contrast, and do a full cost-benefit analysis on her ex-girlfriend before I say anything. *If* I say anything. "She's meeting her ex-girlfriend for dinner tomorrow," I choke out.

Morgan's lips pull together. "Josie? Huh. I didn't know she was back in town."

I nod and stare at my mug. "What's she like?"

Too long of a pause follows. I picked the worst time to hold my breath while waiting for a response.

"I mean, she's a nice woman," Morgan finally says. "I only knew her through town and a few events that we attended. Oh, and I chatted with her once at the animal shelter, when I went with my brother to bring in their hamster—don't ask. But, yes, she's a nice person."

This is not making me feel better. I want to hear that Josie is terrible and evil and rides a broom at night. Not that she's some sweet woman who works with sick animals.

"But, Quinn." Morgan sets her hand on top of mine. "So are you."

I let out a short chortle. "I'm not really that nice."

"Are you kidding?" Morgan's voice rises enough where my head snaps up. "You are one of the most loving, giving, gracious people I know. When you find your people, you love them so hard, with all of yourself. You are smart and brave and funny and hardworking. You are absolutely the real deal." She sits back and gives me a stern look. "And I won't hear you say another bad word about yourself."

I rest my head on her shoulder and sigh. "You're a pretty good sister when Frankie abandons me."

She laughs. "You know she'll be back on Wednesday, right?"

So maybe I do deserve someone. I've always loved my lifestyle, wanted my lifestyle. But since meeting Zoey, I see that I might want something more. My eyes are opening, just a tiny bit, to the possibility that my dating style thus far might have also been a means of protection.

"Listen," Morgan says, cutting through my thoughts. "You are a fighter. Always have been. If you have feelings for Zoey, you go fight for her. Take a chance, tell her how you feel, put yourself out there, okay? Fight for her. But also know your worth."

I reach over and give her a hug. A firm, solid hug, then withdraw. "Thank you." I've used up all my words for now. I need to get out of this kitchen and get some clarity. I grab my mug and march to my bedroom. Inside my room, I pace, and think. Pace and think.

And then I clean. I spend the rest of the day, until the early hours, unpacking everything, organizing, throwing laundry in the wash, hanging everything up, until my room is damn near glistening.

The cleaner the room, the clearer everything becomes. My mind opens, my body shifts, my chest lifts.

I know exactly what I need to do. I just have to put a few plans together first.

TWENTY-ONE
ZOEY

I pin back the loose strands of hair and grab my jacket and scarf. After a freakishly warm fall, the weather has altered and from here until April, there's going to be a constant chance of snow. I lock my door, walk down the alley, and resist peeking into the bakery.

After having a month off from the bakery, something inside me shifted. The urge, the need, the anxiety, to be at the store all of the time lifted. I gave both Luna and Caleb more hours and put an ad out to hire one more full-time staff. In the next year, my goal is to decrease to a solid forty hours a week, down from a gazillion. Life is passing by on a speed train. I don't want to wake up and blink and see that I have missed out on something amazing.

Like Quinn.

While getting ready to meet Josie tonight, I can't help thinking about Quinn. Heck, all I do is think about Quinn. I call or text her so much that I'm surprised she hasn't blocked me by now. But I need to do this dinner tonight. Partly as a test for myself, partly for Josie, and partly for Quinn.

Because I need to be honest with myself, truly honest, and I will only have complete clarity once I meet with Josie.

Orchard's is within walking distance from my place, so I tug on my jacket and stroll. It's still early, only 5:00 p.m., but the orange of the horizon is barely a whisper. And still, all I can think about is Quinn. Maybe I'll call Josie, tell her that I can't make it, and go over to Quinn's place. But Josie's only in town for a short while, she really wants to meet, and I won't ditch out on her, even if she is my ex.

I'm so distracted I don't realize the woman walking towards me on the sidewalk is Josie. Her formerly dark shoulder-length hair is now a fresh, blonde shaggy pixie cut. She's wrapped up in a jacket, ripped skinny jeans, high boots. She looks good. Great, even. *Beautiful*.

And I feel absolutely nothing.

"Hey... you..." Josie reaches her arms out as she approaches, with a soft, almost sheepish smile.

"Hey, Josie. Sorry, whoa, I didn't see you there." I lean into her hug. It's familiar, yet not at the same time, and again, I feel *nothing*. Stepping back, I try to gauge what is happening. Maybe a little nostalgia, or a "hope she's okay," and a little curiosity. Other than that, my cells, my heart, my gut are all at a standstill.

"You look great," Josie says as she stuffs her hands in her jacket pockets. "You look, I don't know. Well rested or something."

"Thank you. I cut back on hours at the shop and am taking some time for myself." I turn toward the restaurant, and we stroll in silence for a few moments.

Josie grips the edges of her scarf in her palm and keeps her gaze on the sidewalk. "Thanks for meeting with me tonight."

"Yeah, of course. It'll be good to catch up." This is all so awkward. I don't know what to say. I've never been good at small talk unless it's a customer interaction. But this isn't that. This is walking down the sidewalk on a beautiful late fall night with the one that I once knew the best, but I no longer know.

The jangle of a dog collar coming towards us has me lifting my head. *Huh*. Colby and Kona are walking toward us on the sidewalk. I wasn't sure if Colby even lived in this town, but if she's taking a random stroll at night it makes me think she might live near the shop.

Josie's eyes snap up. "Ah, sweet golden retriever."

"Hey, Colby." I wave and smile. At this moment, I feel like I know my reclusive customer Colby better than Josie, and I'm thankful for the break in the silence. "Hi, Kona. Are you being a good girl?"

"Hey, Zoey." Colby glances at Josie, and back to me.

Am I supposed to introduce them? Say nothing? How would I even label Josie? *My ex* seems crass. *Friend* seems untruthful. *Someone I used to know* seems like I'm giving away way too much information for a casual introduction.

"Oh my gosh, your pup." Josie's voice rises and she squats near Kona. "Can I pet her?"

Colby grins and rubs the edge of Kona's ears. "Yes, of course. Fair warning, she's a glutton for love. Once you start petting her, she'll beg for more."

"How old is she?" Josie holds out the top of her hand for Kona to sniff.

"Six," Colby says.

"Ah, such a good age. Finally calming down." Josie pets Kona behind the ears, then moves to scratch her under the chin. "Any hip issues yet?"

"No, knock on wood." Colby switches the leash to her other hand. "You have a golden?"

Josie shakes her head. "No, but I'm a vet tech, so I see lots of animals. But in my heart, I've always had a soft spot for golden retrievers."

Colby nods with a soft grin. "They're the most loyal, right?"

Josie laughs and lifts herself back from squatting. "That's the rumor on the street."

My head is swirling at this interaction. This is the most I've seen Colby smile in all the years she's been coming into my shop. I always say hi to Kona and give her a dog treat, of course, but I make a quick mental note to chat with Colby more about dogs when she visits. It's clearly her comfort zone.

Colby steps back, her gaze casting one more time at Josie,

before she nods at me. "Didn't mean to interrupt. Have a good night."

When Colby walks past us, Josie and I continue toward the restaurant. "A friend of yours?" Josie asks.

I shake my head. "No, just a good customer. She's really nice, from the little I know."

"Well, she loves dogs, so she's obviously a saint," Josie says with a smile.

The breeze picks up the tiniest bit and I snug my scarf a little tighter around my neck. We make the most plain, non-intimate small talk during the walk. We talked about Minnesotans' favorite subject—the weather—how the traffic differs from where Josie lives in Minneapolis, and how she discovered an uptown sushi restaurant featured on a Food TV show. I could probably engage more, but my mind is elsewhere. *Quinn.*

In what feels like an hour, but is really less than five minutes, we are finally at the table. After ordering, I squeeze a mist of lemon into an ice water and take a sip. Josie is telling me about the vet hospital she works at, and the surprising amount of snakes that are brought in to be seen, and I promise I'm trying to listen to her, be as polite as I can, and pepper in random questions. But I can hardly focus.

None of this feels right. Being here with Josie is like expecting a certain taste but getting something completely different, something expired and ruined, and then waiting for the inevitable sickness to set in. Josie the *person* is not the sickness. Josie the *relationship* is the expired food. I don't want to be with Josie right now. I don't want to be with Josie, ever. It was clear to me the moment I saw her, and every second sitting here is taking away time from the one I really want to be with.

My knee bounces under the table. Can Josie please say what she needs to say, so I can call Quinn to see if she wants to come over for a movie. Or for a talk. Dammit. I need to tell her how I feel. No more holding back. Time for me to jump onto the frozen lake and see if it can withstand everything before it breaks. I can do this.

"Thank you for meeting with me. I know... it's been a while," Josie says, running her fingers through her shagged hair. "I wanted to let you know I'm moving back to town."

My mouth drops. "Um, why?" *Please don't say it's to get back together.* It doesn't feel good to turn someone down. For the first time since Josie didn't accept my marriage proposal, I finally feel what it was like to be in her shoes all those years ago. The one that has to tell the person, someone you care about, that you don't want to be with them. It feels miserable. But also, needed.

She lifts a brow at my question.

"I mean, I know your family is here, but you were so desperate to move to Minneapolis," I quickly add.

Josie pulls the straw to her mouth. "I wasn't desperate to move to Minneapolis. I was desperate for change."

Well, that stings a little.

"I know that sounds harsh, but I really need to hash out everything, and just... You know what, I'm just going to dive into this." Josie gulps down several long pulls of water. "Zoey, I am so, so sorry about how things ended with us. I was stuck, you know? I'd been in Spring Harbors my whole life, been with you for so long, at my job since I was a teenager, and everything just felt stale."

I can't help a little heat from springing to my chest. "*Stale.* Not stable."

Josie tugs on her fingers as she shifts on the chair, her eyes focused on the table. "I know, I know. I'm sorry. I think I just needed some solitude and self-discovery and to find out who I was without you."

The server comes in at either the best or worst time and sets our salads in front of us. Inside I chuckle—I ordered a Caesar salad. *Caesar.* Made with anchovies. Somehow, when it's blended with cream and lemon, it's delicious, but on pizza it's not. I *have* to remember to tell Quinn this later.

"I'm glad that you took time to learn about yourself." I stab my fork into the salad. "I'm sure that was... therapeutic." Gosh, this conversation is plain painful. I want to scarf down the salad, throw some cash on the table, and leave.

Josie dashes pepper on the salad, then stirs. "It really was. But, by leaving and staying in Minneapolis, I learned everything I need to know. I found myself, what I needed, what I didn't need, and I came to a conclusion."

I take another bite of the dressing-laden crunchy salad.

"I want to give our relationship another try."

I cough. I put my mouth into my napkin and cough so hard that I see a couple of restaurant goers look at me, probably wondering if they'll need to jump up and give me the Heimlich. After swiping my mouth off with the napkin, I toss it on the table. "You have got to be kidding me."

My words are harsh, but not my tone. I can appreciate how hard this must be for Josie, to put herself out like this. I'm struggling with doing this same thing with Quinn, because I'm too scared. But it took me so long to find myself after Josie, and darn it, I really like myself. I like who I am as an independent, as a friend, as a business owner.

"Sorry, I know I just sprung that on you," Josie says, pink now spreading from her cheeks to her neck. "And of course, we can take it as slow as you need it, and rebuild our friendship, and whatever you need to trust me again."

I set the fork on the side of my plate with a clank and look at Josie. Lovely large brown eyes face me. There's an openness to her that I don't remember, but also a sadness. I want to hug her, pull her close, and tell her she hasn't finished finding herself. If she had, she'd know this is a terrible idea.

"Josie." I pause and try to think of my words before I speak. The very last thing I want to do is hurt someone, but I have to be the voice of reason. "I'm flattered, really. It took a lot of courage for you to tell me this. But, um, I don't want to get back together."

Josie pulls her mouth into her lips. "I know this is sudden. Well, I mean I've been sending you letters for almost a year, so maybe not *that* sudden. But, Zoey, what we had is for the record books, you know? It was so special, and I don't think that we'll ever have that with anyone else."

And right there, I know she is wrong. Because it will exist again. I'm cusping on having this with someone else. I just need to be brave. And I suspect that Josie will get there, too.

The paused silence continues to stretch, becoming uncomfortable. Josie pushes the salad around on her plate but isn't putting any in her mouth. Finally, she sets the fork on the edge of the plate and takes a breath. "What's her name?" She's not angry or accusatory. With her shoulders dropping, she's more deflated. My heart hurts for her, for the one I used to love, for the one I still care about. But I'm not going to pretend.

"Quinn." This is the first time I'm admitting this out loud to anyone, and I'm saying it to my ex-girlfriend who once broke my heart. The universe has an interesting way of bringing things full circle. "Her name is Quinn."

The waiter sets down the second course. I use the back of my fork to cut into the pork patty, but I can't eat. My stomach tightens with excitement and nerves, with the urge to flee from this place and rush to the one I want.

Quinn.

It's been Quinn since the moment that fiery redhead stepped into my shop. Quinn, who helped me save my bakery items, let me use her place for a month for prep, who chatted like a pro with my overbearing mother for hours. Quinn, who makes me laugh and knows so much pop culture but not any of the good stuff, who likes fish on pizza and warm hugs and will dance in a crowd of zero with me, even though she doesn't want to, because I need to let go.

It's Quinn.

"Does she know how lucky she is?" Josie asks.

I huff out a breath. "She doesn't know anything... I haven't told her how I feel."

Josie nods. So many expressions pass through her, and I still know Josie. I know her thoughts. There are tears in her eyes, a sad, soft smile, a knowingness that she and I will never get back together. "Why?"

Because I've been too worried about opening myself up again, afraid of becoming a shell of myself again if it doesn't work. "Because I'm scared. When we broke up, it killed me. I wasn't sure I could go through that again."

"But she's worth it?"

I nod. "She really is."

Josie dabs her pinkie in her eye. After a moment, she sits back and folds her hands in her lap. "Thank you for being so refreshingly honest."

I pick up my fork, but I'm not hungry. I don't want to be here. I don't want to waste another single second.

"Go," Josie says, her smile shifting into the crescent-moon shape of sadness. "You don't want to be here with me, and that's okay."

Oh, wow. She really can still read my face. "No, I don't have to leave. We can stay and finish dinner and—"

"Zoey, go." She nods. "It's okay. Do not do what I did. Do not waste even a single second more on the what-ifs. Go be brave and tell her how you feel."

My stomach flutters, joining in my racing pulse. I'm going to tell her how I feel. I'll make her feel safe, I'll see if she will take a chance on something she's never taken a chance on before, I'll tell her we will still be friends if she isn't reciprocating my feelings.

I dig out cash, stand from the table, and pull Josie into a hug. "Thank you," I whisper. "Thank you for being you, and being so wonderful, and giving me the final push I needed."

And then I dash out of the restaurant. The air turned chillier in the time I've been in the restaurant, and a few fat snowflakes start floating from the clouds. I dig out my phone, tug my mitten off with my teeth, and dial Quinn. I'm not wasting another second. I'm telling her everything. Tonight.

No answer. I stop under the streetlight to send a quick text.

I need to talk to you. Are you around?

My pace picks up and I pray I don't trip on a crack in the sidewalk and break my foot again, because nothing is keeping me away this time. My heartbeat thuds against my chest, and now, I'm sprinting. I need to get in the car and drive to her place, or drive to the barn, I need to see her.

When I round the corner, I freeze in my tracks. Everything is in slow motion.

Is this what I think it is? I squint, trying to make out the image. No... it can't be.

It is.

TWENTY-TWO
QUINN

I've been standing in the alley outside of Zoey's loft for an hour, bundled in my jacket, bouncing between my feet, and rethinking everything. Not rethinking that I want to be with Zoey. That, I know. To the deepest part of myself, in a place I didn't know existed, in a place that she opened for me with her smile and kindness and unapologetically positive outlook on the world, I know I want to be with Zoey.

No, what I'm rethinking is not bringing gloves. And a hat. And definitely boots. These tennis shoes are not working in this weather, and who knows why I grabbed those in my rush to leave rather than my work boots that were tucked right next to them in the closet. But after talking with Morgan, and picturing Zoey laughing while splitting a breadbasket and bottle of wine with Josie, adrenaline surged through my veins, and I bolted from the house.

Snowflakes descend from the sky, butterflying to the ground, each one picking up the glint from the streetlights. My breath comes out in a fog. I tug the scarf up to cover my mouth, blink the plump flakes from my eyelashes, and check my watch. I could probably sit inside Truck Norris like a sane human, but then when

Zoey appears, it will ruin what I want to do. Before tingling creeps in my toes, I hop in place to get my blood pumping.

I saw Zoey's call and text message but couldn't answer. This is something that can't be done over the phone, and I have zero willpower. If I picked up, I'd unleash all this pent-up emotion and stumble over my words like a snowball rolling down a rocky hill. This conversation needs to happen in person, where I can see Zoey's face. I need to read the way her eyes flicker and if she chews on the corner of her lip or twists and tugs on her fingers. Or if her mouth curves up in that playful way that I love, or if she is blushing. Or... if sadness and regret fill her eyes that she has to turn me down.

There is no room for miscommunication, not for something as serious as this. I need to assure Zoey if she's not interested, I'll still be friends. The relationship we have is so valuable and unique, that I won't give it up, no matter what. But I also need to be honest with her and tell her I don't know what this looks like. It's scary and I don't want to run, but I'm scared that something will spook me, and I *will* run. Right now, I want to fuse myself with her, but will I always feel like this? This need, this longing, reaches parts of my untouched soul. I need her to be patient and to believe in me, and to hold me when I'm scared and to let me hold her when she's scared. I want to make her breakfast and feed her strawberries and watch old movies and kiss her mouth and run my fingers through her hair and... So yeah. I can't answer her call.

I kick at a small rock, and it flings against the side of the building. When I pivot, my breath halts. Zoey's at the edge of the alley, wrapped in a long brown peacoat. A cascade of chestnut waves flow down the sides of her shoulders, a soft green knitted beanie rests on her head, and she pulls a mitted hand to cover her mouth. Even from a hundred feet away, I don't think I've ever seen her more beautiful.

Now or never. Zoey moves towards me with slow, curious steps, the faint sound of her boots on pavement echoing in the quiet alley. *I can't believe I'm actually doing this.* The streetlamps and alley lights flicker, casting a warm glow in the night sky, and the snowflakes glisten in the light. Butterflies squirm in my belly, wanting to take flight. I swallow. With the slightest shake in my finger, I tap play on my iPhone and cup my hand around the speaker to amplify. The song bursts out, and I hold the phone high above my head.

Zoey's footsteps grow quicker and a wide smile spreads. My heart thumps in my ears, steady and quick. The music echoes against the brick walls, her heels click against the pavement. A few steps in and her curious walk morphs into a determined, intentional speed walk. *Be brave, be brave. Do not chicken out now.* I just need to tell her how I feel and that she deserves happiness.

And so do I.

My heart settles. *So do I.* And Zoey makes me happy.

Her hair bounces with every step, her cheeks pink from the winter air, and God... she's just so beautiful. She radiates a warmth that I crave, that I've been searching for without knowing what I was missing. Zoey is the one I want to be with, the one that makes me think that miracles are possible. She's the one who saw my wall, took a hammer to it, and elbowed her way into my heart.

As she approaches with foggy glasses and a wide smile, she cocks her head at my phone. "Are you Cusacking me?"

I slowly lower the phone.

"With a Chappell Roan song?" she asks.

"It's a lot of pressure!" I smile and tap stop, cutting the music. "I didn't quite realize how iconic that movie scene was, or how perfect that song was for the moment, and I panicked. Had no idea what to choose."

Zoey removes her fogged glasses and gives them a wipe. When she slides her glasses back up her nose, she lifts a brow. "'Pink Pony Club' is... an interesting choice."

"You *love* Chappell Roan." I shove the phone into my pocket. "I debated between this and Nirvana's 'Heart-Shaped Box' because that sounded romantic, but then I googled what the lyrics meant and... well, it wasn't quite the vibe I was going for."

Zoey's mouth twists and she studies my face. *Really* studies it, to the point where the chill I felt before this moment swaps, and I'm dangerously close to overheating.

"So, this is not about trying to make good on your anchovies bet?" she asks, her voice more timid than I've heard before. "You're trying to be... *romantic?*"

Yes. *Trying* being the operative word here. *Failing* is probably a better word. For someone known for being chatty, I'm currently forgetting all my words. Christ, this is so scary. My mouth is dry, and I'm about two seconds away from sticking my tongue out to catch some of the soft fluttering snowflakes to replenish some moisture.

"Romantic? Did I say that? Where did that word come from?" My voice is unnaturally high and skittery, and I cringe at the sound.

Zoey tilts her head, rightfully so.

"I'm sorry. God, what is wrong with me?" Why am I being so weird? My thoughts are all over the place. I have so many things I need to say, but none of them are taking the shape I want. I suck in a sharp, cool inhale. "Did Josie want to get back together?" I pull my lips into my mouth and hold my breath waiting for the answer.

Zoey tugs the top of her jacket a little tighter. "Yes, she did."

My snow-covered world and Christmas-miracle dreams crumble. *Please say you didn't say yes. Please say you're not thinking about it.* I want to shake Zoey by the shoulders. Maybe Josie is a perfectly lovely human, but I want to be with Zoey. *I want to be with Zoey.* My lips tremble.

Run. Run away now. Save yourself and potential heartache.

"Are you okay?" Zoey takes a step toward me and lays a mitten-covered hand on my arm.

I blink off the snowflakes from my lashes. "Please don't get back together with Josie. I mean, not unless you want to, but oh my God, I hope you don't want to. I just... I feel like I have so much stuff to tell you. How you make me feel, and that I think about you so much, like *so much* that I wonder if I'm obsessed, and I want to be like you. Your kindness rubs off on me, and makes me want to be nicer to people, and I promise you I'm actually not that nice, so this is a huge deal."

The words are an avalanche, roaring from me, tumbling, and I can't stop. Everything in me bubbles to the surface. The time pressure of Zoey slipping through my fingers, that I might be too late, weighs on my chest.

My chin quivers, but I power on. "And you are just so inspiring. Do you know that, Zoey? You inspire me to be a better person. No matter what, promise me right now that if I say what I'm going to say, and you think differently, we will stay friends. Because I want you in my life, okay? In any way you'll have me..."

The rambling is embarrassing, not at all how I wanted this to go, but my thoughts are scattering like pine needles in a tornado, and I cannot grasp on to any single one with even a sliver of coherency. Zoey's quiet, still, her cheeks rosy, but her smile... Her smile's soft and comforting.

"Would you ever take a chance on something else?" We're outside, but there's still not enough air to get this all out. My pulse pounds in my head, rings in my ears. "Would you take a chance on me, you, us?"

"Yes."

Wait, what? One simple word, delivered with a smile. Said so quickly, no hesitation, like she expected it. Did she even hear me? Does she understand exactly what I'm talking about?

"Yes?" I croak, searching her eyes behind the misted glasses, the curve of her lips, the way she inches closer to me. "On which part? I just threw a lot at you, like a ton, and I want to make sure we are clear so there's no miscommunication—"

Her mitted gloves cup my cheeks, the soft wool fibers tickle my skin, and she pushes her lips into mine. Gentle at first, a pillowy soft kiss, but enough where my knees nearly give in. "Yes." Her gaze pins me before she presses her mouth back onto mine, a little stronger, a little longer. Her kiss is like warm brown sugar on a chilly day, and I'm officially melting. "Yes to everything."

Yes? Like yes, yes? This is too easy. My heart has officially left my body and is moving into some dreamlike winter wonderland. I'm in a snow globe that a toddler is shaking, and everything feels scattered and surreal. Her smile reaches her eyes, her lips curve up. I blink. Is this real? "Um, I don't want to question this, but I'm questioning this. This all seemed too smooth, and traditionally, you know, things in my life are not smooth."

Zoey steps back with a soft grin. "Were you hoping for resistance?"

For the last hour as I paced outside of her loft, I had visions of how we'd play out this conversation. I imagined she'd run into my arms and just say yes. I replayed it over and over in my mind. But I didn't really think it would happen just like it did. Maybe I'm in some sort of lucid dream and any moment now I'm going to be nudged awake. "No, I mean, of course not. I just... What's happening here? How is this just so easy?"

Zoey's eyes dash between mine. "I left Josie at the restaurant to come find you," she says with a soft voice. "I called you. I texted you, too."

"I know. I'm sorry. I knew I'd break if I talked to you on the phone, and I wanted to tell you this in person." I tug on the edges of Zoey's scarf, and she tiptoes near me. "Why did you leave Josie?"

Zoey looks down, the redness in her cheeks getting stronger. "I needed to find you. I wanted to see if *you'd* take a chance on *me.*"

My heart leaps and locks in my chest. *She* wanted to know if *I'd* take a chance on *her?* A million times over, yes. The snow, the stars, the moon, everything is in alignment. Zoey and I want the same thing, feel the same thing. There is no misunderstanding. Nothing has ever felt so right. I pull her into me, kiss her, harder this time, breathing in her vanilla and honeysuckle scent. Hands wrap around my waist, dragging my body into hers. Snow falls between our lips, on our hair, combating the warmth I feel with a burst of chill.

Zoey pulls back, and gives me a look I've never seen before. A switch has flipped. A devilish, glorious gleam in her eyes, a hike in her eyebrows, and a long, leisurely gaze runs from my toes to my mouth to my eyes. "Upstairs?"

Oh God, it's happening. *It's. Happening.*

I grab her hand. "Upstairs."

TWENTY-THREE
QUINN

Adrenaline courses through my veins as I rush upstairs with Zoey. Once inside her loft, she rips off her mittens and tosses them against the wall, kissing me, shrugging off her jacket, tugging off mine. She tosses her glasses on the table while I kick off my shoes, stumbling, my heart racing. *This is actually happening.* Zoey's lips are so soft and delicious, but firm. She slides her tongue over me, her breaths heavy, her hands gripping me. She's kissing me like she's starving, like she's been waiting years.

My jacket knocks over something with a loud thump when I toss it, but we don't stop. I want more. I want to canvass her body with my fingers and breathe her in and taste her skin. God, she smells so good, tastes so good, and the need to be closer to her intensifies. Shallow pants leave my mouth. My pulse pounds in my chest, a steady thud that grows stronger, more intense, more desperate. I cup her cheeks, fist her hair, inhale everything about her. Just from the kisses, the foreign emotions, I feel myself slowly come undone. I'm not going to last more than a few minutes.

Zoey spins me around and presses my back against the wall, and... Holy hell, who is this person? She leans back and meets my gaze. Her clean, crisp blue eyes have darkened, and something nearly feral has taken over. The sweetness is gone. She looks like she wants to devour me. Her hands glide down my side and tug up my shirt. My heart pounds against my rib cage. Fingertips swipe against the skin at my belly, and goosebumps fly up my arms.

I hold her tight, pull her into me, needing her closer. Her body is so warm, so open, so ready. She moans against my ear, dragging her lips across my neck, kissing the slope below my ear. Her mouth doesn't leave mine, hardly at all. A bolt of electricity rushes through me, a current that is firing all my cells, springing me to life. Her lips are so full and strong, her tongue moves against me, owns my mouth and... What does this all mean? Is this it? Is this what people talk about when they have so many feelings, and being with someone special, and emotions, and—
Shit.

I pull back.

Immediately, she stops. Her lips are red, swollen, wet with kisses. Heavy breaths heave against her chest and her gaze dashes across mine. "Oh, gosh, okay, oh yikes. Sorry, I just, with our conversation, I thought... Oh no... Are we good?"

I drag my hands down my face. What is my problem? This is the type of sex that I love, that I crave. Hot, fiery. The kind where everything inside me burns to the point where I need to unleash, and now, I'm literally frozen. "Yes, we're totally good." I drop my hands from her waist and pull in a few calming breaths. Zoey steps back with a crease forming between her brows.

"Did I do something wrong?" Zoey asks, her eyes growing wide.

I grab her hands and swipe my thumb against the smooth skin. "No, no, of course not. You're... perfect." Words choke at my throat. "I'm so totally up in my head right now. I'm sorry."

Leaning against the wall, I release her hands and calm my breaths. Never once since I was sixteen and first had sex has something like this ever happened. I've never stopped midway because of nerves. *Nerves*, for God's sake. This is my realm. With sex, I'm like on a mission control operation. There is a goal. Make the woman orgasm, get myself off, clean up, and go home. It's what I do, and I'm a master at it. I don't think, I do. And now, I'm thinking. A lot. Too much.

"Quinn? Talk to me." Zoey lays a hand on my shoulder and dips her head to meet my gaze. "We don't have to do this. Really. It's totally okay."

Ugh. I want to do this, so bad. My legs are practically quivering already from her kisses alone. I picture her, us, more than the bedroom, more than this moment. A future. A low pinch starts in my chest. "No, no. I *want* to do this. Like so bad I can hardly stand it. Zoey, you are incredible. So kind, so thoughtful, so fucking beautiful." My words are failing me. But I need her to understand, and I can't explain it properly. "I do this. Like all the time. This is who I am. But until you..."

Zoey takes a hesitant step back. "Until me, what?"

Trembles overtake my body. I exhale, heavy, through my nose, and try to push past them. "Until you, it felt different. It wasn't *this*... and I'm so scared for *this*." My body and brain begin to splinter. An ache to touch Zoey, to taste her, to feel what she feels like pressed against me, fights against this brick wall in my heart and I don't know how to reconcile them. I don't know how to sleep with my best friend and kiss her and feel the satiny smoothness of her skin, while still having all her other parts—the one I want to call at night, the one I want to watch movies with, laugh with, dance on empty dance floors with. How do I combine all the parts I love about her with all the parts I crave?

"You're shaking," she says softly. "Come on, let's sit on the couch."

Her fingers intertwine with mine and she leads me to the living room. When I sink into the cushions, I sigh. I love this as much as I hate it. I want to be with Zoey. This is not a question. This is not my fear, not what I'm running from. But *how* to be with Zoey is a totally different question.

As Zoey holds my hand, she rubs a gentle thumb against my inner wrist. The feather-soft tracing makes my skin spark alive and I lean into the touch. She doesn't push me to talk. Instead, she continues holding me, letting me think and process. Silent moments fall between us until I finally take a sharp breath. "I'm scared." I tuck a leg under my butt and shift to face her. "This isn't me. I don't know what you've done to me, but I've changed since coming back here, since meeting you." I nibble on the corner of my lip and take another breath. "I've always just had sex. That's it. I've never had... this."

Zoey tucks a lock of hair behind her ear. "What is this?" she asks. When I don't answer, she leans forward and cups my face. "What is *this*?"

Her eyes are reading my soul, burying into me, seeing all my darkness, and she's still here. She's not running, she's not making me feel like shit, she's not doing anything but listening.

My chest feels tight. Christ, do people do this in the real world? Talk about feelings and fears? It feels like I'm opening my diary and just waiting to see if Zoey will look past all the ickiness or if she'll flee. It's suffocating and frightening, but Zoey is worth it. To the deepest part of me, I know Zoey is worth me living in the fear. I push out a shaky breath. "I'm terrified of these feelings. They're so, I don't know, raw. Real. And so fucking scary. I've never had them before and don't know what to do with them."

A soft grin passes, and she drops her hands from my face. "I'm scared, too."

My chest lifts. "You are?"

She nods and tugs a pillow into her lap. "I've had these feelings before. And they're beautiful and wonderful. I thought I was going to marry these feelings, you know? When Josie and I were together, I was convinced it was for life. And when it ended, I knew, I just absolutely knew, that I would never have this again."

Maybe I am the most self-centered person in the world, but it never occurred to me that she is scared, too. She's comforting me, supporting me, and it should be the other way around. Zoey's navigated a broken heart, learned to overcome, opened herself up again. I'm the one who has never had this, and I'm scared. Zoey must be petrified.

I peek up into those warm blue eyes, absorb the way Zoey is looking at me with want, and intention, and care, and I want to fold myself into her. "I'm scared of real."

"I'm scared of real, too," she says. "But if it's real with you, then I want to try."

Her eyes dip to my mouth, and I know that look. The lust is obvious. But there's more, something deeper. She's giving me a peek into her soul, a gift, one that I think she's given to very few people. And in this moment, I decide. I'll accept the gift.

The couch dips below me as I move forward, cup her face, and bring her to me. I'm slow, diligent, purposeful, as I press my mouth against hers. I inhale the cherry on her lips, the taste of sweet orange and passion and promise. She moves against me, her hands caressing my arms, and slips her tongue against mine.

My body melts. With every swipe, breath, kiss, I drop. My defenses, my fears, my insecurities. Her fingers tug at the edge of my shirt, and my belly quivers. She lifts the fabric, softly, hesitantly, her fingers sweeping against my skin.

The urgency pushes both of us, stronger, firmer, and Zoey deepens the kiss. She pulls my bottom lip into her mouth, then releases. My breaths increase, my pulse picks up speed. This is really happening. This moment, this feeling, I want to remember every second.

She grips the bottom of my shirt and lifts it over my head, leaving me only in my tank. "Oh my gosh..."

The look she's giving me as she takes me in makes my mouth water. Lust and want and need, and my body fires to life. She murmurs against my skin and fills my neck with kisses. Her mouth grazes across my shoulders, my collarbone, and the tingles are set free. When she pulls back, her eyes read mine. "Um, can we take this to..." She's shy. The Zoey-vixen from when we first stepped into her place is gone, at least for now, and reality has set in. I can see what she wants. I know her, and she can't say it.

I do it for her. "Let's go to your bedroom."

Without a word, she hops from the couch, grabs my hand, and

leads me there. The hall light illuminates as we walk to her room. Every step is slow, intentional, filled with unspoken words. Nothing is rushed, hurried, nothing is the heat of the moment. We both know exactly what we're doing.

In the bedroom, Zoey sits on the edge of the bed and brings me in between her legs. Her hands fan underneath my tank, her fingertips slide against my skin. I sink into the touch and loop a finger through her silky hair. She tugs up my shirt, lays a trail of kisses against my lower belly and pulls back up. "Is this okay?"

Let's get this out of the way. I've had a consent conversation with every single sexual partner I've ever had. It's important. Critical, even. But with the way I feel right now, Zoey could dominate me from here to Atlanta, and I'd be the happiest woman alive.

"Zoey. I want it all. You can do anything you want, anything you're comfortable with," I say, heat flushing my chest. *Please do everything*. My senses are heightened, hungry, but I don't want to spook her. "My safe word is 'dragon fruit.'"

A small giggle escapes. "That's an interesting safe word."

"Right? So, there's no confusion." I grin. "For real, though, I'm just going to call this out. I want to sleep with you. Like so bad that I'm practically shaking. But I recognize that this is all really new for you, too. So, you can lead, go as far as you want to go, stop when you want to stop. Anything. Okay?"

Rose blooms her cheeks. She glances down and seems to chew on the inside of her cheek. "I, um, I haven't been with anyone for two years."

An almost underlying shame, or shyness, laces those words. But to me, they're amazing. Zoey is controlled and measured, and this is a gift that she's letting me know this part of her. How am I this lucky? This beautiful creature wants to be with me. She knows my ins and outs and still wants to share this part of herself with me. "It's okay. We can take it as slow as you need, or stop completely, or anything. Whatever you want, truly. I'll still be here in the morning, still whatever—"

She lifts herself from the bed and kisses me, hard. Her mouth moves against mine, hungry, and breathless. "Can we stop talking now so I can put my mouth on your huge, perfect tits."

Oh my God! Zoey just said the word *tits*, and I am officially dead. We both rip my tank off, she pulls down my bra, my tits fling free, and her mouth latches on. It's so quick, so sharp, and pleasure rips through me. I bite back a moan as her fingers dig into my skin. The sensation of her mouth on my body, sucking and licking my nipples, make my knees shake. I cup the back of her head, bring her closer, as goosebumps skate across my skin.

Pleasure rushes through my veins. Her mouth is magic, I'm moaning, she's moaning, and we're both practically clothed. "I've wanted these in my mouth since I met you..." She hums against me. Her fingers work my breasts, massaging, tugging, squeezing. "Lie on the bed."

Well, holy shit. That husky tone makes my insides curl. Electricity buzzes in the air. The sweet, shy kitten is gone, overtaken by a fierce lioness who knows *exactly* what she wants. I practically throw myself onto the mattress and scramble up to the pillow.

Zoey straddles me. Her long hair cascades down her arms, her eyes glazed with hunger, her grip on my skin is needy and searching. God, she's so beautiful. She's wiggling against me, squirming and moaning, releasing sounds I've never heard come from her. I'm so turned on that I beg myself not to come early.

I grip the bottom of her shirt. "Can I take this off?"

"You can take *everything* off," she says as her hands work to unclasp my jeans.

Oh my... I rip the shirt over her head, and a sheer black bra meets me. All my blood rushes to my center as I take her in. Her skin is so delicate, pale, powdery. The outline of her nipples pushes against the fabric. I trail my thumb and fingers against her skin, and her eyes close.

"Yes, more," she whispers.

Her breasts are so much smaller, more delicate, than mine, and I want to worship every part. She reaches her hand behind her back, unsnaps her bra, and throws it into the wall with a soft *ping*.

My hands, reach up, cup her, fill themselves with softness. "Zoey, shit. You are so perfect."

She's twisting her hips against me, and I lift mine to meet her. I need release and friction. I need tits in my mouth, my tongue on her body, to feel every part of her. The heat between us builds as hands and mouths explore and connect. Hesitation, gone. Uncertainty, dissolved. Replaced with need and hunger. My pulse surges, thuds in my ears, in my chest. I slide my hand up her hips under the skirt, and my fingers hook the band of her underwear. Rapid, choppy breaths leave her mouth as I guide my palm to her center over the thin fabric.

I want every part of Zoey—her brilliant mind, her humor, her sweetness, her tiger. Everything. I want everything. I want to taste her, to feel how silky and smooth she is, to hear the noises I can draw from her.

Her naked chest lifts and drops in heavy spurts. She hops off me, her skirt fanning the bed. "Take off your pants."

This commanding tone is so different, so freaking sexy, and I oblige. I take off my pants, throw them to the side, and she climbs back on top. She buries her face into my chest. Her tongue swipes and swirls against me, she sucks and releases. I lift my hips, try to touch myself, but she's on my lap, and as hot as she is, as this is, I need some friction, or I'll pass out.

"You're beautiful, Quinn. Your skin, your body, your everything..." She moans as she sucks and squeezes.

Still on top of me, she slides one hand behind her, reaching between my legs, and keeps the other one at my breasts. My skin is starving, begging, anxious for her touches. It may have been years since Zoey's done this, but I swear, *I* feel like the virgin.

"I want to see all of you," Zoey says, her tone dark and husky. "Will you show me all of you?"

Not yet. First, she needs to be taken care of. "Let me make you feel good, first." A trail of goosebumps skitters up her arm with my words. I cannot wait to make her feel the way she makes me feel. I want to see her come undone and moan and shiver underneath me.

The edge of her skirt trails her pale thighs. I tug down until I free her hips and skim my hands across her belly. Her skin is so smooth, so soft, and the need to explore all the parts of her consumes me. She shimmies out of the skirt. I roll over and guide her underneath me. Her scent perfumes the air, takes a hold of me, and my body crumbles. I kiss her silky skin, starting at her forehead, her lips, her neck. I trail my tongue on her jaw and press my mouth to her shoulders. My hand moves, cups her breast, and she moans against me. Her fingers tug at my curls, her mouth moves, connects with mine. I cannot believe this is happening. It's all so real and simultaneously surreal, and I want to pinch myself. She lifts a leg, hooks it around me, and flips me on my back.

"*Holy shit,*" I say, breathless from the surprise movement. Zoey is much, much stronger than I gave her credit for. My pulse pounds in my ears. The sight of nearly naked Zoey moving against me is almost too much.

I start to tug down her underwear and she holds my hands steady. "Not yet." Her voice is husky, deep, how I've never heard her before, and my God, I can't even. My mouth waters. My fingers itch to be inside her, to make her move, to show her how beautiful she is. But she, right now, is the dominant. My whole adult life, I've been the one in control in the bedroom. The roles are reversed and it's *so freaking hot.* My skin is starving, and every touch, swipe, lick she feeds me shreds my defenses.

She pinches, touches, squeezes, makes me squirm. My body trembles, the anticipation of release building to a dizzying degree. "Do you like this?" she asks. It's not seeking permission, not really. It's a command. And I want to collapse.

My vision clouds, hazy and dazed. She grabs my hand, pulls two of my fingers into her mouth, and swirls her tongue. *Oof.* Having a topless Zoey on top of me, a glistening of sweat beading on her chest, her mouth and tongue swirling against my fingers, and I begin to shake. *Hold out. A little longer.* I cannot, under any circumstance, orgasm too quickly.

Zoey removes my fingers from her mouth, and slides them

down her chest, her smooth belly, above her center, and she hovers. "Show me what you can do with your hands."

I'm dead. It's so much and not enough, and *my God*, can she be any more beautiful? I hover above her center, rub her with my fingertip, softly at first, until I hear her moan. Her eyes close and hips rock. And then I dip a finger and *ohhhh...* We both moan. She's so silky, so perfect, I'm so desperate for her to know how beautiful she is. I move against her, hold her tight with one hand, add another finger. My heart pounds against my chest.

I build my rhythm, steady and full, as she rocks against me. The sounds she makes fills me, but I'm greedy. I want to hear her scream. Her slim legs bury into mine. She grips any available flesh, sporadic, unhinged, searching for relief, and I can't breathe. This is the most beautiful, most perfect, most mouthwatering moment of my life. I cup her ass, hold her tight, until she whips her legs off and rolls to the side.

"Oh God, are you okay? Did I do something?" I ask, frantic, searching her eyes.

She shimmies down on the bed, and glances up with a playful, seductive grin spreading across her pink glistening cheeks. "I need to feel you in my mouth."

Holy hell.

She hooks her fingers around my underwear, slides them down my legs, and tosses them onto the floor. And now, she takes her time. She lifts my leg on her shoulder. Kisses start at my ankle, my calf, the side of my knee. Her fingertips graze my skin leaving a cascade of goosebumps, and the air locks in my chest. I never, ever, want to move.

"You're beautiful, Quinn, so, so beautiful..." She moves closer, higher, her mouth presses against the delicate, sensitive skin at my inner thigh. Her breath warms me, makes my skin tingle, makes me move against the mattress. Higher and higher she climbs, and her mouth is so close, so close... *ah...* right there. Her tongue slides against me, swirling and gentle sucks. She slides a finger into me, then two, matching the tongue. *Damn...* Two years at least since she's had sex and she's owning every part of me. I feel shy and timid and worshipped. I'm in heaven. This is heaven. She moans against me, the vibrations making me blink away stars.

Everything builds. Slow, steady, then increases. She's reading me like no one has ever read me. Less pressure, more, steady, her mouth is perfect. My hands fist her hair and tug, and she pushes, more, harder, giving me exactly what I crave. Pressure builds inside me, I'm burning, shaking, and my insides tense.

"It's so good. I'm close. I'm so close. Don't stop." I'm not even sure if I'm making coherent sentences, and I don't care. My breath is labored, shallow, rapid. My legs quiver and she keeps going. She's right fucking there.

Ahhhhh. My body clenches, tight, and waves engulf me. I rock against her, and she coaxes the orgasm from me, my heartbeat screaming against my chest. She lies, unmoving, against my leg, waiting for me to calm. It might be freezing outside, but in here the air is heavy, hot, our skin sticky. My pulse slows, my breaths even, and I twirl her hair around my fingers. Recovery doesn't take me long. Much quicker than I've ever had before. And when it does, a near feral response kicks in.

"Roll over," I command, matching Zoey's intensity from before.

She immediately obliges.

As I move my lips down her skin, I marvel at these feelings. I may have done this hundreds of times before. But never in my lifetime have I ever felt like this.

TWENTY-FOUR
ZOEY

The bed barely makes a creak as I leave. In all fairness, I slithered out of it like I'm on some covert operation hidden behind enemy lines. But I still held my breath the entire time, only releasing my lungs once I reached the bathroom. Quinn has pushed herself to the limit, both physically and mentally, at the farm. And at night, I'm giving her no rest. I'm not even apologizing for it, either. Not really, anyway. Although, last night, I did ask her if we needed to take a break to let her rest. Luckily, she looked at me like I'd asked her to chew on a spiked pinecone. But I did draw her a sudsy bath and bring her a sandwich, first.

And then devoured her after.

After nearly three years without sex, and finally connecting with someone like this, I'm famished. Insatiable. And Quinn is the one who fills me.

The farm is close to opening, one week away, and I see how the pressure is wearing on Quinn. Red eyes in the morning, yawns at night, heavy breaths while she sleeps. So, the fact that she's typically gone before I even wake up, and today she slept through my alarm, tells me what I need to know.

After my shower, I creep back into my room, and take it all in. My new life. The scent of Quinn's coconut shampoo lingers in my room. I want to bottle it up and take it with me downstairs. Quinn's a goddess. She's lying on her stomach now, her bare back exposed. Crimson hair splashes against the white pillow with a burst of color contrast. She lifts and lowers with each heavy breath. My mouth was on her all last night and still I salivate for more. As much as I want to leave a trail of kisses down her spine and one sweet smooch on her perfect round tush, I don't. I grab clothes from my closet and tiptoe from the room to get dressed in the guest bedroom.

At the front door, I quietly put on shoes when bare feet patter against the hallway hardwood floor. I look up and... *Ah*. I know it's been barely a week since we officially got together, but this feeling, this all-encompassing tingle that charges each cell with electricity and shoots heat everywhere, I never want it to leave. Every day since the day in the alley feels new. I'm seeing my friend, my best friend, in a fresh, beautiful light. I will never get enough.

"Good morning," I whisper to a sleepy-eyed Quinn, and lift myself from the chair. I used to think denim-overall-wearing Quinn was my favorite. I was wrong. Naked, messy hair, pink sleep marks imbedded into her cheeks, wrapped in my sheet, is my favorite Quinn.

"Are you leaving already?" Her voice carries the raspy edge of exhaustion. She crosses the room and cocoons herself into me, laying her head against my chest. I wrap my arms around her, kiss the top of her head, and breathe in the remnants of her conditioner.

Her body relaxes into me as I hold her. While so many things in our relationship haven't changed—we still have movie night, we still disagree about food, we still share very different pop culture memories—so many things have. The sex, the *phenomenal* sex, I may add, and the teenage level of make-out sessions of course is different. But it's the hugs. The cuddles. Quinn seems to have this almost frenetic need to touch me, like she's making up for a lifetime of not being held. And I love it.

And while she's making up for all the snuggles, I'm making up for all my celibate years. At some point, we're going to be imprinted on each other and our skin will fuse together like a graft. But until then, I'll soak up every ounce I can.

I kiss the top of her head. "I have to go to work."

"Aren't you the owner?" she says, then peels herself away. She yawns into her palm and slinks into a chair.

What I would give for a full day off to do nothing but be with her. Someday soon. The holidays will be over, I'll take some time off work, and we'll do takeout for a week. I tug a jacket over my arms and button up. "If you stay up here in my loft, I'll come up as much as I can during the day."

She groans. "I have to go to work, too."

"Aren't you the owner?" I ask in the same teasing tone. When she lifts her head, I lean down to plant a soft kiss on her mouth.

"Whoever thought entrepreneurship was a good idea works for the devil," Quinn says as she tugs the bed sheet around her folded arms. "Want to quit, sell everything, and drive around the country in a beat-up VW van with a solid nineties music playlist?"

"I'm in." I wrap her in my arms one more time, and her head rests against my belly. This is heaven. Do I really need to be at the bakery today? I mean sure, Thanksgiving is six days away, but maybe the prep for the pie can wait and the community can go somewhere else this year. "I have an idea..."

"Oh, I love your ideas," she says, her head snapping up to meet my gaze.

I giggle. Sure, we haven't been together long, but we're making up for lost time. So, I *know* this look. The sparkle that highlights the tiny amber ridge around her jade-and-moss-colored irises. The red blooming across her cheekbones. The way her chest lifts the tiniest bit. She's thinking about "Petunia's Box," my nickname for my toy box. And trust me, I think about that box a lot, too. But I'm not thinking about it this time.

"Well, not that exactly," I say.

"Boo." She puts her head back on my stomach.

I still want to do that, but first I want us to do coupley things. Outside the bedroom. Petunia's Box can be for dessert. "How about after work tonight, we have a date night. I can make reservations, we can have some wine, I can do dirty things to you after—"

"Yes," Quinn says. "Immediately, yes."

I giggle, kiss her once more, tell her to go back to bed even for just a little while, and walk down the stairs to the shop. The second I step into the bakery, and I'm hit with that familiar, tangy scent of raw dough, my brain shifts into business mode. Less than a week until Thanksgiving, and there is only so much prep I can do for the vast orders of pumpkin and pecan pies we have to fill. I love my job, so much, but this year I wish I could spend more time with Quinn at her farm. Luna and Caleb have put in more hours this week to give me a bit of time off to help Quinn, but I need more. I miss Quinn even when she's lying in my arms.

As I start loading the display case with the items the morning baker made, all I can do is think of Quinn. At what point is this excessive? No matter what I'm doing, I'm picturing her face and smiling. Even when I picture her in my shop this past summer, angry about blue cookies, I'm happy.

Snow falls outside the window, and I take a moment to watch the flakes descend and melt into the sidewalk. One major thing I've realized since being with Quinn is that I didn't need her, or anyone, to be happy. Yes, I've wanted to find a mate, and yes, I think Quinn is the one I want to be with long term, but I'm not any happier per se. My happiness has just shifted. I feel the same way as I did with Josie, but also different somehow. More confident, more controlled, more centered.

I'm so dang lucky. And I never want to forget this.

TWENTY-FIVE
ZOEY

The analog clock on the wall finally reaches two. One more hour, and I'll close up the shop, prep for tomorrow like my life depends on it, and get ready for tonight. Even though I told Quinn I was going to make reservations, Luna gave me a great suggestion for an alternative. I cannot wait to put it into motion.

The doorbell jingles and I glance at Colby and Kona strolling in. "Hey, guys," I say, coming around the counter to pet Kona. "Is Kona loving the snow?"

Colby nods and tucks the leash into her palm. "So much. All she wants to do is run. Has no care in the world that us humans get chilly." She cocks her head at me. "Something looks different about you. The stress of the holidays must be fading."

Well, I am destressing at a frantic rate every night. Not that I'll say that to a customer. "Oh, well, I think I've been exercising more these last few weeks, and that has done the trick." Oh gosh, I don't know how she sees it on me, but Colby gives me a look that makes me blush. She absolutely thinks I'm full of baloney. "And you are very observant."

A soft grin passes her face. "I don't chat with a lot of people, so I tend to notice... nuances. Well, that exercise program seems to be working. I'm glad you found an activity you can enjoy."

I shouldn't be dying inside the way I am. But before I break into a giggle or blush any higher, the bell jingles and I peek up at Mrs. Pinkerton stepping in wearing a puffy down coat, fur hat, and her Pomeranian wrapped in a sweater.

Kona's tail wags furiously and the impatient whimper of wanting to play starts. Mrs. Pinkerton's dog starts yapping, loud, cutting through the noise of the chatting customers. I don't think that the two dogs have ever been in here at the same time. It's obvious that Kona wants a friend and Mrs. Pinkerton's dog wants to attack.

"It's okay, Kona. You're a good girl," Colby says in a calm voice. She steps in front of Kona and strokes her fur. "We'll come back," Colby says to me. "I'll take Kona around the block."

I shake my head. Colby should not feel like she needs to leave this place because a seven-pound demon is here at the same time. "No, you don't have to do that. I can't imagine Kona hurting that dog."

"No, she won't," Colby says with a small frown. "But the little ones like to bite the bigger ones, and my girl here doesn't deserve that. It's okay, I'll be back in like twenty minutes."

Mrs. Pinkerton's dog yaps and snarls, while Mrs. Pinkerton blissfully looks at the display cases. Seriously, does she not have eardrums? She's acting like the dog is singing. I love dogs. I really do. Someday when things settle down, and I can devote proper time to an animal, I'm getting one. And really, the Pomeranian's not the issue. Mrs. Pinkerton's obliviousness is the issue.

And then... everything seems to happen in slow motion. Colby moves to the door, the little dog leaps from Mrs. Pinkerton's arms, yapping as she tears across the bakery. Kona's barks are loud and urgent, ready to play with a new friend. Mrs. Pinkerton's singsong voice barely makes a dent as she calls out, *"Oh, Peaches... come here."* A kid screams bloody murder in the corner, a mom scolds their child, a man in the corner watches the scene unfold. I scurry out from behind the counter, when Colby positions herself between the little dog and Kona.

"Hey, stop!" I call to the dog as if it will listen to me.

Mrs. Pinkerton claps at the dog but barely moves, and a good-natured chuckle leaves her mouth.

My face grows hot. The little dog lunges, teeth bared, toward Kona. Colby scoops up the Pomeranian with more fire than I've seen from her before. She has a leash in her hand, the little dog in her arms, and her body blocks Kona as much as she can. She plops the dog in Mrs. Pinkerton's arms and storms out of the shop. I give her a sympathetic nod, turn to face Mrs. Pinkerton, and something in me snaps. *Enough.*

I march over to Mrs. Pinkerton and the dog, who is still yapping in her arms.

"Mrs. Pinkerton." I breathe out the shakes from my voice. "I love you coming in here and am so happy you enjoy my shop." *Don't say sorry, don't say sorry.* Channel my fierce, independent inner goddess and be firm. "But dogs must be on a leash in order to enter."

Mrs. Pinkerton turns and faces me, her eyes narrowing just a bit. A long moment passes where I think she's waiting to see if I'm kidding or going to back down. I'm not.

"Well, Peaches really doesn't like wearing leashes." She bristles.

She absolutely, positively, flipping bristles. Oh, no... Nope. This is not fair. She must not think this is okay, right? Her dog is a terror, and sure, it's not the dog's fault, that rests on the owner, but *come on.* My neck prickles with tiny sweat beads and I'm twisting my apron so hard it may snap.

"I can understand that Peaches doesn't like that very much. But these are the rules. If Peaches can't wear a leash"—I swallow back the boulder lodged in my throat—"then Peaches is no longer allowed in the store. I'm so sorry." I'm cutting myself a break for apologizing on this one, because this is hard and doesn't feel very good.

"Well, I never..." Mrs. Pinkerton turns on her heels and stomps out of the store.

My cheeks burn so hot I'm not sure if I'm considered feverish. The customer to my left looks at me, and I'm worried she's going to stomp out, too. Instead, she leans forward and says, "Thank you, Zoey. My toddler has been too scared to come in here since a few months ago when that dog barked at him in the stroller. I really appreciate you saying something to her."

The heat dissipates from my body. "Thank you. I needed to hear that." I glance at Luna ringing up orders. "Be right back."

She nods, and I rush into the kitchen to fully exhale. A moment later, I grab my phone and press call as I move back to the office.

Quinn answers with a heavily breathed "Hello."

"Hey," I say. "Did I catch you in the middle of a workout?"

"Ah, sorry, no," she says, a slight strain to her voice. "Just up on the ladder."

I slump into the office chair and sigh. "Seriously, you shouldn't answer your phone when you're on a ladder. I promise I won't think you are up to something nefarious if you send me to voicemail."

A small chortle sounds from the phone. "I will *always* answer your call."

She says it sweetly, but there's a finality in her tone that I know she's serious. *Swoon.* I roll a pen across the table with my palm. "What are you doing?"

"Oh, you know..."

I do, in fact, know. Or at least I have a really good idea. Quinn finished setting up her shop a few days ago. And it's *perfect*. From the Santa stand to the calligraphy signs pointing to the free hot chocolate and marshmallows, to the s'more stand, she transformed the previously bare barn into a truly spectacular winter wonderland Christmas shop. Quinn is ready.

But at night after I'm done at the bakery and head out to the barn, Quinn does the same thing for hours—shifts a product a few inches to the left, then to the right, then stands back and stares for a while until she returns it to its original position. Besides the first day I met her, she's only snapped at me one time, and that was two days ago when I told her that all the shifting of products in the world is not going to make or break her shop. In hindsight, I thought I was being helpful. She did not.

She's burnt out, nervous, and not only navigating a new relationship, but a *first* relationship. Thankfully, when we're alone, she lets herself fall and I hold her until I'm convinced she's rested. But for her own sake, I feel like I need to force her to take a break.

"Everything okay?" she asks.

"Yep. Do you have two minutes for a quick story?" When she says yes, I tell her about what happened with Mrs. Pinkerton.

"Damn... What have you done with my gentle, sweet, passive girlfriend?"

Girlfriend. She said the word. Oh my gosh, she said the word! I've thought it, felt it from the moment we kissed in the alley, but didn't want to totally spook her. And now, I'm beaming. I'm literally beaming so wide the light is probably ricocheting from my teeth and bouncing against the walls.

"Although..." Quinn says, "you're not always sweet and passive..."

Oh, that huskiness in Quinn's voice. And now heat flushes my body. She's right, though. Quinn has unleashed something almost feral in me, and my sexual inner goddess is exploding. Yes, we have sweet, romantic, beautiful sex in my bedroom. But I've also been on my knees behind her in the shower, pushing her into the wall, with her wrists bound in my hands, seeing how loud I can make her scream using my tongue along with a waterproof dildo.

A man's voice calls out in the background at the farm. "I have to go," Quinn says. "The crew is here to help me move the precut trees. Tonight, I want to hear every single detail of how you were a badass with Mrs. Pinkerton."

"Let's just say after all that even Chuck Norris himself wouldn't bring in an unleashed dog." I laugh and roll back on the office chair. "But seriously, I just told you the story."

"Nope, I want the full exclusive. How you felt, how she looked, if the dog bit you, everything," Quinn says. "I miss you."

My smile grows. "I just saw you a few hours ago."

"You know what I mean."

I do know what she means. Having the luxury of spending every waking moment with Quinn this past fall while my bakery was closed is something I'll never take for granted. But now, she's in the heart of her busy season, which will stay busy leading up to Christmas, and our time is limited. Thank gosh she's slept over every night since the first night, or I'm not sure I could handle it.

"Don't forget to save your appetite for tonight," I say.

"That will not be a problem," Quinn says, with a chuckle. "But I'm so curious what you have planned. Do I get a little hint?"

"None. Just wear something nice, and I will pick you up at six."

"You know I can drive over to your place, right?" Quinn says. "Pretty sure I'll be sleeping over anyway."

"Pretty sure you will, too." A smile inches across my face. "But tonight, I'm giving you a proper date. And I cannot wait."

After we hang up, I settle back into my chair and tap my fingers against the desk. As far as girlfriends go, Quinn is not fussy or high-maintenance; she has a go-with-the-flow mentality about how we spend our time together. But just because she is complacent does not mean that I can slack. I look around my office. Think, think. I need to have a wow factor tonight.

When I step out of the office and into the kitchen, I stop in my tracks. I rush into the fridge, scour the racks, and my insides start to tingle.

I know exactly what I need to do.

TWENTY-SIX

QUINN

Thank you to whoever invented waterproof, weatherproof, Quinn-proof winter boots. I have no doubt had these bad boys not been developed, I'd have a raging case of frostbite and perhaps a broken toe by now.

The snow on the farm is beautiful. It drips from the pine trees, lights up like tiny crystals in the sun during the day, it smells clean and fresh. But after four hours out here today, making sure all the precut trees are in the right spot, *again*, and doing the final touches on the outside decorations, I'm freezing.

Even though it's early afternoon, I turn on all the outside lights, step back, and try to picture opening night. Will there be a line of cars wrapped down the county road? Will children be chasing each other, screaming in delight, fat like abominable snowmen stuffed in their snowsuits? Will couples hold hands and stroll the property and pick out their very first joint Christmas tree? The day is so close, I can almost taste it.

My phone buzzes in my pocket. Zoey again? My heart skips a beat until I look at the screen. My sister. Not that I don't want to talk to Frankie. It's just that I *always* want to talk to Zoey.

"Go inside," Frankie says when I answer.

I would not put it past Frankie that she has security cameras adorning my property to make sure I'm not doing something dumb. Like standing outside four hours straight looking at the same stuff I've been looking at for the last week. "How did you know?"

"I didn't," Frankie says. "But now that you've busted yourself, can you please go inside so I can talk to you without your teeth chattering?"

The snow and gravel crunch under my feet as I make my way back into the barn. As Frankie asks all of the usual mother-hen questions, and I give her an update on all things farm-related, I step inside the barn and a warm gush of air hits me. I shrug out of my jacket and take a seat on the folding chair.

"So, Morgan says you haven't been home for almost a week," Frankie says.

My mouth is uncontrollable. It immediately quirks into a grin. "Morgan likes to lie."

Although, Morgan is not completely wrong. I haven't slept there since Zoey and I got together. But I was at home yesterday to shove some more clothes into an overnight bag, but Morgan was gone.

Is this normal? Is this what other people feel like in relationships? Warm and buttery, but also tingling inside, like you're getting constant zaps of luscious currents anytime you picture your partner. Since being with Zoey, everything is more vibrant, more colorful, sweeter. Even the snow-filled gray days are prettier. "In all fairness, though, I've spent almost every other second at the property. It's almost ready."

"Zoey told me it is ready."

My head snaps up. "Jesus, did you call my girlfriend?"

"Oh, so *now* we're getting somewhere," Frankie says. "Girlfriend, huh? Is this official? Did you have the whole 'let's go steady' conversation?"

I lift myself from the chair and cross the room to the coffee pot. "No one under the age of sixty uses that term anymore." I drain the last of the liquid into a mug and lean against the counter. "It's just... perfect. She's perfect."

Frankie is not a swooner. But that is the only way I can describe the *aww* sound that releases over the phone. "I knew it. Can you please, for once, finally admit that I knew something? It would make me feel so good inside if you would utter three tiny words to me. Call it an early Christmas present."

I know the words she wants me to say. And normally, I refrain. But even with the stress of setting up the shop, I'm darn near dancing on the insides so just once, I'll give in. *"You were right."*

"God, that feels good! I mean, really, have any other more perfect words in existence ever been said? I'm going to savor this for a while."

I hate that I'm grinning. I'm sure somehow Frankie can see it over the phone. "You are seriously annoying. Do you need anything else, or can I get back to work?"

"Nope, nothing else," Frankie says. "I switched my morning flight to the red-eye tonight, so I'll hopefully see you sometime tomorrow."

"Awesome. I need your muscles out here once you're rested." We chat for another moment, then we drop. I finish the rest of the coffee in my mug and start my rounds. As I stroll by the display shelf, I examine each item and confirm a price tag is attached. I do a dozen mock sales, verify the register is working, and swipe my credit cards. Approved purchase. *Good.*

I cross the room to wiggle in the Santa chair, step on top of it, and shake to validate its sturdiness. *Good.* I continue through the room, check the ornaments on the artificial tree and the wreaths. In the supply closet, I recount the paper cups and marshmallow supply, and exhale. Outside the window, the snowflakes grow heavier.

Okay, okay. Mother Nature is nudging me to take a break, go back to Zoey's, and get ready for my date. I stuff my hat and gloves in a bag, gather my empty lunch container, and check the weather app for the fifth time today.

My breath hitches. *Snow.* A ton of snow is on its way. This forecast clearly changed from this morning when it said mild flurries with minimal accumulation. Now it says some blustery conditions and moderate accumulation. I refresh. *Shit.*

Everything is going to get canceled. Ruined. The opening weekend will be a disaster, no one will come. The streets will shut down, I'll lose my business, and my life as I know it will be over. I pinch the bridge of my nose and punch out a breath.

Now that I've let my little downward spiral of fear tailspin away, I slip my phone in my pocket and take a full, calming breath.

Everything is *fine.* We live in Northern Minnesota. There has never not been snow on Thanksgiving. It's part of the magic of the area we live in. How many tornado watches and warnings did we have this spring and summer? So many I lost track.

Things will be okay.

After I close up shop and hop in my car to head back to town, I only check the app one more time as I roll up to a stop sign. I allow myself one more little freak-out, then push away the negative thoughts. This is what I do. Quinn Lee, master's degree in Freaking the Fuck Out Over Everything. I always expect the worst. I did it when I moved to Minnesota, and things are turning out fine. Perfect, even. I did the same thing when I bought the farm, when I didn't think I could set my shop up in time, when I thought Zoey wouldn't love me.

I mean, not that she *loves* me, loves me. She probably loves me as a friend. Because I love her as a friend. But now we're not friends, which means that we're more than friends which means I love Zoey. Do I love Zoey?

Holy shit. I think I love Zoey.

Is this too soon? Nope—I'm not doing this, either. I'm not going to dissect and overanalyze every single thought and feeling, nor am I going to listen to any sort of negative stereotypes that I'm following a long lineage of proud lesbians who've U-Hauled. Zoey and I spent months getting to know each other. Besides Frankie, I've spent more time with her collectively than any other human.

I know what I know.

My breath strangles my throat. I bite my mitten off and toss it to the side, tug off my hat, and lower the temperature in the truck. *I love Zoey.* After the heat settles into my skin, there's part of me that is filled, a lightness and heaviness that is wonderful and scary and all consuming.

I love Zoey.

TWENTY-SEVEN
ZOEY

When I pull up to Quinn's house a little after six, I kill the engine and take a deep breath. Everything tonight needs to be perfect. The expectation of giving someone their first real date is a lot, and I want it to be memorable. I double-check myself in the vanity mirror and swipe a pinkie underneath my glasses to catch a few rogue mascara flakes. I grab the flower bouquet resting on the passenger seat, step up the front porch of Quinn's house, and knock.

When it opens, my breath halts. How is this my girlfriend? Quinn's hair is full and bouncing, the fresh coconut conditioner scent reaching my nose. She's wearing a long, fitted winter skirt, knee-high boots, and a button-down that is popping her cleavage enough to make my mouth water. If I could just bury myself into her chest from here until eternity, I'd die a very, very happy woman. "What? Oh my gosh, look at you. Quinn Lee, I think you might truly be the most beautiful woman I've ever seen." There's a playfulness to my tone, but I'm dead serious. This woman steals the air from me.

"Did you bring me flowers?" she asks when I hand her the bouquet. She brings the pink and lavender roses to her nose, closes her eyes, and sniffs. "These are beautiful, thank you."

She presses her lips softly into mine, probably not wanting to smear any of our lipsticks. But right now, I don't care about messing up hair or makeup. I want to ravish her in the bedroom, cave-woman-style. Dinner can wait.

I follow Quinn to the kitchen where she digs down a vase from a cabinet and fills it with water. "I cannot wait to show you every-thing I have planned for tonight," I say.

A grin tugs at her lips as she stuffs the flowers inside the vase. "I am both curious and kind of terrified."

"Terrified? Why?"

Quinn shrugs. "I've never gone on a date like this before. What if I say or do something completely inappropriate?"

"I hope you do," I say with a grin.

After she adds the flowers, she leans her head on my chest and wraps me in a hug. "Thank you for everything. It's already a perfect evening."

I kiss the top of her head. "We haven't even started, yet."

"I know." She pulls back and plants a kiss on my mouth. A little fuller, a little stronger, and grips me tight into her.

Fifteen minutes later as my windshield wipers fight off the snow, I pull the car up to park alongside my bakery.

Quinn dashes a glance between me and my shop. "Did you forget something?"

"No, you'll see. Come on." We hop out of the car and dash to the entrance. I jiggle the keys into the door, step inside, and hold the door open for Quinn.

Her eyes grow and she takes a sharp inhale. "Zoey..." A soft grin tugs at her lips as her head moves slowly, her eyes scanning every inch of the space.

This is the *exact* reaction I'm looking for.

For the past week, I've been decorating for the holidays, so I've already strung the white lights, and put up the artificial tree in the corner. But after I closed shop today, Luna and I tore around this place to turn it into a five-star-worthy restaurant. Dozens of flame-free candles scatter the space. With the blinds closed, the candles and white Christmas lights cast a beautiful soft glow around the bakery.

In the middle of my shop, I pulled one of my round café tables into the center, covered it with white linen, added a vase of flowers, and a beautiful place setting—crystal wine glasses, white-and-gold plates, water glasses, linen napkins, and silverware.

"Zoey, this is perfect," Quinn says as I pull out her chair. She smooths her skirt under her bottom and slides in. "It's absolutely beautiful."

My grin overtakes my face. "One second, I'll be right back." I swing through the kitchen doors, and trot over to Luna, who's just pulling items out of the oven.

"Hey there," she says, setting the pans on top of the stove. "Perfect timing."

"Everything smells amazing." I check over her shoulder at the bubbling food. "And looks amazing. Wow, you've really outdone yourself. Is everything set?"

"Yep. Food is ready, wine is corked, dessert is prepped. You are officially ready to impress the hell out of your lady." She plates up the food onto a tray, then tugs off the oven mitts and tosses them to the side. "I'm going to sneak out the back and leave you two be."

Luna is staff, not a friend, and that is the only reason I'm not giving her a big, fat hug right now. After I came up with the idea to have a private meal here, she offered to cook, saying it was the perfect opportunity for her to get some practice for her dream profession. Someday, Luna's going to leave me to open a catering business. And based on the way everything looks and smells, she'll do amazing. "You are the best. I cannot thank you enough for everything."

Luna nods with a smile, picks up the envelope of cash I paid her to cater tonight, tugs on her coat, and sneaks out the back.

I use my butt to open the swinging door, holding the large tray of food. When I set it in front of Quinn, she dips her head into the savory steam and pulls in a breath. "God, this smells like heaven. Is this chicken Kiev?"

"Yes, and grilled brussels sprouts with prosciutto and balsamic vinegar," I say and start dishing onto her plate. "And mashed potatoes, because obviously."

Quinn's eyes are dancing at the food, and it looks like she is two seconds away from drooling. Once I'm done filling her plate, I scoop my own, then fill her wine glass. Quinn's cheeks are rosy and darn near glowing, with an almost innocent look. Seeing Quinn have a first real date makes me want to do more firsts with her.

"Cheers," I say and tap my glass against hers. The Chardonnay that a customer recommended to go with the heavier dinner tonight is delicate and a little tart and easily slides down my throat. "Happy first date."

A blush spreads across her freckled cheeks. The flame-free candlelight casts a pretty, soft glow, and I swear I could sit in this moment forever. She cuts a piece of chicken and takes a bite. "Oh my God, this is so good." She adds another bite before she finishes chewing the first one. "Okay, tell me every single thing about what happened with Mrs. Pinkerton."

We spend the rest of dinner talking about the day, the Mrs. Pinkerton story, and memories of Thanksgivings growing up. As I take a second helping of the most creamy, buttery mashed potatoes I've ever had, and make a mental note to tell Luna how delicious they are, Quinn chats about how the holiday has been for her in the past. "Frankie and I had this favorite Chinese restaurant not too far from our place that stayed opened during Thanksgiving, so we'd gorge on egg rolls and sesame chicken," she says. "Not a lot different from how we did it when we were younger."

The tone is so matter-of-fact about never really celebrating Thanksgiving, and I bite back the urge to force my traditions on Quinn. There's still a fragility to this relationship, and the last thing I want to do is smother her. But next to Christmas, Thanksgiving is my absolute favorite holiday. The food, the family, the full bellies after lunch. I help my mom in the kitchen all day, and we make a ridiculous amount of sides, from tater-tot hotdish, green bean casserole, stuffing, and candied yams. I bring pies from the shop, and the house is full of not only family, but friends and neighbors.

So, I'm really swallowing back the urge to ask Quinn, again, if she wants to join me for Thanksgiving. When I asked her last week, she was noncommittal, and that pesky little insecurity gremlin keeps edging its way into my brain, thinking I'm pushing this too fast.

When Josie and I broke up, and I went to counseling, a recurring theme was that I was terrible at communication. My eyes dip to my plate. I take a quick breath and stiffen my back. I refuse to allow my lack of communication get in the way of what Quinn and I have. She, we, us, are worth fighting for. If I'm being too pushy, I need her to tell me. Not me blocking myself. "Can I ask you something?"

The smile drops from her face at the serious tone. She lowers her glass to the table. "Of course. Everything okay?"

I nod. "Last week when I asked if you wanted to come to my family's Thanksgiving, was that too pushy? I know we just got together, but it seemed so natural. And... it's super informal. Like sweatpants and Vikings sweatshirts and there's a revolving door of guests that traipse through and—"

Her soft hand touches mine and stops me. "I am so sorry if I gave you that impression. God, I'm glad you said something. No, not too pushy. At all. I'm sorry if I blew off the invitation." She removes her hand. "I'm freaking out more than I thought I'd be right now about the farm, and that is the day before I open. I just didn't want people to count on me being there, and if something happened last minute and I couldn't show, I didn't want to seem disrespectful to your parents."

Oh, for Pete's sake. *Duh.* "This makes perfect sense." I pick my knife and fork back up. "Well then, we'll make a different time where we go out on snowmobiles. It's almost a family tradition. Turkey, pie, nap, then snowmobile races."

"Wait," Quinn says, stabbing a fork into a brussels sprout. "You drive a snowmobile?"

"Sure do," I say, loving the shock on her face. Every time I think Quinn knows all there is to know about me, or vice versa, something else unravels. "I keep it at my parents' house, but we all have one. I'll have to take you out at some point. I'm sure my mom will want to go with, too. But she's a speed demon so be prepared we will never keep up."

Quinn's mouth drops open. "Debbie? No, no way."

"Oh yes," I say, cutting a slice of the chicken and dipping it into the sauce. "She takes no prisoners. And she's competitive, too. She'll absolutely tease us for driving like grandmas."

"Debbie. Huh. Who knew?" Quinn takes a bite of potatoes, then rests her fork on the side of the plate. "I'm bummed I can't be there. But I will love you forever if you save a big fat plate of turkey for me. With an obnoxious size of all the sides. Don't think I can't eat it all. I can and will." She giggles and lifts the glass to her mouth.

I will love you forever. She said it lightheartedly, a joke really, in the context of the conversation. But I'm latching on to those words for dear life and dissecting every syllable. "You will love me…"

Quinn's smile drops, and a seriousness flushes her face. She dips her eyes to the plate and her throat rolls with a hard swallow. "I *do*… love you."

She may have lobbed the words softly, quietly, a hesitation and fear laced in the tone, but the words land with the weight of granite. I can see the vulnerability in her eyes, the moss green highlighting against the light, the anticipation, the hope that someone loves her back. Before she can take it back, say she was joking, pass it off as an aloof comment, I reach across the table, and intertwine my fingers in hers. I rub my thumb across the satiny skin on top of her hand. "I love you, too."

A long moment stretches between us. There is nothing that needs to be said right now. We both know the gravity of the situation, the intensity of the moment. My guess is she is feeling the same as me. Trepidation, mixed with this luxurious, velvety warmth knowing that this is something special, beautiful, something to be grateful for.

Another moment passes when I finally let go of my grip, polish off my glass of wine, and eye her through the flickering light. Opening night is so close, and I know she's stressed, but she has everything ready. Time to take her mind off of the shop. "Ready for dessert?" I ask.

"I'm *always* ready for your dessert."

I push back my chair with a small squeak against the floor and hold out my hand. She lifts herself, interlaces her fingers in mine, and lets me lead her to the kitchen.

Inside, the space is dimly lit. Quinn's gaze travels the white tablecloth draping the stainless-steel prep area, with a water bottle, several spoons, and a blindfold.

"A blindfold?" Her brow arches.

Oh, I can't wait for this. I pat the top of the countertop. "Sit."

Quinn immediately hops up on the counter and faces me with her legs dangling off the table.

I wrap the blindfold around her and tug the back into a bow. "Can you see anything?"

"Nope," she says and plants her palms on the counter.

My mind is walking through all of the gloriously naughty things I could do with my girlfriend. But right now, that will have to wait. I grab the tray near the stove and cross back to her. I scoop up a small amount of dessert with a spoon. "Open your mouth."

"Oh God, you're dreamy when you're domineering like this," Quinn says, then parts her mouth.

I deposit a tiny bit, and she swallows. "Tell me what you taste."

"Mmmm." She licks her bottom lip. "Chocolate."

I sweep her lips with mine, then give her another bite. "What else?"

Quinn savors the sweetness, rolls it in her tongue, then swallows. "Vanilla."

"Good." With my other hand I lift her skirt up to her knee. Her breath hitches and her knees fall open. It's going to take all my willpower to go slow. I give her another small taste. "What else?

"Um... berries."

I lift the skirt a little higher.

"Raspberries."

And a little higher. I brush my thumb against the outside of Quinn's soft, smooth thigh. Her chest rises and falls with quick breaths. She licks the outside of her lips and inches closer. Oh... this is fun. Seeing the anticipation, watching her breaths increase, feeling her lean into me. Warmth spreads inside me. I add a small amount of whipped cream on her mouth and kiss it off. Her lips part, push into me, and I melt from the sugar on her tongue. I don't want to rip myself away, but I do.

I use the corner of the spoon to cut into the next dessert and place it in her mouth. "Now, what do you taste?"

A moment passes. Her head tilts to the side. I give her one more little taste. "Cinnamon."

I unbutton the top button of her shirt.

"And... um... cream."

Second button, removed.

"And... and... cardamom?"

I'm practically salivating watching her squirm against the table. Her anticipation feeds into mine. "Very good. That one was a hard one." I remove the final three buttons, tug her shirt past her shoulders, and skim my fingertips across her chest. My pulse kicks up, my need to be closer to her starts to consume me.

Quinn's hands reach out, finds me, and she pulls me between her legs. When I tug on her bottom lip with my thumb, she leans forward, mouth parted, searching for me. I press my lips onto hers, move against her, inhale her taste and scent.

When she leans back, I want to take in everything. The way her cheeks flush, the way her freckles sprinkle her face, the way she squirms and shivers with every touch. She is so utterly perfect.

I take my time and indulge, spreading dessert on her mouth, letting her taste it, then licking it off. I swipe a little on her neck, then kiss it off. When I lower her bra strap and kiss the skin, goosebumps skitter across her arms. I tug the bra all the way down and her breasts spring free. Quinn's breath is heavy against my ear, and her fingers dig into my hips. I dip my finger into the chocolate, spread it across her nipple and lick it off, slowly, lusciously, as her moans fill my ear.

"Zoey," she whispers between heavy breaths. She lifts the blindfold a little, looking sheepish. "I don't want to stop. But... unless you really want to sanitize this table, we better move this upstairs."

I chuckle, step back, and pull her bra back up. "This is a very fair point. I don't think I fully thought this through."

Quinn pulls me in for another kiss, then releases. After she buttons up, she hops off the table. Once we throw on our jackets, I grab her hand and practically sprint to the end of the kitchen.

"Wait!" Quinn drops my hand, runs back to the table, and grabs the blindfold. She grips it with a devilish grin. "We are *so* not done with this."

TWENTY-EIGHT
QUINN

My fingers spread the blinds apart and I peek out the window. I close them. I peek. I close them. I peek—

"If you do that again..." Zoey says, tugging the bed sheet up to her naked chest and rolling onto her side. She props her elbow on the mattress and rests her head in her hands. "Looking at the snow is not going to change anything."

I exhale. I know, I know. She's right. But we are three days away from opening day, and the snow is piling on. What if a snowplow doesn't clear the roads, and I can't get to the farm, and I need to check things and...

"You're ready for opening day. Even if we get stuck in a snowstorm until then, you can open," Zoey says, patting the mattress. "Come back to bed."

My shoulders loosen. Just because Zoey is being logical, and I know she's right, doesn't mean that this message is transferring to my brain. I peek one final time, then crawl back into the warm bed sprinkled with Zoey's sleepy, dewy scent.

What am I thinking, wanting to leave this, her, the bed? Being with Zoey is heaven. Every time I think things can't get better, they do. The date night a few nights ago tipped things over the edge. As much as I love this, her, being with her, the anxiety of not being able to check my farm is still fierce. "I'll lie here for a little while, then I'm going to head out to the farm."

Zoey chews the bottom of her lip and a deep crease cuts between her brows. "The roads are too bad to drive right now. Let's just hold tight, okay? You can hang out with me today at the store. Or rest. I can feed you cupcakes in bed."

Normally, her smile can get me to do anything, but not today. "Okay," I say, but I know I'm lying. We are so close to opening, and what if something happened overnight? I don't have the luxury to *not* check on the property.

When Zoey steps into the shower, I open up the weather app, and swallow. A blizzard is heading our way. *A blizzard!* Unbelievable. I press my palm against my forehead and breathe out a shaky breath. Am I prepped for a blizzard? Sure, the barn has been there fifty-plus years and has probably seen a lot in its day, but still...

Okay, I'm just going to go there, super quick, confirm things are still standing, that none of the signs knocked over in the wind, and then come back. I can spend the rest of the afternoon helping Zoey prep for her Thanksgiving pie rush, and the rest of the night snuggling with my girlfriend.

After Zoey goes to work, I take a quick shower, pack up all my winter gear, and rush outside. *Jesus.* A short gust of wind hurls a mound of snow at me, and I spin my back at it until it stops. A heap of snow covers Truck Norris. After I hop in and start it, I swipe the brush across the windshield and windows. The snow is heavy, flakes barreling down, and I'm blinking it away like I'm in an avalanche.

Finally, I cautiously pull out of the alley. This area hasn't been plowed, and the piles are thick, but the truck pushes through. Snow pummels against the windshield. Even though the wipers are at the highest speed, they're barely keeping up.

It's okay, it's okay. I can do this. My pulse thuds against my chest. I did learn how to drive on these roads, but it's been probably a good fifteen years since I drove in a snowstorm. Just take it slow, easy, and if I start skidding, just turn my wheels into the direction of the skid.

Wait... right? That doesn't make sense. Wouldn't that mean I'd end up going in a circle? The last thing I want to do is whip a shitty in the middle of an intersection. My breath shakes against my rib cage. *I'm okay. I got this.*

I creep to a stop at the empty intersection. The sound of a snowplow's loud scrape against the pavement jars me. I turn and look out all the windows and finally see its blue flashing lights. This is actually perfect. If I follow this guy, I'll have freshly plowed streets the whole way.

Sadly, the plow turns in the opposite direction.

The wind howls so loud it shakes the nearly unshakable Truck Norris. Gusts of snow whip against my truck. The light turns green, and I inch into the intersection. My knuckles have surpassed white and are moving toward nearly translucent with my death grip.

I lean as close as I can to the windshield, squinting to read the street signs. The town is gray, muted, and covered in a white blanket. I can't make out trees, cars, houses, or much of the road. Am I over the line, in the other lane, in the right spot? Near the ditch? I think I'm close to the middle, and hope to God that if a car is coming my way, we'll see each other and avoid a disaster.

A faint outline of a red light pops into view. *Shit!* I press on the brakes a little too quickly and tailspin into the street before skidding to a stop. My pulse races, tears against my chest, and I freeze. I rest my head back on the seat and exhale.

What the hell am I doing?

My heartbeat slows a little bit as I turn around. This is dumb. I'm being ridiculous. I'm putting myself at danger, at risk, for this compulsion that's eating away at me. Even if I got to my farm, which right now seems highly unlikely since I've made it less than a mile out of town, there is nothing I can do.

Slowly, I turn around and drive back to Zoey's. When I finally pull into the alleyway and kill the engine, I release my grasp on the steering wheel and shake out my fatigued hands. I hop out of the truck, slam the door with a heavy thud, and traipse to the bakery.

The door jingles when I push it open. Zoey's gaze snaps to me and she wrings a towel through her hand. "Hey... what are you doing?"

I tug off my gloves and shove them in my jacket pocket. "I tried to go to the farm, but..."

"Quinn, *noooo*." Zoey's voice is a cross between scolding and concern and I don't know what's worse. "You can't drive in conditions like this. It's barreling down out there. We're supposed to get a blizzard."

I know! Obviously, I know. My pulse has barely evened out since arriving back at the bakery. I breathe through my nose and close my eyes. The very, very last thing I want to do is snap at my perfect, sweet, delicate girlfriend, but nerves have crawled up my neck and have me locked in a chokehold. "It probably wasn't the smartest decision, but I just needed to check on my place."

Zoey crosses her arms. "I get it, but you have to think of safety first. Driving like this is reckless. Seriously. You can hurt yourself, or someone else. Please, please promise me you will never do this again."

My face heats, and I push out a heavy breath. "You of all people should understand what this is like. What if there was a storm before your opening day? Would you have just not checked it out? I have a four-wheel-drive truck and a survival kit, okay?"

I don't like my tone. It doesn't feel good, and I know that Zoey is coming from a place of love. But sometimes I don't think Zoey understands. Yes, she's set up her own business. And she knows how difficult it is to do something like this, solo. But she's imbedded into the town. The community is practically an extra limb. And she has a strong family support system, with the kind of parents people dream about.

I have Frankie. That's it. There's no one to fall back on, no parents I can borrow money from, no grandma who's still alive that I can lean on. So, sure I know it was dumb to attempt to drive in a budding storm, but I needed to check on my second home, my livelihood, my dream.

Zoey steps over to me and wraps me in her arms. "You're shaking."

I didn't realize it until she said it, but she's right. I'm not sure if it's from gripping my steering wheel so hard, or the realization that I did something not very smart. Her warm honeysuckle and vanilla scent engulfs me, and I lean into her embrace.

The wind roars against the building. A large branch tears from the tree and cracks against the window and I flinch so hard I feel a pop in my neck.

"I'm going to lock everything up," Zoey says, releasing me. "No one's coming in and I sent the staff home an hour ago."

While she goes into the kitchen and returns with a container to save the items in the display case, I stack chairs on the table, then grab the broom and mop. Twenty minutes later, we head back to the kitchen where the counters overflow with pie supplies.

Yikes. That is a very overwhelming pile of product. "Need some help?"

"Are you sure you don't want to go rest?" Zoey asks, but I can see in her eyes, that yes, she would love the help.

After I tie my hair into a tight bun and wash my hands, I follow Zoey's instructions. It's methodical and precise, and after a while I lose myself in the motion. Being with Zoey, baking, building, makes me forget about everything outside. A little. With no windows, it's quiet in the kitchen, and I can't see the outside. So, for now, I'm going to pretend that everything's okay.

Even though something in my gut tells me that everything is definitely not okay.

I roll over in my bed and run my hand around the cool, wrinkled sheets. One second passes, then two, then... "Quinn?" I bolt upright and blink into the darkness. Oh no... I click on the lamp and glance around the room.

"Quinn?" I call out a little louder, but silence meets me.

She wouldn't have... right? I hop out of the bed and shove my glasses on my face. My footsteps are heavy against the hardwood floors as I rush from room to room. In the bathroom, the kitchen, the living room, I'm met with nothing.

It's 6:30 a.m. but feels much earlier. In the living room, I open the blinds and look at the alley. Truck Norris is gone. My stomach twists. Quinn is gone. What time did she bolt from here? I didn't even feel her leave the bed.

Granted, we were both exhausted. After prepping all of the pies, the storm was so loud and fierce last night that it took a bit for us to fall asleep. It rattled the windows and shook the building for hours, before it finally stopped. Thankfully, it was quick, if relentless.

I rush back to the bedroom. Where did she go?

Obviously, something is wrong. I could sense it last night. Sure, at some point the sex has to slow down, but Quinn only gave me one small kiss, then rolled over to snuggle a pillow instead of me. Did I push things with her too quickly? No. Maybe? I don't know. Or is this about me chatting with her *again* last night before bed about how dangerous driving in these conditions can be? When Quinn stepped into my bakery and said that she'd tried to go to the farm, I almost choked. She's lived in New York for all these years, without a car. Does she remember about black ice? How to prevent skidding? What the heck would she have done if she actually made it to an unplowed county road?

I grab my phone to call her. The call goes directly to voicemail. I send a text, but it shows undelivered. *Oh no...* I push my palm into my head. I want to go after her, but that would be ridiculous. What am I supposed to do? Drive out to her farm, which is where I'm assuming she went, and check if she's okay? I can't. Even if I want to, I can't. I have almost two hundred people coming in today to pick up orders, and only Luna is on staff.

I try one more text message and it goes undelivered. She didn't block me, right? Wait, no. I'm not doing this. Now is not the time to be overbearing or insecure. Something most likely happened with the cell towers.

After getting ready, I brew a large pot of coffee, fill a Thermos, and go to the shop. Yes, of course I'm worried about Quinn, but she's an adult and if she wanted to leave, that's her choice. The MnDOT folks around here are spectacular. The streets are already plowed, there is no wind, and besides massive snowbanks filling the holding spots, no one would know we had a storm last night.

I tuck my hair into a bun and get to work. Today is going to be a long day. The shop itself is closed except for the half-priced goods left over from yesterday, and folks coming in to get their orders for Thursday. I check my phone one last time. No new messages. I push out a quick breath, then stuff it back in my pocket.

Time will probably fly by quickly with the revolving door of folks coming into my shop, but I cannot shake this dark, icky feeling churning in my gut. Where is the line between caring and overbearing? I do not want to overstep and turn into my mother, and yet, if something happens to Quinn, and I'm the only one who knows she's not answering her calls, I'll never forgive myself.

Forget it. I'd rather be overbearing than regretful. I dial Frankie, who answers with a groggy voice. "Hey, it's Zoey," I say. I feel like I'm the student barging to the teacher to tattle. "Have you heard from Quinn?"

"No... I thought she was with you," Frankie says.

I take off my glasses and pinch the bridge of my nose. "She was, but when I woke up this morning, she was already gone. And I'm probably being paranoid, but she's not answering any of my calls and I'm worried."

"Did you guys have a fight?" Frankie asks.

Did we? No, not really? But something was definitely, definitely off. The energy of the entire evening was gloomy, and the fact that she didn't wake me up this morning shows that there's clearly an unresolved issue. "No. I don't know. I mean, nothing big or dramatic or anything."

Whispers and shuffling sound in the background. I hear Frankie tell Morgan what I've just said to her. "Okay, Morgan said the cell service is spotty right now, and unless Quinn's on Wi-Fi, she probably won't get messages or calls. So, let's just give it a bit. If you don't hear from her in an hour, let me know, and Morgan and I will head out to the farm and see if she's just busy with cleanup or something."

My shoulders relax. I thank her and get back to work but am distracted. Thankfully, Luna is handling ringing up the customers, so I don't have to fake a smile, and I'm in the kitchen packaging. The minutes that should be rushing by are slogging.

Something is wrong. I can feel it. I pause packaging and pull up the Department of Transportation website and scour for anything on accidents. I check the news, social media, and our community website, and nothing. No reports of any accidents. But this feeling is not going away. What if Quinn is in a ditch? What if she hit her head and is trapped in a car and will freeze to death? Everything in me claws at my skin. Should I call the sheriff? Have him do some sort of welfare check? Is that unreasonable? My face turns hot, and a ring starts in my ears. I can feel this to the deepest part of my bones. Something is very, very wrong.

Another five minutes pass, and I can't take it. I text my mom to see if I can borrow her Jeep. The road conditions might be terrible out in the country and I'm taking no chances with my little sedan. How am I going to figure out a time to go out there with hundreds of people coming into my shop today? Maybe my mom can help package while I do a safety check.

I package up an order when my phone vibrates in my pocket. I nearly drop the box to grab it, and my heart leaps into my throat at Quinn's name splashed across my screen.

"Oh my gosh, are you okay?" I ask when I answer.

"Zoey..." Quinn's shaky voice sounds through the receiver. Raw, gut-wrenching sobs boom through the phone, and my heart breaks at the noise. Her breathing is quick and choppy, and I freeze, waiting for her to speak. "Everything is destroyed."

THIRTY

QUINN

I'm crumbled into the corner of the barn, my teeth rattling, partly from the chill, and partly from the crying. My jacket is snug around my body, my knees are against my chest, and I'm sobbing into my hands.

When I pulled up here this morning, and saw what happened, I simply dropped to my knees in the snow. Two windows busted out, glass everywhere, the display case blown to bits. Mason jars with the firefly lights tipped over, some broken, some cracked. Ornaments shattered against the floor. The Santa photo op station ripped to shreds. Snowflake bulbs broken, the artificial trees tipped over with shattered lights. Everything... ruined.

"Quinn, what happened?" Zoey repeats.

I sniff hard and try to breathe out the cries. I thought I had cried it all out, but apparently, I hadn't. The second Zoey answered, it rushed forward. When I woke up this morning, I was so restless, and the sky was eerily calm. Like the blizzard had torn through the town, ravished the streets, then came to a dead stop. Zoey was so peaceful tucked in the bed, and I couldn't sleep. So, I'd slithered out of there and took off for the farm.

I probably could've left a note, but I thought I'd text her on the way. I tried and it wouldn't connect, then called, and it wouldn't connect. The roads were all clear in town, but the moment I took a turn outside of the city limits, I dropped the phone and concentrated on not getting in an accident.

Each downed tree, dead branch, and heavy snowbank I passed kicked my anxiety sky-high. It took nearly two hours to make the twenty-five-minute drive. I couldn't even get the truck onto my property. I had to park on the side of the road and hike the rest of the way.

"Quinn," Zoey says again, softly. "What happened?"

A choked sob releases. "Two of the windows broke and glass is everywhere and everything is broken... and it's all... over. I can't open my store. It's all ruined." Another guttural sound releases and I bury my head in my hands. I can't believe this happened. My dream, my livelihood, everything is destroyed. Gone, in a snap.

Zoey's saying something on the other end, but I can barely make it out. Finally, I pull in some calming breaths and rest my head against the wall.

"I'm so sorry, Quinn. I can't believe this happened," Zoey says. "Why don't you come back to my place, rest for a bit, and we'll figure something out."

I almost want to laugh. There is nothing to figure out. Opening day is less than forty-eight hours away. The day after Thanksgiving is the busiest day of the year for Christmas-tree farmers. Black Friday is not just for retail stores. If I miss out on this, I'm missing out on half my business for the year. *The year.* My head pounds with a headache and I push my thumbs into my temples.

"Quinn. Can you hear me? Come back home, okay? I promise we'll figure this out."

I sigh and swipe my hand under my chin to catch the tear dribbles. "The roads are so bad. In town they're great, but out here they haven't cleared them yet."

"Then I'm coming to you," Zoey says.

"Absolutely not," I snap. "It was stupid enough to put myself in danger like this, but there's no chance in hell I'm putting you in any danger. If the roads don't clear out by tonight, I'll just sleep here. But please, promise me you won't."

Silence meets me.

"*Zoey*. Promise me." I stiffen against the wall. Right now is not the time for Zoey to try any heroic shit. Now is the time for me to wallow in my grief and watch my dreams sink.

"Fine," she finally says, and my body relaxes. "But you are a planner and an organizer. Make a plan."

"I can't! I have one day. *One*. It's impossible. Even if I could fix the windows, the products are destroyed." I loosen my scarf and stare at my broken store. No matter how hard or fast I work, I can't get this place back in order. A cry locks in my throat, but I breathe it out.

"Please don't lose hope," Zoey says, her voice cracking.

I know she wants to take this heartache away from me. But she can't.

My dream is gone.

"I'm going to go," I say. "I'll call you later and let you know if I'll sleep here or if the plows come."

A heavy sigh releases on the other line. "Okay. Be safe. And I love you."

These words are the only thing that make a crack in this awful day. "I love you, too."

I straighten my legs in front of me, rest my hands in my lap, and my shoulders collapse. *Fuck*. I absolutely cannot believe this happened. But Zoey is right. I need a plan. At least for tonight, if I have to stay here, I need to figure out a way to not freeze to death. With the two windows busted out, I turned off all heat. But maybe if I put up an industrial packing blanket in the window, I can block the cold air from coming in and just eat the cost of reheating this place for the night.

I drag myself from the floor, grab the ladder, and hammer the blankets tight into both windows. Glass crunches under my feet as I move across the room. I grab a broom and start sweeping. I sweep, cry, sweep, cry.

With no wind, the physical movement, blankets covering the windows, and the heater kicking back in, the barn begins to warm. I snap a hefty black garbage bag in the air, stuff it into a trash can, and start clearing piles.

A bulb ornament that looks unbroken rests beneath a table. I squat and reach for it. "*Ouch. Shit.*" Great. Just what I need. I scurry over to the sink and wash the cut, then grab the first aid kit. Once I'm bandaged up properly, I go back to work. An hour goes by, then two. I need some air.

I throw on my jacket and walk the property. Tears stream as I pass by the homemade signs. Anyone seen Rudolph? is missing the *R*. Where did Mrs. Claus put my boots? is cracked in half. I swipe at tears with the back of my glove, then drag it back to the barn to fix for next year—*if* there is a next year. Right now, I don't think I want to try this again.

God, how did I get here? I left New York, my career, my home, for this. Did I make the right choice? Maybe I should go back to New York and start over again.

Stop. What am I even saying? There is no Zoey in New York. Or Frankie. Or Morgan. There are not the nice people at the coffee shop, or the slow traffic, or Lake Superior, or the church ladies who show up to help build a stockpile of goodies for someone they don't know. Nope, I'm not doing this. Enough feeling sorry for myself. I move my shoulders back, lift my chin, and continue moving around the property.

After I gather all the broken signs, which were less than half of all the signs, I start shoveling the wraparound porch. My muscles burn, my breath is heavy, my heart thuds. I should be feeling better with the physical exertion, but I'm not. I wish I could be all positivity and sunshine like my girlfriend, but this is disastrous.

I move to the back of the porch when faint zipping sounds echo across the valley. It grows quickly, gets louder, and it sounds like it's coming up the trail to my property. *Freaking snowmobilers.* Sounds like a herd of them. I swear I'm not a violent person, but if they're on my property, I'm installing a barbed-wire fence and they can deal with the consequences.

Okay, fine, perhaps murderous thoughts are not the best, but this is private property, and my trees are delicate and... *Ugh!* They are definitely on my property. By some miracle, the seedlings were still standing when I checked earlier, and if these asshats do anything to harm them, I'm not in the mood to play Minnesota-nice. They will absolutely be receiving the full pissed-off Quinn Lee New York treatment. I toss my shovel and stomp to the front of the property and... *Wait, what?*

What's happening here? Several long moments pass before I fully take in the scene. And when I do, my chest lifts. It not only lifts but soars all the way to the moon. Zoey, Frankie, Morgan, and Debbie hop off the snowmobiles and remove their helmets. Right behind them is a lifted Jeep that smashes through snowbanks with ease. Zoey's dad waves from behind the steering wheel as a mountain of supplies rattle against the Jeep windows.

I rush over to Zoey, but before I can say anything, all of them wrap me in a group hug. The strong, healing power of these five people, supporting me, lifting me, holding me up when I can barely hold myself, fills me and I start bawling. Zoey grips me as tight as she's ever held me, transferring all the care and love I need and pulling my worries away.

When I pull back, I scan their faces. "I can't believe you guys all came."

Frankie claps her hands together. "Where do you want us first? We're all here, ready to be bossed around by you for as long as it takes to get this place back in shape."

My mouth drops open. I don't think... I don't know. Is this even doable? Wasted time? Worth it? "What about Thanksgiving tomorrow? Zoey, Debbie, you guys have all the prep today, right? And you'll be so tired and—"

"Now, don't you even worry about that for a second," Debbie says, planting her gloved hands against my shoulders. "Thanksgiving is about being around family and friends, and right now we are around family and friends. If we're too tired, I'll order pizza, and we will save it and do it next week. It'll be fine. I promise."

My lips tremble. Behind Zoey's fogged glasses, her eyes are encouraging. She wraps her arms around my waist and squeezes. Behind her, her dad is smiling. And to the side of him, Morgan gives me a firm nod and a wink. "Do you all actually think we can do this?"

"Absolutely we can," Zoey says. "Look at us. A force to be reckoned with, if I do say so myself. Just point us where you need us. What you're doing here is special, Quinn. The town is going to love it."

My heart bursts from my body. I have never felt anything like this before. This rock-solid, unfaltering support and belief in me and what I'm trying to do. I rest my head on Zoey's shoulders and take a breath. "Thank you all so much. I literally don't know what to say."

"Which never happens, so let's all recognize this for the miracle that it is," Frankie says and groans when Morgan nudges her elbow into her side.

"We got you, Quinn," Morgan says, tugging her hat a little snugger on her head. "How about we head inside, and you show us where to go?"

After we grab the supplies from the Jeep, and everyone stomps through the snow toward the barn, I tug at Zoey's arm. She pauses and turns to me, her eyes sheepish. "I know, I know, I promised I wouldn't come," she says. "Don't be mad, okay? This isn't about me not listening or respecting what you say. This was about me and my selfish need to help."

My God, she's amazing. I don't know what I ever did in my life to deserve someone like Zoey, but here she is. Plopped right in my lap, a gift from the universe. I wrap my mitted palms around her red cheeks and pull her into me. I kiss her chilly lips, warm them with mine, then fold myself into her. "Thank you for not listening to me."

She kisses me on the top of my head, then grabs my hand. "Come on. Let's make this Christmas miracle happen."

THIRTY-ONE
ZOEY

Holy bananas. Quinn was not exaggerating. This place is destroyed. The phrase "it looks like a cyclone hit this place" has never rung truer than now. Blankets cover two of the windows, broken outdoor signs lie across one of the tables, the tree is knocked over and ornaments litter the floor. Pine needles, towels, and embroidered items scatter the entire place, and broken lights dangle from the ceiling. And this is *after* Quinn spent hours cleaning. Yikes.

The display is... Oh boy. I swallow back a bit of a panic but soften my face when I look at Quinn. "Okay. Wow. Okay." Well, these are not the helpful or comforting words I intended. I shrug off my jacket and snow pants and take a deep breath. "We absolutely got this. What's first?"

Quinn shifts into her executive assistant mode and starts directing like a champ. Morgan and Frankie move to pick up all items on the floor, my mom creates an ornament triage space to scour what items are fixable or should be tossed, Quinn and my dad leave to get plywood from the supply shed to board up the broken windows, and I'm going to sweep, vacuum, and then mop to make sure we have all the glass shards picked up so no one cuts themselves.

I take a quick moment to check in on Luna, who assures me she has everything under control at the shop. I'd packed all the pies before I left, so she only has to ring up customers. I even told her that she could just take everything in the display case back to her house for Thanksgiving, so she didn't have to worry about selling and boxing those items. I felt terrible leaving her there alone to handle the customers, but I needed to be with Quinn. My shop is important. But Quinn is my everything. The choice was easy.

A few hours into working, my mom brings out PB&Js and potato chips and makes everyone sit and take a break—which is good. It's past dinnertime and we haven't slowed. I gulp back nearly a bottle of water and wipe my mouth with my sleeve. My gosh, this is a ton of work. And there's still so much to do. But we're making progress.

Morgan steps over to me and Quinn and takes a seat in a folding chair. "How do you feel if I start fixing up some of the merchandise that we think is salvageable?"

"Perfect," Quinn says and twists off the water bottle cap. "Frankie and I can put the tree back up. Zoey, do you think you and your mom can make sure all the price tags and things are on the unbroken products?"

"Definitely." I crunch into the sandwich and swallow. "Do you have another string of lights? After that, me and my dad can replace the broken one hanging from the beams."

We finish our food, and then we move. Besides the distinct sounds of metal scraping pavement from the snowplows clearing the county roads outside the shop, we work in almost complete silence. There is no laughter, no joking around, just six people on a mission to save a dream. Once the cleanup is over, we sit assembly-line style and start fixing all the merchandise we can. Hot glue guns and paint are spread across the table. While Morgan, Quinn, my mom, and I work on the artistry, Frankie and my dad go to the machine shed to fire up the Bobcats to clear out the winding drive. When Quinn told Frankie she could drive one of the Bobcats, Frankie nearly sprinted across the room to throw on her snowsuit.

It's 2:00 a.m. before we finish everything, and Quinn finally calls it. The exhaustion in her is so deep I can see it across the room —red eyes, yawns, sluggish movements. But underneath all of that, there's hope. She smiles at me as she tugs on her coat and grabs her keys. Everyone else piles into the Jeep for the ride back home, but Quinn and I walk down to the edge of the property, arms linked, to grab her truck.

The damage was terrible. Really. But also, more salvageable than we all thought. After working for hours, we saved nearly seventy-five percent of the items. The night is quiet, the moon bright overhead as we walk down the path to the truck. Quinn tucks herself into me and nestles against my shoulder like I'm the fuel she needs to move along. And I love it. Together, we make a great team.

Tonight, all of us were part of something bigger than ourselves. We helped save Christmas for the tree farm.

THIRTY-TWO

QUINN

I can't breathe. I want to breathe. Air right now would be good, welcome, exciting even, and yet, I cannot breathe.

"You need to breathe," Zoey says as she steps up behind me and nuzzles her head into my neck.

"Is it that obvious?" I ask, kissing her on the forehead.

"Your face turning blue is a dead giveaway." She steps back and grabs my hand. "You got this. Everything is going to be great."

I have all of my fingers and toes crossed that she's right. After the storm two days ago and working yesterday into the wee hours of the morning, I've officially done everything I can do. My shop, although not perfect, is pretty darn good. The plywood across the windows was not giving off the comfortable homey vibe I wanted, so this morning I stapled bows across all of it to cover.

But really, it's not about the plywood. It's about wondering if my yearlong effort to transform the farm, the advertising, social media, and hand making all these items will pay off. If people will love this place the same as I do, if my tree farm will generate some beautiful memories, if kids will have a good time.

The creak of the barn doors opening sounds behind me and a slight breeze whooshes in. "Ho, ho, ho!" a loud voice booms.

If I knew Zoey's dad just a little bit better, I'd run over there and give him a big hug. After the Santa I'd originally hired called me last night to cancel because of a terrible case of food poisoning, I nearly panicked that I'd have to get into the suit myself or bribe Morgan to do it. But within five minutes of telling Zoey what happened, her dad stepped up to the plate. And not only that, but Debbie also begged to play Mrs. Claus. Problem solved.

"Red really suits you," I say. "I think you should take Debbie out for a night on the town wearing this."

He pats his round, jolly belly. "I think that's a good idea. Maybe I'll see if we can squeeze in the back seat of my car—"

"Dad, nope. Please for the love of everything, do not finish that sentence," Zoey says with her hands up. "My stomach is already fragile enough from the pizza last night. I can't take much more."

The pizza. I felt terrible that I ruined Thanksgiving for Zoey's family. After not returning home until close to 3:00 a.m., it didn't surprise me that everyone was too exhausted to make a feast later that day. Debbie cheerfully claimed that Sunday was as good of a day as any to celebrate Thanksgiving, and it was all about being with loved ones, not which day the date fell on the calendar.

If it wouldn't make Zoey and me sisters, I swear I'd ask them to adopt me.

"Quinn, come take some test shots," Frankie calls from the photo shoot area. "Zoey, I'd love to get a few of you in here as well."

Zoey and I cross the room to the "Santa Station." I sit on the large red chair and pat my thighs. Zoey grins, slides onto my lap, and wraps her arm around me.

"Tell me everything you want for Christmas," I say, breathing in her warm scent. Out of respect for everyone in here, I ignore the deep urge to slide my hand on her ass.

"I already have everything I want," Zoey says, then leans into my ear, "but if you're not too tired tonight, let's bring back that blindfold and I'll give you one of your presents early."

"I'm not too tired tonight." I giggle and ignore the groans coming from Frankie. I tip my head up and meet Zoey's lips.

This really is more than I could've ever dreamed. We snap a

few pictures, and Frankie checks the exposure and setting. Morgan is in the kitchen area brewing the coffee next to the hot chocolate, and Zoey's parents are in the corner adjusting their outfits.

And me? I'm holding my girlfriend and taking in the moments before—hopefully—chaos hits with a mad rush of customers. If I can squeeze one more Christmas miracle out of this year, my hope is that I have customers, and those customers leave here smiling.

Two hours later, the beautiful chaos hits.

The temporary crew waves in the cars like air traffic controllers, lining them up to park near the barn, and the overflow area—which I never dreamed we'd have to use. As Christmas music fills the shop, Frankie works the crowd, completely in her element, cheering on the kids to smile with Santa and snapping photos. Morgan is at the register, chatting with customers and wrapping up their merchandise in heavy paper and festive bags. Zoey is in the kitchen area, smiling widely, serving up cookies and hot chocolate to the guests. And me? Well, I'm running around everywhere like a baby goat who just realized they could actually run. I dash to one area, then to another, then to another. Every single one of the twenty temporary crew showed up on time, and if this keeps up, I'm definitely handing out holiday bonuses. They're helping customers drag wrapped trees to cars, adhering them Griswold-style to their cars, and directing traffic.

"More marshmallows?" Zoey asks as I wiggle behind her and dig in the cabinets.

"Yep. Here I thought I bought enough for the season, but I think we're going to go through them by the end of the weekend," I say, grabbing three bags and an extra box of graham crackers. This is the *best* problem to have. The bonfire and s'mores stand are a huge hit, and sticky-fingered children are running around wiping their hands in the snow. "Instead of date night later, I think we need to make a Costco run."

"Oh, that's still a date night. Who doesn't love Costco?" Zoey grins and greets a guest.

At the bonfire behind the barn, I drop off the supplies and

hand out water to the crew member who's diligently making sure the fire stays hot and no one burns themselves. I run back inside, grab a tray of hot chocolate, and make my rounds to check on the rest of the crew and give them a little hot cocoa reprieve.

The crew member giving hayrides waves at me from the tractor as parents and kids climb on the trailer and settle on hay bales. As the huge tires crunch against the gravel, soft, gentle snowflakes begin to flutter to the ground. I stop where I'm at and give myself just a moment to watch them float against the white lights strung across a few of the trees. With the activity, and kids running, the fire, and the joy filling the air, I feel like I'm in a real-life snow globe. Joy fills me, starting in my soul and moving to my heart. A warmth that I've always wanted, that always seemed just a stretch out of reach, I'm finally touching.

This is happiness.

I *love* Christmas time.

The day flies by. I'm outside more than inside, but don't even have time to get cold. So many customers stop me and marvel at my place. They tell me stories of coming here when they were little, and how I tapped into something deeply nostalgic. Kids stop me and ask if they can come back and meet Santa again and have more cookies. Families have me take pictures of them with their cell phones, and more than one person has given me a hug.

We were supposed to close at four because it's getting dark, but cars are still rolling in. Sadly, for their safety, I finally tell my crew that we cannot let anyone in past five. Day one, and I have to turn away customers. *Turn. Away. Customers.* I cannot believe this is real life.

When we finally, officially, close up shop, I thank everyone profusely and send them all home. After hugging Zoey's parents, Morgan, and Frankie, I close the barn door and collapse into the large Santa chair.

Zoey wriggles in next to me and lays her head against my chest. "What a day, huh?"

What a day, a year, a life. Things I thought were impossible turned possible. Leaving New York and moving home. Starting and launching my own business. Revamping an entire tree farm into something beautiful and inspiring.

Finding love.

My chest fills and I hold Zoey tight against me. She tips up her head, her eyes searching mine, and a gentle grin passes her face. "Where's that mistletoe you promised me earlier?"

I cup her cheeks and plant a kiss on her beautiful plump lips. "I don't need mistletoe to give my love kisses."

Her warm grin fills me. She snuggles back into my chest, and I take a deep, cleansing breath as everything around me settles. Against all odds, something I never thought would happen, happened.

I found my Christmas miracle.

THIRTY-THREE

QUINN

Six months later

Fresh, warm spring air just hits a little different than regular air. I step out onto the barn patio in my gown and take a deep breath. *Wedding Day*. My heart is racing so fast that any moment now I'm going to get dizzy. I can't believe today is actually here.

I touch the side of my hair and then drop it. The hairstylist warned me to stop poking at it, but I hardly ever wear my hair up, and it feels a bit foreign. I have so many bobby pins holding my curls in place that I'm worried I won't remove them all tonight and I'll accidently stab Zoey in my sleep.

After a phenomenal Christmas season, I took several weeks off in January to decompress. My beautiful love even made a New Year's resolution to cut her days down to four days a week by March, and she did it. Four days! She hired more staff and bumped up Luna and Caleb's hours. Not that Zoey was ever worried about money, but when I officially moved in with her in February, cutting her costs by half, I think it gave her the extra breathing room she needed to not be at her place daily.

A butterfly lands on the railing, its wings fluttering in the sunlight. I'm trying to take this as the omen I need to confirm that today will be perfect. It *has* to be perfect.

The farm is beautiful, and ready for the ceremony. White lights, linen-covered tables, fresh flowers on every table. The ceremony itself will be small, only a handful of family and friends, but that doesn't mean I wanted to skimp on any details. The brides deserve nothing but the best.

A click of heels sounds behind me, and I turn around. Will Zoey ever not take my breath away? I see her every day, I live with her, and after Christmas ended, I was in her shop more than my own. And yet, my breath hitches and locks in my throat every time she's in my path. "Wow, you look beautiful."

"Thank you." She smooths down the fabric of her purple strapless gown and does a little spin. "You look stunning. Your sister picked out the best maid of honor dress ever for you."

"*Morgan* picked out the best dress ever," I say with a laugh. "God love Frankie, but pretty sure she didn't even know I was part of her and Morgan's wedding party until I planned the bachelorette festivities."

Obviously, I'm joking. I never, ever see Frankie nervous. It's not part of her DNA. But when she told me she was going to propose to Morgan, and wanted me there to take pictures, I watched the ring box shake in Frankie's trembling palms as she got down on one knee. Everyone cried. Frankie, Morgan, me. It was a beautiful moment, and one that, hopefully, someday Zoey and I will have for ourselves.

So yes, Frankie was involved in the wedding planning, but Morgan is a wedding coordinator, and way more of a type A personality than my sister. I think even if Frankie had an opinion on a color scheme or songs, she probably would've kept them to herself.

The sun beams down, highlighting the chestnut in Zoey's hair, and the turquoise in her eyes. She stands next to my shoulders, looks out into the property, and takes the same deep breaths as me. "How's your sister doing today?"

"Today, she's good. Yesterday, a little nervous. But now that the day is here, she is cool as a cucumber." I wrap my pinkie around Zoey's, and she curls her finger into mine. "Morgan on the other hand..."

Zoey chuckles. "It's got to be hard for her to give up the control like this. Think she can let go and enjoy the day?"

I nod. I'm sure it is hard for Morgan to let go, but when she asked Zoey to manage the caterers today, and Zoey quickly agreed, I knew Morgan felt at peace. "I do. She left today's details in very capable hands."

"Yeah, she did." Zoey grins. "I'm going to kick booty and take names."

I laugh. "I love your feisty side."

Zoey glances at me, a seriousness taking over. "I love all your sides."

My heart blooms. I go to rest my head on her shoulder and whip it back. Dang hair. I want to kiss her, but the makeup artist also warned me about not ruining my makeup until after the ceremony. I guess I'll settle for linked pinkies. For now.

"When we do this, I say we elope," Zoey says. "Just me and you. Somewhere tropical. Messy hair. No makeup. No shoes. We'll just let the warm sand sift through our toes. What do you think?"

When. She said *when.* I knew "when." I've thought "when." Once I decided to open up to love, once I found love, Zoey was instantly a "when." Never an "if." But I've never heard her say it. Not like this, not so sincere, so matter-of-fact, so casual.

Screw the makeup. I lean in and give her a kiss on the mouth, and let everything about today, this last year, fill me, complete me, make me whole. I pull myself back and smile. "Sounds perfect."

A LETTER FROM THE AUTHOR

Hey there!

Thanks so much for reading *Any Girl But You*. I loved having you learn more about Quinn and Zoey, bringing back Morgan and Frankie from *The Ex Effect*, and bringing in Josie and Colby, who will all be characters in the series. I had so much fun writing this book and creating this fictional town in Northern Minnesota which is heavily influenced by some of my favorite areas in this state—Two Harbors, Duluth, Grand Marais, and Lutsen.

As I continue to write my sparkly, upbeat romances celebrating queer joy, I'd love to keep you posted about my new releases and bonus content. Please sign up for my newsletter. I promise I won't spam you or sell your info.

www.stormpublishing.co/dana-hawkins

I'd be so grateful if you liked this book and wouldn't mind leaving a review. Even a short review can make all the difference in encouraging a reader to discover my books for the first time. Thank you so much!

I consciously choose to write stories where coming out is not an "issue" and that being LGBTQIA+ is nothing to "overcome." Creating a world where my characters live in a safe, affirming, cele-bratory space while navigating their relationships and real-life issues fills my heart. I am keenly aware the queer community continues to live in fear and is subject to discrimination, violence, anti-inclusive legislation, and more. I write novels that create a reality I want to be a part of—a hate-free world.

Thanks again for being part of this amazing journey with me! Please stay in touch—I have so many more stories and can't wait to share them with you.

ACKNOWLEDGMENTS

To my spouse, "My Forever." You are my everything. Thank you for putting up with my goofy ways and laughing when I'm sure you want to cringe. Truly, I don't know how you still give me smiles after all these years.

Jennifer Gatewood. My severe dependent relationship on you continues! Thank you for always being so willing to read my things, jump on a call, critique my work, and guide me. My shoulder-shimmying partner forever! Truly, having you in my corner through all my projects means more to me than you will ever know.

S. E. Reed. I love you! (Yes, I am screaming this.) Your unwavering support, friendship, and encouragement over these years has grown to something I never expected. Thank you for supporting my dreams no matter how outlandish they seem to be. I'm so happy to have you in my world.

To my kiddos, Tanner, Kiki, and Joey. I don't care how old you are, I will still steal hugs any time I can. I adore you all so much.

To Erica Dusha. Thank you for calming my chaos, always.

To Esther Dusha. You are the best mom ever. Thank you for your unwavering support and for always reading my pages! I know you will catch any error that slips through the cracks.

To Emily Gowers and the Storm team. Thank you so much for your support, encouragement, and for giving me a forum for my words through FIVE books. Five. Never in my life, when I had a call with Emily a few years ago, did I think everything would change as much as it did. Thank you for giving me such a great home.

To "Team Jenna." You all are the best teammates I could ever ask for. Thank you for creating such a supportive space.

And to my agent, Jenna Satterthwaite. Book #2 between us done. One thousand more to go. Thank you, a million times over, for your kindness and leadership. You are the perfect champion in the corner, leading the way with grace, intelligence, and kindness. I am so very lucky to be on your team.